"In Andrés N. Ordorica's majestic novel, the emotional and intellectual life of Daniel de La Luna, a first-generation college student, is rendered beautifully, deftly. Belonging, for Daniel, is complicated by familial grief and self-doubt, but a heart-shattering first love spurs him to cross and to erase the borders between him and those who love him. I'm especially moved by his bond with his Abuelo, which is impactful, instructive. Novels this well-written remind us reading is an intimacy, an immersive experience that enriches us beyond measure."

—**Eduardo C. Corral**,
author of *Guillotine*

"In *How We Named the Stars*, Andrés N. Ordorica has crafted a radiant and deeply moving novel about the beauty and pain of love—for our partners, our families, and ourselves. An impressive emotional tour de force, and an extraordinary debut."

—**Christopher Castellani**,
author of *Leading Men*

"Love and loss, freedom and security, sex and identity—Andrés N. Ordorica's *How We Named the Stars* explores the desires and fears that live within us, that surface despite our attempts to tame or quiet them. In Ordorica's thoughtful prose, time becomes a character through which we come to learn the value of what can be gained when we allow ourselves to be vulnerable to our deepest longings. The story of Daniel and Sam will be with us for years to come."

—**Eloisa Amezcua**,
author of *Fighting Is Like a Wife*

"With *How We Named the Stars*, Andrés N. Ordorica has written an intimate, necessary story of first love, first loss, and the promise of new beginnings. This empowering novel is required reading for anyone struggling to uncover their most authentic self."

—Zak Salih,
author of *Let's Get Back to the Party*

"*How We Named the Stars* is a novel of first love and last rites. Ordorica captures perfectly the challenges of building a life out of experience, out of allowing ourselves to feel everything. A beautiful tale of friendship and the comfort found in stories of the past and in the arms of elders, living and dead."

—Richard Mirabella,
author of *Brother & Sister Enter the Forest*

"Andrés N. Ordorica has captured the crushing isolation of navigating an elite college for the first time, all while experiencing a powerful, yet unattainable first love. Named after his family's late uncle, Daniel wrestles with the continued impact of loss even as he finds glimpses of comfort. This novel is an extended meditation on the relationship between joy and grief, and how it can bind and heal both a life and a family."

—Analicia Sotelo,
author of *Virgin*

HOW WE

NAMED

THE STARS

HOW WE NAMED THE STARS

a novel

ANDRÉS N. ORDORICA

TIN HOUSE / PORTLAND, OREGON

EPIGRAPH CREDIT: *Waiting for Godot* copyright © 1954 by
Grove Press, Inc.; Copyright © renewal 1982 by Samuel Beckett.
Used by permission of Grove/Atlantic, Inc. Any third-party use
of this material, outside of this publication, is prohibited.

First US Edition 2024
Printed in the United States of America

Manufacturing by Sheridan
Interior design by Beth Steidle

Library of Congress Cataloging-in-Publication Data

Names: Ordorica, Andrés N. (Andrés Nicolás), author.
Title: How we named the stars : a novel / Andrés N. Ordorica.
Description: Portland, Oregon : Tin House, 2024.
Identifiers: LCCN 2023038758 | ISBN 9781959030331 (paperback) |
ISBN 9781959030485 (ebook)
Subjects: LCGFT: Queer fiction. | Bildungsromans. | Novels.
Classification: LCC PR6115.R426 H69 2024 |
DDC 823/.92—dc23/eng/20230822
LC record available at https://lccn.loc.gov/2023038758

Tin House
2617 NW Thurman Street, Portland, OR 97210
www.tinhouse.com

Distributed by W. W. Norton & Company
2   3   4   5   6   7   8   9   0

For my grandfather Filomeno and for Serena.

VLADIMIR: Do you remember the Gospels?

ESTRAGON: I remember the maps of the Holy Land. Coloured they were. Very pretty. The Dead Sea was pale blue. The very look of it made me thirsty. That's where we'll go, I used to say, that's where we'll go for our honeymoon. We'll swim. We'll be happy.

—Samuel Beckett, *Waiting for Godot*

HOW WE
NAMED
THE STARS

PROLOGUE

If you asked me, I'd tell you: Cetus, the sea monster—which would no doubt prompt questions charged with panic and intrigue. It's not a pretty myth, but I'd explain how the Aztecs knew the constellation as Axólotl. Perhaps, being native to México, that pink salamander with its sweet face would be more reassuring to you. The truth is, both origin stories are dark—scary, even. In the Greek myth, Princess Andromeda was offered up as a sacrifice for the monster Cetus to devour in hopes this act might bring an end to Poseidon's wrath. Xolotl, who inspired the lizard's name, was god of fire and lightning, a guide for the souls of the dead into the underworld.

If you asked me to explain why I chose this constellation to be yours—which of course you would, being you—I'd say that although darkness can be scary, it also can be profound. I'd say, *Imagine a blacked-out room, completely void of light. Now imagine striking a match. Although the room is mostly dark, full of so much unknown, it's also full of so much light.*

Even if you looked at me with a face that screams *You're certifiably insane,* I'd say, *See how inviting that single flame is, how brave it must be to burn brightly, even when alone in such darkness, even when it's faced with such pain.*

I'd say, *That's you.*

You'd no doubt protest, call me dumb, tell me to be quiet, might even say, *Please shut the fuck up.* You'd make some argument about how you're not bright enough to be a star, let alone luminescent enough to be a collection of them, enough to make up a whole constellation. But I'd counter this argument, pushing past your self-doubt. All my real feelings would pour out: you aren't just a constellation, you're a galaxy, a universe to me. But knowing you like I do, well, of course all this honesty would be too much. It would make you retreat, like a clam, and it would be a lot of work to get you to come back out of your shell.

But no matter these imagined protestations, I still see you as the god of fire. When I look at you, watching you in all our quiet moments, an electricity runs through my body, a spark that only you can bring about. Around the fire, orange-red flames bouncing off your copper skin, I imagine you as a bearer of light: someone who deftly moves between shadow and revelation, navigates both darkness and truth, holding those dark black eyes of yours shut—your hands snaking through the midnight air, your body aligning with the beat of your favorite song playing softly from a speaker. All I want is to be near you.

As the logs continue burning, smoke seeping into hair and clothes, I witness you at your brightest and fullest—the brightest and fullest you have ever been in the short time I've known you. Tonight, I want to tell you this. Tonight, I want to grab my camera, take a photo, and say, pointing to the screen, *This is you. Can't you see how I see you?* But I fear that rousing you from this moment of joy, from the comfort enveloping you, might break the spell. Between the fire and drink scattered around our feet, there is enough to keep you warm, but still I long to hold you close—long to offer up some of my body's heat. Perhaps it's the drink allowing these thoughts to unfurl, or perhaps it's something that's been building for a while now. But I stay quiet all the same, letting the stillness of night take over, allowing you to dance freely under the October sky.

As you continue dancing, I hold the six letters of your name close to my chest. Looking up at the firmament, at these gods of vengeance who produced all this beauty around us, I begin to pray for you. I don't know who I'm praying to, but I pray you might remain in the light always, be this free, be this happy, that you might never know darkness. I then close my eyes, allow my body to sync with your movements, and whisper each letter, releasing them one by one into the night sky:

D   E

            N   I

    A   L

You're singing to yourself now, an almost mantra, and, I kid you not, I see lyrics buzzing around us like the letters I've let go of. Inching ever closer to your light, I join you. Together our movements grow more erratic, more urgent, as we move and shake with newfound purpose. Guided by something carnal, a yearning for truth and a desire to be our realest selves, the most honest versions. I will stay like this with you for a few more hours, dancing around this burning blaze just as man has done since the dawn of time. When he used to fall asleep under the stars, seeing them as nothing more than blank pages in which stories would unfold, in which myths and legends would be written.

PART I

DAY ONE

AUGUST 23, 1989

Sometimes I dream of another life, one in which leaving this town does not scare me. I feel a call inside me as deep as a canyon. Animal-like, instinctive and knowing. Often it comes in the form of silences. Like in the dark of night when I wander home alone, drunk from the bar, I will be walking under lamplight, kicking up the dust of the road, and I'll hear it. It brings me to a complete standstill. The voice will often tell me how there is something bigger out there. Something bigger than what I've grown up believing. But to get to where I need to go, I must be willing to face the unknown. With only the streetlamps as my witness, I call out to ask what that unknown is, but I never get an answer. The voice goes quiet, leaving me to wrestle with what I need to find.

—D.M.

Sam's dead.

Those words have followed me for six weeks now, across borders and many time zones, over thousands of miles, and still they haven't shifted—the weight of their truth still very much bears

3

down on me. I've spent most of today's first flight staring out the window, my mind returning to the weeks before we met, when we were nothing more than words shared online. All this traveling, these layovers, are starting to surface more and more memories; how our story began only twelve months ago, when I was making this journey for the first time, dashing around airports wondering what freshman year of college would be like. Now here I am, returning to Ithaca as an almost completely different person. But of course, you know that already.

Today, while traveling across this vast country, above cities and states I know nothing of, I thought about the night I answered that strange number only to hear your mom's voice, brought to me through telephone lines and satellites straddling man-made borders. As I heard her words, I retreated to our happy times, like when I'd spot you from across the quad darting between classes; the thrill of knowing you were happy to see me, how you'd run over just to smother me in a hug before darting off once more—it was safer there in our past than in my present.

Between her crying and frantic breathing, I didn't really put two and two together. I was too lost in the past, buoyed by all our adventures, hours of conversation, how I felt whole in your company. I couldn't hear what she was telling me, didn't want it.

"I'm so sorry, sweetie. I'm so, so sorry to have to tell you like this." Her tears poured through the phone, starting to flood me with sadness.

You're wrong, Martha, you're so wrong, I thought. But she wasn't.

"Sam's dead."

Please don't judge me, but after I heard those words I started to forget things almost immediately. It scared me, honestly. In the days that followed the phone call, all sorts of memories—big and small, important, superfluous—just started evaporating into the ether. As hard as I tried, I couldn't stop them. Time was working against me, and so I needed to work fast to remember what I still could.

What hurt the most was when I started to forget your voice, what it sounded like to hear you say my name aloud; started to forget how hearing you say my name was a way of seeing myself as I had never seen myself—someone free from how my family saw me—and how you gave my name new meaning, new weight. No longer was I my parents' son, my grandfather's nieto, the bearer of a deceased uncle's name. I was Daniel.

I was your Daniel, at least for a time.

It's strange to think we knew nothing about each other before moving in together. We had sent three, maybe four, messages over Facebook that summer, always straight and to the point: *What's your major? Where you from? Do you drink?* They seemed essential enough questions for understanding what we were both getting into. I always responded promptly: *I'm Daniel. I'll be an English major with a hopeful minor in creative writing. I am from a small town in Northern California (you won't have heard of it).* A few hours later, you responded: *Nice to meet you, Daniel. I'm Sam, pre-med student. From SoCal – just outside Orange County.* Followed by: *I have a cousin in Sacramento – you anywhere near there?* I responded: *About an hour away in the middle of some farmland.* You sent a quick, *LOL, well nice to meet you – speak soon, bro.*

I remember being afraid of you before we met. I spent hours studying your strong jaw, golden shoulder-length curls, that perfect smile in your Facebook profile—all of it belonged to the face of a man I feared might reject me. Having never had many male friends, I didn't expect great things, and the fact that you were an athlete only added to my pessimism. You looked like all the guys who tortured me in the hallways of high school. I tried not to dwell on this fact too much in the lead-up to my arrival, but the fear was still very present. In my final days at home, I went out with friends to say goodbye, and all of them seemed thrilled at the idea of college on the East Coast, of dormitories and roommates. With each goodbye, I could sense their need to hear a boundless thrill in my voice, but all I could muster was mild optimism that it would all turn out okay, that you would be okay. That I might be wrong in my prejudgments was all I could hope for.

I arrived the day before you for an induction given to latecomers, those who hadn't already flown or driven to visit the University of Cayuga during the admissions process. The campus in Ithaca, New York, was like nothing I was used to, with its old brick buildings and white-columned entryways, bell towers and pristinely manicured lawns. All their colors overwhelmed me: those deep greens, copperish reds, and the crystalline-blue sky above the lake sitting in a basin below us. I had entered a world of privilege, and by day one was already doubting my ability to survive.

During this induction I met Rob and Mona, who, on that first day, also scared me. They had a confidence and worldliness that I lacked. Still, we stayed fixed to one another while being guided along by a campus rep pointing out fact after fact about our elite East Coast school.

"He is kind of hot, right?" Rob asked as we meandered side by side.

"The tour guide in the MC Hammer pants?" Mona asked. As she spoke, she was simultaneously checking out two Korean girls near the front wearing Chanel outfits and Miu Miu backpacks.

"Yeah, like in that kind of 'I know I'm hot but I'm not going to make it a thing' kind of way."

"I wouldn't know, Rob, I'm into girls. How about you ask him?" she said, pointing to me with barely any interest.

I was horror-stricken as Rob homed in on me, and immediately felt sweat trickling down my back. I hadn't told either of them I was gay; how had Mona known? I thought about running away before Rob could ask for my opinion, disappearing into another tour group, never to speak to either of them again.

"What do you think, Daniel?"

"I . . . umm . . . well, he . . . seems *nice*."

"Nice?"

"Yeah, like nice."

Mona smiled at me before turning to Rob to say that "nice" was certainly a good quality to look for in a partner, but before she could go on, he cut her off to clarify that he was only implying he'd fuck the guy, not date him.

"I mean, come on, Mona. It's like day one of freshman year. I'm not going to chain myself to monogamy straight out the gate. Don't you agree, Daniel?"

"About what?"

"That, like, now isn't the time to settle down. Now is the time to get some D, or V, or—" Rob looked at me. "I don't know what you're into, truth be told."

"I'm not . . . quite . . . so experienced," I said, praying that being frank would put this all to bed. However, the screams my words elicited from both Rob and Mona were so over the top that every person in our tour group, not to mention every person who happened to be on the quad just then, suddenly looked to us in either intrigue or annoyance.

"Shut the fuck up! Are you, like, a virgin?" Rob said, sotto voce.

"Yeah, but like, I don't really want to talk about it," I said. "It's not like some weird religious thing or whatnot. I just . . . haven't gotten around to it." In many ways that was the truth.

"Hey, no shame, Daniel. It is 2011, for God's sake. We need to be more sex positive as a society and not judge anyone no matter where they are on their journey," Mona said. She had the fervor of a street minister, or a Tumblr influencer. "Right, Rob?"

"Totally—no shame, man."

As we continued through the rest of induction day, I thought about where I was on my journey. In all honesty, I had no clue. But here I was grouped with these two loud, well-meaning but overly self-assured peers of mine, fearing what their questions had implied. Worse, what their understanding of me might be because of what

7

they hadn't seemed to need to ask. Had they read me as gay? And did that mean that you, or others I would soon meet, might read me as gay? These questions followed me as I made my way back to our dorm, praying sleep might bring comfort and clarity.

I awoke to complete stillness the following morning. Most students had yet to move in or were dead asleep after a night full of illegal parties I hadn't dared join. In my bed, with the rays of sun through the window heating up my skin, I felt safe and well rested. I lay there taking in the quiet views before me, and looked at the clock. It was 10:00 AM, far later than I had meant to sleep. Suddenly I heard voices and sat up very still, trying to remember if I'd locked the front door. I quickly dressed and exited my room, only to be met by three new faces sitting on the couch. You were exactly how I remembered you from Facebook. The other two were older, a man and a woman, possibly in their early fifties, well dressed, with features similar to yours. Your parents, I quickly realized. You smiled at me before getting up.

"Oh my gosh, hello, I'm so sorry, I must have missed my alarm."

"Hey, dude, no worries. We just arrived."

I stood there awkwardly, not knowing what to do.

"I'm Sam, by the way. Sam Morris. And these are my parents, Martha and Ed, or Mom and Dad, as I like to call them," you said. When we shook hands, I felt every muscle in your long arm move with purpose.

"Daniel de La Luna. Nice to meet you all," I said, nodding to you and your parents in turn, like someone interviewing for a job.

You had already brought in all your luggage, and your parents were taking you to run errands. It would save me a trip on the bus, so I gladly accepted when they invited me to join. I remember you were keen to get the shopping over with and so ushered us all out the door. As we zipped down through the city center toward Cayuga Lake, your mom began listing off all the things you'd need for your new college life. Your dad occasionally offered affirmations along the lines of "Yes, honey" and "Martha, what would we do without you here to set us right?"

You only half listened to her, instead focusing more on your phone. I tried to see what you were doing, who you were speaking to—a girlfriend, possibly. But when I glanced over, I saw you were just catching up on the previous night's MLB games. With you busy on your phone and your parents deep in planning, I allowed myself to take in the outside views of the lake, the trees, the city, trying to position myself in this new world of mine.

Once at the shopping center, I struck out on my own, not wanting to infringe on your time with your parents, but was soon interrupted by my phone ringing. It was my mom, likely checking in as I hadn't spoken to her since arriving in Ithaca. My mind felt muddled, heavy with too much thought, and since I couldn't feign the positive hopefulness I knew she wanted to hear, I ignored the call and made my way to the toilets. It seems ridiculous now, but at the time I felt so alone in all these changes, changes I had brought about. I mean, I'd chosen to go to school on the opposite side of the country. I'd told everyone I could do it, told everyone it was my biggest dream, that I could not imagine anywhere else in the world for me, but I was already feeling like maybe it wasn't going to work out. A new life, a new home, a new roommate. What proof did I have it would be okay?

As doubt crashed down upon me, I rushed into a stall and sat on the dirty toilet seat, closing my eyes, letting myself be still for a few moments. I let my mind be transported back to senior year of high school, back to the day that specific letter came through the mail—the look on my parents' faces, the tears Abuelo cried, the joy of translating those life-changing words:

It is with great pleasure that we inform you, Daniel Manuel de La Luna, that you have been accepted into the University of Cayuga as part of the incoming class of 2015. You will be enrolled as an English major in the College of Arts & Sciences. Your acceptance includes an unconditional offer of full financial aid for tuition fees as well as room and board (see further details below). We look forward to welcoming you in the fall . . .

We held hands and jumped up and down in our humble living room, St. Joseph on the mantle, a crucifix and painting of La Virgen de Guadalupe on otherwise sparse walls watching over us. The Holy Family, too, were basking in our jubilation as our eight feet clattered against the tile floor. In the reflection of the TV screen, I could see how free our bodies were that day of all the things chaining us to the ground. It wasn't just Daniel Manuel de La Luna who'd gotten into Cayuga, but my entire family.

When I opened my eyes, I felt less sad. For now, at least, reliving the memory had helped. I left the stall and washed my hands, then headed back out in the direction of Target, where I immediately proceeded to bump into your mom—or, more so, she bumped into me. She was trying to text you and not watching where she was going. I smiled nervously and apologized even though I hadn't done anything wrong. Though I thought she'd turn around and continue on her own, she began instead to walk around with me, offering running commentary in each aisle of the homeware section.

"Those towels are lovely. I have them in lavender in our downstairs guest bathroom."

"They do look nice," I said as diplomatically as possible, mindful of the eighteen-dollar price tag. "But I think I'll do a little price comparison before committing."

"Of course. So responsible," your mom said, impressed by what she perceived as maturity.

"Wish my son were more like you, Daniel. I swear Sam thinks money grows on trees. What else is on your list?"

"Just a few things. Trying to be sensible, you know, until, umm, my stipend kicks in."

Your mom smiled sympathetically as she led us to the snack aisle, where she began building a small mountain of food—necessary, she said, because you had a voracious appetite. Eventually she coaxed me into adding a few things just for me.

"So, Mrs. Morris, did you go to college on the East Coast?"

"Please call me Martha, and, to answer your question, no. I went to USC and then Stanford."

"California girl through and through."

"West Coast, best coast, as they say," she said, smiling again as we reached the end of the aisle. "And what about your parents, where did they go?"

"Well, actually, I'm a first-generation college student. My parents finished high school back in México but never got around to going to college as they had me quite young."

"They must be so proud of you—the University of Cayuga no less," she said, patting my shoulder. "Sam tells me you'll be studying English."

"Yes," I nodded. My interest in English seemed, at least to me, to pale in comparison to the fact that she was a medical doctor.

"A man who loves the written word, brilliant—and what is your favorite book?"

"That's difficult to say, but the book that made me want to study English was Hawthorne's *The Scarlet Letter*. I was so engrossed in it senior year . . . in Hester's story. That a writer from over a hundred and fifty years ago could move me like that . . . It just fascinated me, and made me want to explore literature even more deeply."

"I hear the passion in your voice . . . I truly think Cayuga is going to be an amazing place for you to expand your horizons."

"I hope so, ma'am."

We had made our way to the cash register when she got a call from your dad. Apparently, you two had hunkered down in the food court to enjoy pretzels. She insisted I go join you and took what few school supplies I had managed to budget for before sending me away.

"No cash," she joked, "and I get double points on every dollar when using my American Express."

"Really, Martha, I can't let you."

"It's nothing, Daniel. Trust me. My treat," she said as the cashier started ringing her up.

I felt a pain in my side because in reality, it was not nothing. All this newness was so much to me, too much, but to survive the day, I knew it'd be easier to smile and say thanks rather than draw out the moment any further. I had no more fight in me. "I appreciate it," I said as I left your mom to it, praying the whole shopping trip would soon be over.

"We didn't know what to order, so we got one of everything," your dad declared, proudly pointing to the table covered in every available flavor of pretzel when I arrived.

"And you think you'll still be hungry for lunch later?" I asked.

"Daniel, here is something you need to know about my son: growing up, we called him the human garbage disposal. Food will never go to waste with Samuel in your life."

"And yet I still have a six-pack, old man," you said, patting your stomach with a thunderous thud.

As I sat down and tucked into a pepperoni pretzel, you both began discussing Cayuga's rankings in various sports. As you spoke, you kept one eye on me, your father oblivious to this watchful gaze. Even now, looking back, I can't say whether you were inviting me in or studying me, but I took the opportunity to join the conversation.

"So, Mr. Morris, did you go to USC like your wife?"

"No, Martha and I dated long-distance throughout college."

"Oh, so where did you go?"

Your dad grinned before continuing, as if I had missed out on some obvious clue. "Cayuga, actually. Class of 1983 . . . I came for the scenery but stayed for the vet program."

"Dad always said that he was obligated to come to Cayuga since our family originally hails from New York," you added, in between bites of a cheddar-dipped pretzel.

"The best schools are the historic ones over here. Don't get me wrong, I love California, but I am glad to have graduated a Fighting Osprey," he said, before you both unashamedly dog-barked "Fighting Osprey" in the middle of the food court.

"Go Ospreys," I whooped, my emaciated school spirit falling flat. Your dad stared at me, unsure how to follow up. I was mortified, and would've done anything to evaporate into oblivion. But then you laughed, like really laughed, and I learned how beautiful your smile was. I mouthed, *Thank you*, as your father shifted gears and began to dissect your first-semester schedule. I could feel your eyes again, but this time I just listened, giving myself a break from small talk. I studied the table, the paper plates stained with cheese, cinnamon sugar, and tomato sauce, the bright overhead lights. Anything to stop me from returning to your gaze, those eyes that intrigued and scared me all the same.

Afterward, we joined your mom in the parking lot. Though I thought we might just return to campus, we drove down to the lakefront instead to enjoy a late lunch of hamburgers. To my amazement our conversations flowed easily, and I began to find my rhythm. I was able to charm your parents with my nerdy, bookish knowledge, and they shared their reading recommendations with me. Your dad even offered me tips as a Californian who'd be facing his first East Coast winter soon. Your mom sat there happily taking it all in, studying me, this young man who would be spending lots of time with her one and only son.

After lunch, your parents dropped us back at campus. Unloading the car was a military operation; your mom had packed things strategically and would only let us take what she handed over. I remember how you carried the crates of drinks all stacked on top of one another, your muscles tensing from the weight but your face easy-breezy. The plastic bags dug into my fingers from all the snacks you'd finish off in the next few weeks, but I soldiered on. I left you upstairs to start the unloading process and returned to the SUV to find your mom standing by the trunk with a big grin on her face. "Now, Daniel, I don't want you to get upset with me."

"Why would I get upset, Mrs. Morris? I mean Martha."

"You left your list behind with me, and so I just decided to get some things for you," she said, handing me the sheet of paper.

"Oh no, you really shouldn't have. What do I owe you?"

"Daniel, you owe me nothing."

I looked at the trunk of the car full of so many things, things meant for me, and all I could think of was how these boring but practical things were evidence of your mother's kindness, but also a reminder of what I could not do for myself: a reminder that I did not come from money, that I did not have a safety net to protect me in my new adult life. I thought of my parents, the shame they might feel at knowing someone else had to help their son out. Even if your mom's gesture came from a good place, the contents of the trunk still represented what they'd never be able to give me. Again, it was just stuff, but it meant so much, too much even, and I felt tears trickling down my cheeks, everything I had been holding in all day finally breaking through.

"Oh sweetie, there's no need to cry. You have enough to think about with starting your first year, and making friends and having fun, and I know you're going to do wonderful things here. You're going to make your parents so proud."

"I really don't know what to say . . . I mean . . . it's a lot . . . today . . . all of it."

"I know sweetie, I know."

She hugged me, and I tried to say more, but all I could do was relinquish myself to what I needed most just then: someone to hold me and let me know it was going to be all right.

"You have a great year, Daniel, and if you ever need anything, we are here for you. Honestly, think of Ed and me as your new Cayuga parents, and all I ask of you is that you please, please, watch out for my sweet Sam. Love that kid, but he is going to give me an ulcer—someone has to look out for him!"

I promised her I would, and I meant it.

When we returned to join you in the dorm, you and your father had set up a small TV and were watching the Giants versus the Astros. AT&T Park was glistening in the late-afternoon sun as the camera panned out, showing the Golden Gate Bridge and the blue but cold Pacific Ocean. Your mom gave your dad a look, promptly getting him up. We said our goodbyes and they headed off, back to their hotel, leaving us to finish assembling a storage unit and clearing away boxes and suitcases. As you kept an eye on the game, I half listened while all these thoughts fought for my attention. Before me was a man I barely knew, who on paper was my opposite, and now we were left alone together: two strangers thrown into the wild unknown of academia, tasked with making sense of adulthood and building a new life.

But what could we talk about, beyond the basics we'd already covered? How would we get on? What if you were exactly how I saw you on the surface: some perfect, upper-middle-class all-American jock who'd snuff out whatever quiet brightness I held within me? But then I thought about your mom, who'd only just met me but had treated me with such love on a day I felt so alienated, and I had to believe the apple did not fall far from the tree.

"Everything good, man?"

"Yeah, sorry, just thinking about classes starting next week and all."

"Crazy, right? Like, my God, we're actual college students," you said. I watched as you looked around our new place, taking in the living room, the small kitchenette that divided our separate sleeping quarters. It was a makeshift version of adult life, an in-between space, blank and longing for us to add our color. Yours was a face full of hope, a face that did not share the dread that was starting to consume me again.

"Does it scare you?" I asked, surprised by the openness of my own question.

"What?"

"I mean, just all this newness coming at us—does it overwhelm you?"

You stared at me as you considered these questions. I feared you might be sizing me up, seeing my concern as a form of weakness, a slight against the confidence you exuded.

"I think I'm more excited than scared. I'm ready for something different. You know?"

"That's a good way to think about it, I guess."

You offered me a tender smile, nodding gently, before bending down to grab a twelve-pack of Yuengling, strategically hidden behind storage containers and luggage.

"How about a toast? To starting our new lives as part of the class of 2015." You handed me a can, attempting to bond us in this new friendship.

"Here's to something different for both of us."

"To something different," I repeated, looking straight into your eyes.

As I nursed the rest of my beer, I thought of all the ways I might actually become different. I thought of the Daniel who had first arrived on campus for induction, only a day ago, and then imagined him months from now, what he might get up to, how he might evolve. On the flight over, I had promised myself to be bolder in those first few weeks and try new things, to be someone other than the unconfident person I'd known myself to be, to learn to open up to others.

"It's going to happen."

"Huh?" I asked, in a daze.

"Watch, dude," you said, pointing to the little television.

We both turned to the screen. It was the bottom of the ninth, bases loaded, and I was confident most of Northern California, including my family, was glued to their screens as well. Just then Brandon Belt swung his bat, sending the ball flying toward the Pacific. The stadium crowd went wild as we jumped up and down in our dorm, cheering alongside them, beer spilling everywhere. We hugged each other as if we were there on that field instead of in our small living room, here on the other side of the country, on the cusp of a blossoming friendship.

SEPTEMBER

SEPTEMBER 9, 1988

*I turned nineteen today. I am unsure how to feel about it. Amá
and Apá threw me a party and Luis and the boys came, along
with every family member of mine living in a hundred-kilometer
radius. My sister even invited her friends. The boys loved having
high school girls in attendance. Xochitl was there, and we danced
even though I would've been happy just watching the others
enjoy themselves. Still, she held me close and whispered softly
in my ear all the things she wanted to give me for my birthday.
Her small hands tried to hold as much of my muscled back as they
could. It felt as though if she could only grab something of mine,
she might be able to hold on to me a little longer. I was respectful,
and knew it was more the tequila than her speaking. But still, I
feel like she must know I will never give her what she needs. She
must know she is not who I was wishing for when the candle's
flame was blown. You see, as we danced along to the rhythm of
the cumbia, it was not her pressed up against me, but the weight
of another I've yet to meet but often return to in my dreams.*

—D.M.

It was a few days into September when I walked sleepily into our living room cum kitchenette. I still hadn't adjusted to living with someone new and so, in my tired state, was surprised to find you up with a cup of coffee. You smiled at me and whispered, "Good morning," with such warmth, it startled me. It seemed you had already welcomed me into the fold of your life.

I sat down on the couch, and you asked me how I took my coffee. I told you two sugars and a small amount of creamer. You joined me with two cups in hand, and both of us sat, knees tucked up against our chests, looking out at the lush green treescape outside our window. I asked you how you were finding it all— Cayuga, I clarified—and you told me it was exactly what you'd hoped it would be.

"Something different," I said.

You laughed. "So you remember?"

"Yes."

"And you?"

I wanted to tell you many things. I wanted to tell you how it was like learning to walk again, learning to speak, like being in a body I was not used to; how it overwhelmed me, people asking me all these questions: What did I think about this book? What did I think about this article? What was my opinion on the state of the world? All around us people were consuming and producing knowledge and asking so much of one another, but all I wanted was time to find my footing.

"I'm enjoying the scenery," I told you, blowing on my cup.

"It's beautiful, isn't it? I grew up with my dad's stories of college life, but being here on my own . . . I'm glad to experience it as he did, but also with my own eyes."

We would go on to create a routine of these mornings. Me zombie-walking into our living room, you always greeting me with a coffee while laughing at my inability to be a morning person. You'd usually push me in a playful way before taking your seat on the couch. I'd stay fixed, sipping my coffee and smiling brightly inside.

But, in those early days, I was so scared our dynamic would come crumbling down at the first sign of you displaying ugly, stereotypical masculine behavior. However, you were the opposite—caring, thoughtful, and extremely funny. When we sat together watching TV, or as I read a book and you messed about on your laptop, you'd always find a way to make me laugh or include me in what you were doing, and I cherished those moments so much. They mean even more now that they're lost to time, because just then you were what kept me afloat in a changeable ocean. I remember, not long into the semester, in my Intro to American Theater class, we were studying a play by Suzan-Lori Parks when the professor picked on me to answer his question.

"And Daniel, what about you?"

"What do you mean, sir?"

"I am interested in your perspective as an international student. What do you think of this portrayal of the United States in Parks's *Topdog/Underdog*? Does it feel authentic?" His voice was so earnest and direct.

It took me a few seconds to understand what he was getting at, this dramatic allusion to the American Civil War and racial injustice, and he wanted my opinion . . . but as the outsider? I remember he just kept staring at me like I was holding his class up, inconveniencing his lesson plan. My neck was clammy, my throat dry. My face hurt from the embarrassment.

"Well, I was born here in America, so . . . I don't really have an international perspective to add to the discussion," I mustered.

"Oh, yes, well then as a minority, being Hispanic and all. For you, what does America look like in this play? Does it align with your American dream?"

Everyone just sat there looking at me, waiting for my answer. No one intervened, no one said, *Excuse me, sir, that's kind of a fucked-up question.* I looked around and it dawned on me: I was the only one, the only person of color there, and I was meant to speak on behalf of the great minority, but my mind was blank.

"Umm . . . I'm not sure," I said in complete defeat.

"That's fine, but please, in the future, actually participate in the discussion," he said, quickly moving the class along.

The truth is, Sam, those early days were full of moments like that one, but no matter how often they occurred I never got used to them. I hadn't yet learned to stand up for myself. But I knew I had to at least appear as if I was enjoying my life, so I put on a positive front. I did my best to keep everything inside when you and I spoke, and treated calls home like minefields; my job was to get to the other side of each one unscathed.

"How are you enjoying college, mijo?"

"It's great, Mom. I'm so glad I came to Cayuga."

"That's amazing, Daniel. I'm praying for you always. Every day I wake up and ask our Lord to guide you to what is good and right. I just know he is doing it, mijo."

"I love you, Mom. Thank you for your prayers."

She'd pass me to my dad, and I'd continue the pretending.

"Hello, mijo, how is the weather? How's life?"

"It's beautiful, Dad. The trees . . . I've never seen so many shades of green. I wish you could come visit. I think you'd love all the hiking trails and the lake, the one the university is named after . . . it's like an ocean."

"It sounds wonderful, mijo. You deserve to see the world."

Then he'd pass me to my grandfather, my final hurdle.

"Daniel, are you there? How are your classes, mi nieto querido?"

"I love them, Abuelo. I feel so lucky to be studying what I want. I feel like this is where I belong."

"I'm so proud of you, Daniel. I know your grandmother and your uncle are watching over you always and are just as proud."

"I feel them, Abuelo. I feel their love."

"I'm so glad to hear. I love you so much, mijo, and miss you immensely."

I was never lying to them, but I was never telling them the whole story either. I was never able to share those moments of embarrassment, of being told implicitly: *You are the outsider, and it is our job to remind you of your place in the world.* I didn't tell them how I felt alone, like I was drowning in dark waters. And then there was you, always happy to see me, always so kind. I didn't want you to think of me as sad or a downer.

After the incident in my American Theater class, I began hiding in my room. You'd knock on my door and try to lure me out with coffee, but I'd ignore you, no longer joining you on the couch. I developed tunnel vision and became hyperfocused on proving to my English professors that I deserved to be at Cayuga, but to the detriment of my other classes. At the end of September, my advisor Naomi called me into a meeting. Too many professors from other departments had spoken to her about me missing deadlines or not showing up. I felt like a child being reprimanded, but this was real life, with a degree worth fifty thousand dollars a year on the line.

"Daniel, this is not what I expected from that excited man I met back in August!"

I tried to think of a defense, but all that came to mind were the doubts I'd been having.

"I'm not sure if I can manage—maybe the rigor of Cayuga is proving too much."

"No, I don't buy that crap. Sorry for being real with you, chico, but we're not playing that game. You were one of the top students admitted to our English program. I won't let you throw it all away without a fight."

"What if it isn't about the coursework—what if I just don't make sense here?"

"Why wouldn't you?"

"Come on, Naomi . . . you must know."

"Because you're Mexican? Because you're first gen? Are you really going to let them win? Let the 'man' push you out and make you feel like you don't deserve to be here?"

"Maybe it was easier for you?"

"¿En serio, Daniel? Hello, you are speaking to the first Black professor in our school's English department. The first tenured Afro-Latina in the school's entire two-hundred-year history. You think I got here without having to deal with shit time and time again?"

"You make it sound like I'm taking the easy way out."

"Well, are you?"

"I just don't know what to do. I have no one to turn to."

"That's not true—you have me, and together we will find a way forward. First off, you're going to start going to your other classes again. I can't fight for you if you're not showing up. ¿Me entiendes?"

"Sí, Naomi. I do, I promise."

"Then you're going to start coming to see me once a week. I don't want to hear any excuses, tengo que hacer this or that—no, we are going to check in with each other regularly. And one final thing: we are going to get you enrolled in the honors program for next semester."

"What? No, I can't. The school wouldn't let me anyway. They said my high school transcript wasn't compatible with the academic caliber of the honors program."

"Well, that's some classic Cayuga bullshit. Again, Daniel, you are too smart for those intro classes we have for remedial students. I'm not going to let this place keep ostracizing Black and brown students like this. Tell me: Why are you my smartest advisee, and yet not in any of my honors seminars? Tell me why every Charity, Cassadee, and Chad are always in my classes, wasting my time by not even doing the work."

"I dunno . . ."

"Yes, you do."

"Because Cayuga is wack?"

"¡Mirálo! He's getting it. Gracias a Dios," she said, making the sign of the cross for show. "So, what I'm going to do is get you into that program, and what you're going to do is remember why you are here: because you are smart and capable, and you are going to change the world. You're just finding your footing, Daniel, that's all this is . . . growing pains."

I came home that evening feeling better than I had at the start of the day. I appreciated Naomi's directness, her ability to see me in a way that I struggled to see myself. When I arrived at our dorm, you were there on the couch, and before I could hide away in my room, you called, "Hey, dude, how are you?"

"I'm okay," I said wearily, embarrassed by how I'd been avoiding people. "And you?"

"I'm doing pretty good, but what's happened to our morning coffee chats?"

"Life's just been, I dunno . . . a bit much. I've been too caught up in my own world."

"That's okay, glad you're here now." You paused. "How was your advisor meeting, by the way?"

"It went well. She isn't kicking me out of the university. So that's good."

You smiled, but your face looked concerned, and so I sat down, unsure why. All I knew was I didn't want to hide that night. Something was saying I needed to be with you. All of a sudden you stood up and said you had an idea, and this is how we ended up on a long evening stroll, with a six-pack of cider in hand. You guided us to a hill near the campus art museum. From the top of it, you could see Cayuga Lake in the distance.

You pointed to the moon, which was bright orange, reflecting off the dark waters below. You loved astronomy and began to explain the meteorological phenomenon that allowed for this kind of a moon. Something about the relative position of the sun. You then asked me what the translation for this moon would be in Spanish. I did not know if it had its own name, so I told you, "Luna de sangre."

"Wait! How did I not clock your last name means 'moon'?"

"Yeah, strange, isn't it? Like, have you ever met a white person named James Sun or Megan Star?"

"It's incredible. I mean, 'Morris' is hardly inspiring."

"You're right, I'd rather be a Luna than a Morris," I said, joking.

As I took in my family's namesake, so beautiful and unreal with its bright orange-red, I could feel your eyes on me. I started to get the feeling this walk was meant for more than just getting me out of my room.

"Daniel, can I ask if everything's all right?"

I turned to you, afraid. "What do you mean?"

"If I'm being honest, dude, you've been super quiet the past few weeks and I don't see you going out much. Just want to make sure you're not feeling upset or something? Sorry if I'm reading the situation wrong, but I couldn't not say anything."

I felt exposed by your candor even as I appreciated it, the way you had thrown me a lifeline. I also was intimidated by your bravery. I didn't understand how someone my own age could so easily reach out to another person.

"You know, my whole life I thought if I could just get out of my small town, I could be happy. Like if I aimed for something as big as the University of Cayuga, then maybe, just maybe, I could show my parents that all their hard work was for something. I spent all of high school working toward this idea, an idea I thrust on myself." I paused. "But what if that isn't true?"

"What do you mean by 'that'?"

"What if aiming for such high places won't end up making me happy? What if none of it matters at the end of the day?"

"I'm not sure I know the answer, Daniel, but I think you seem pretty fucking brilliant."

"Really?"

"Yes, like honestly. I see the books you read, and you're always writing things in your notebooks, and, like, you just seem so aware of what you want."

I started laughing uncontrollably, amazed to hear an impression of me so opposite to how I saw myself.

"You think I know what I want?"

"I mean, kind of. Like you just seem to love words and reading and, like, I think that's awesome. I mean, I sometimes wonder if I'm pursuing pre-med because I want to or because of who my parents are, but here you are, someone who found something of your own. That's just so awesome to me."

"Thanks, Sam. I don't think I've ever thought of myself as someone truly in tune with what he wants, but it's nice to hear all the same."

"Can I ask you something else?"

I downed my cider, unsure what you were about to say, but nodded for you to go ahead.

"You don't want to leave Cayuga, do you?"

"No. Trust me. I think I've just had a rocky few weeks, but honestly, there's nowhere else I would rather be right now."

You smiled before pulling me into the crook of your arm for the manliest of hugs.

"Good, because if you did, I would kick your ass. I'm not having my roomie ditch me five weeks into the school year."

I stayed tucked close to you for a while longer, as we finished off our bottles of cider.

Sitting there that night, under a blood-orange moon, I started to feel a sense of peace. You and Naomi had both noticed me floundering in those waves of great change and, instead of making me feel ashamed, had reached out to help. I was beginning to see help as a form of love, a type of kindness we all deserved. I didn't yet have all the answers to all the questions weighing on my heart, but my mind was less consumed by a fear of not fitting in. It was like Naomi said: this was all just a bit of growing pain. As we sat on that hill, my heart was pulsing from the now-obvious truth of why I wanted to stay at Cayuga. It was not because of ambitions of greatness, or because I needed to prove myself, but because I wasn't ready to leave the company of the man sitting next to me. In that moment, you were unknowingly helping me to make sense of what it means to belong. With the warmth of your body against mine, under the guardianship of our luna de sangre, I couldn't help but feel I was exactly where I was meant to be.

OCTOBER

I have this idea that if I could just get away from here, I might be free. In another city, I imagine there is a version of myself who is a lily floating along a stream, unrooted but blossoming. Birds will come to me and sup on my nectar, they will take what they need and I will gladly give it to them. I will be free. I will float with aimless purpose. I will be happy. I will find him, this other version of myself, and I will learn to be whole.

—D.M.

Come October, the weather started to cool ever so slightly. By this time, halfway through the semester, the college admins had approved my honors program application thanks to Naomi, who remained on her larger mission to improve the experiences of all students of color at Cayuga. Getting into the program offered me a sense of calm I hadn't expected. The tension in my body began to ease as I unfurled into a Daniel who was more present in his life. A Daniel who now understood he was capable and worthy of his place at Cayuga. This sense of belonging carried through from my weekly meeting with Naomi to our dorm room, from the way

I breathed in the autumn air to the songs I listened to on my iPod, underscoring my movements. I was grateful to be alive and looked forward to getting home each day so you could see how positive I was feeling. But something was off one afternoon when I arrived back. Normally, you greeted me with such mirth and enthusiasm. You were never not happy to see me when I walked through the door. But that day, as soon as I entered the dorm, I could feel something was different.

I dropped my backpack on the floor and went to fill a glass of water before joining you. From the safety of the kitchenette, I was able to study your face, which was busy reading something on your laptop. Your forehead was lined with angry furrows, your shoulders heavy with tension. It shocked me how you held none of that lightness I was used to.

"Are you all right?" I asked as I turned off the faucet.

You quickly registered my presence. "Sorry, dude, just dealing with some bullshit stuff right now."

"What's happened?" I said, taking a seat next to you while still keeping some distance between us.

You didn't reply.

I was nervous this silence might be you finally revealing your true self, a self I'd feared: a mean, angry man. I didn't understand how guy friends were meant to be. I wanted to get up from the couch or wait for you to come to me, but I also wanted to be brave enough to reach out then and there, just like you had done for me a few weeks earlier. I was stuck, indecisive, and I think you sensed my unease and so reined in your emotions bit by bit. After a few minutes, you began to speak, explaining how your fall break plans had fallen through because Michael and Josh, two of the guys you were supposed to be going to Boston with, were on academic probation. The two of them were in serious trouble with your soccer coach, and this meant you were now days away from having to spend your first fall break doing fuck all.

"Wow, I'm really sorry. Honestly, that fucking sucks, but how bad can they be doing only two months into their first semester?"

"Our coach is a hard-ass. So anything less than his version of 'passing' means they could be cut mid-season, and they're two of our best midfielders."

Your words meant very little to me, but I suspected, based on the anger and passion with which you spoke, that losing these teammates was not an option. I wanted to help cheer you up by generating ideas for alternative plans, but you brushed each aside: Did you have any family you could visit? Did you have any friends at other schools on the East Coast? Could you fly home to California for a few days? You met each question with the same response, by shaking your head and muttering "Not really" or "No." After a while, I left you to sulk on the couch and went to my room to read. You sent me a text asking if I wanted to go to dinner with you later. This made me laugh. It was good to know you could be moody and hormonal. I wrote back immediately: *Sounds good, lazy ass!*

SAM: *Ha, leave me alone. I'm allowed to be a Debbie Downer every once in a while.*

ME: *You better buck up. I won't have you ruining tonight's fine-dining experience.*

SAM: *Tonight's meatballs stroganoff? Promise to get my act together.*

Two hours later, you came out of your room freshly showered and in a better mood. You were saying something to me as you pulled on a hoodie, your creased abs exposed in the moment. I quickly turned so as not to gawk at you so openly. As you came closer to me, I could smell sandalwood and sage. It was the scent of your favorite bodywash, and even now, if I smell it when passing people on the street, I think of you.

On the walk over to the dining hall I told you about my plans to meet up with Rob and Mona for lunch soon. I had bumped into Rob and his boyfriend earlier in the week, and he'd invited me to grab sushi with them all. I was grateful to have good news to share with you, so you could see I wasn't all alone and had made an effort to connect with people, no longer defaulting to hiding in my room.

It was just as we were joining the line for dinner when you sprang an idea on me. "How about we go camping?"

I was so caught off guard between the dinnertime rush and the surprise, I didn't have a chance to formulate proper thoughts.

"Go camping? Are you crazy? Fall break starts on Wednesday— we don't even have a tent!"

You registered the doubt in my voice and quickly began to share your Google findings. You were so excited, like a child on Christmas morning, as you ran me through how it would all work.

"We can rent camping gear from the rec center on campus. I already asked Josh if we could borrow his Subaru. There are some campgrounds near Seneca Lake, so it will at least feel like we got away even if it's not that far."

I struggled to process how we were going to go from having no plans to sharing a tent in less than thirty-six hours. I'd been at peace with my own staycation plans and now you were offering me an alternative.

"Come on, you don't want to waste your break here," you insisted, blocking me from getting to the drink fountain. "Please, dude. I don't want to just do nothing all week."

I looked at your face and could see how much you wanted me to say yes. I thought back to those difficult weeks in September, my feelings of unsettledness, and how there was now someone who wanted my company, to root himself in my presence. I didn't know what our trip would look like, how we'd fill the many hours alone out there in the forest, but I needed to try, I told myself; I needed to be open to this opportunity. Now it was my turn to do something for you. And so I said yes.

You hugged me so tightly you nearly knocked over my tray. But I didn't mind, because being held by you was everything. It was, I was starting to realize, one step closer to what I really longed for but could not yet say aloud.

Two days later, we pulled up to our campsite just off Seneca Lake. It was less than a forty-five-minute drive from campus, so not an actual road trip, but it was nice to get away all the same. The parking area was oddly quiet, I thought. I wondered whether we'd happen upon any other campers while there. That pervading quietness had the potential to be either relaxing or incredibly boring, and only time would tell which version we'd get.

You parked the car in a stretch of forest surrounded by trees. You told me it was ideal, as it wasn't too far from the showers and toilets but was far enough to not be disturbed by the few other campers. As you breathed in the fresh pine air, you told me how happy you were, and I knew I was happy because of your happiness. As we unloaded the car, we started to take stock of our supplies. We ran through the list of items multiple times until it dawned on us both. "Shit. We forgot the pillows."

I checked and double-checked before finally admitting that even after all our careful, albeit last-minute, planning we had forgotten this one essential item. You brushed it off as a minor annoyance before moving on to pitch the tent. I was hopeless, having never gone camping before in my life, so I started to organize the groceries based on the meals we'd be eating, and then went to fire up the grill for lunch. I heard you calling from behind me.

"Want a beer? Should be cold by now."

I walked over to the ice chest to get out two bottles. In front of me were tall maple and oak trees still very much full with leaves. All around us summer was clinging on, fighting off any October chill. It reminded me of back home but was much lusher. From my small town, I had views of the snowcapped Sierra Nevadas with their towering cedar and pine trees, but always from a distance.

I was used to long stretches of dry fields of golden grass coupled with occasional walnut and almond groves. I didn't know nature could be so green. I didn't know autumn could feel so alive.

"How's the tent coming along?"

"Your palace awaits you, my lord," you said, smiling at your quick handiwork.

It was cozier than I'd anticipated. You might remember how our sleeping bags were basically on top of one another. In the corner you'd placed two pillows fashioned from spare hoodies and random towels found in the trunk of Josh's car. I doubted they'd been washed, but I was touched all the same by your ingenuity. We both sat down with our beers to take in our new temporary home, with the forest as our front and back yard. When you plopped down next to me, your legs were almost sticking out of the tent. We laughed together for a good while before returning to silent contemplation, until you asked, "Do you like being the big spoon or the little spoon?"

There was only an ounce of jest in your voice, and I was paralyzed with fear, not knowing how to respond. I didn't know if it was a trap. Again, I think the anger you'd possessed earlier in the week caused me to behave more cautiously around you. But you simply sat there smiling and watching me as I took too big a sip of beer and choked a little. I struggled to catch my breath. All the while I felt your eyes on me, waiting for a response, waiting for me to make the joke all right.

"Not sure," I finally mustered.

"We'll just have to see then," you said, not missing a beat. "Got to take a leak. Be back soon."

And just like that you were up and out of the tent, leaving me to finish my not-quite-chilled beer, pondering whether I was in fact the little spoon in our friendship. You took awhile to return, so I got up to start on lunch. While prepping things, I couldn't help but replay what had just taken place, turning each word over like an archaeologist examining his dig site. What had prompted this question? Did you ask other friends these kinds of things? You arrived just as I was flipping the hot dogs one final time, saving me from my overthinking. You propped our camping chairs in front of a little stream, and we ate the hot dogs along with half a jumbo packet of cheese puffs. By the end, we were both orange messes and had to wash ourselves in the icy-cold water. Feeling the chill on my hands was exhilarating. The water ran crystal clear, and you told me it was because it was so fresh from the underground springs feeding Seneca Lake.

"Should we go exploring?"

"There's a gorge trail we can follow. Might be nice for photos," I offered.

"Engagement shot?"

"Something like that, Sam," I said, rolling my eyes.

You squeezed my shoulder and went to lock up our stuff in the tent while I filled our water bottles and packed granola bars for the road. Everything was rich with cinematic color and overwhelmed each of my senses: The air sweet with trees full of foliage and moss. The sound of the waterfalls flowing alongside us. The green leaves holding on from an unseasonably warm fall. I stopped every few minutes to take photos. You were patient with me even though I know you wanted to get to the waterfall at the end of the trail. In the viewfinder of my camera, the light hit the rock formations in brilliant ways, bouncing off the white-gray of the stones. I asked you to pose next to a boulder and you obliged, mimicking a young Arnold Schwarzenegger, biceps bulging. You, as tall and powerful as a tree.

"Do you want a photo?"

"Sure, I guess," I said coolly, while joy was screaming inside of me.

You took a photo of us together, and then told me to pose by myself. I felt strangely shy in front of you. But I let you direct me.

You asked me to extend my arms as wide as possible, trying to capture just how big the gorge is.

"You look good," you said while scrolling through the photos. "Your smile makes you look very happy."

I was happy, and now, looking back, I am grateful I have these memories of you, that I can remember it all with such vividness. Wherever you are, are you remembering it the same way? How the birds flew overhead, weaving from branch to branch, following us as we hiked up the path. How the squirrels scaled trees, chasing one another. Everything had its purpose and understood its seasonality and temporality in that place. Just like us.

We made it halfway along the trail and happened upon the majestic Rainbow Falls. There was no one else around, so you ran up and down beside the rushing water, screaming at the top of your lungs as the mist from the falls sprayed you. I snapped photo after photo of you, laughing all the while from your infectious elation. You eventually tired yourself out and walked over to me. To my surprise, you grabbed my hand and placed two quarters inside it, whispering softly for me to make a wish.

I held the quarters in my palm. I was overcome then, as I was each time you touched me in those first few months, by a sensation of newness. It was like meeting myself for the first time, a person whose body could both give and receive affection with people beyond family. I was starting to see myself as someone who might want to hold other men's hands, kiss their lips, even learn how to move together, as one connected body. And even if I hadn't yet found someone to do any of that with, I was beginning not to hate myself for wanting those things. Looking back, I think it was because my body finally felt at peace. In the safety of those green woods, I was learning to be okay.

As I walked closer to the rushing waters, light poured in through the roof above us, made from an overhanging rock and the canopy of trees. I closed my eyes at the stinging brightness and turned around, so my back was to the waterfall. I took your request seriously and thought about everything I could wish for in that moment, everything I might have wanted to come true. I counted, "One, two, three," before tossing the coins over my shoulder, and continued to keep my eyes shut, choosing to listen to the sound of their metal hitting rock face. The clanking was swiftly drowned out by flowing water, and, deep down, I knew that what I wanted would come to fruition eventually. In the midst of all the natural beauty, God was telling me that what I wanted and what I needed would collide into each other when the time was right.

Later that evening, we sat around a fire polishing off a twelve-pack of beer, and you had the idea to make after-dinner s'mores. The sky was a dark purple, which allowed the stars to shine brightly; you were glowing red-orange. As you roasted the marsh-mallows and I assembled the graham crackers and chocolate, we discussed our favorite things from the hike.

"The waterfall was incredible."

"I know. Every time the spray blew in the wind, I could see dozens of tiny rainbows."

"Kind of makes you wonder if that's how Rainbow Falls got its name," you joked.

I rolled my eyes before continuing. "I just kept thinking all day how green it is compared to back home."

"It reminds me a lot of Yosemite, where I went camping all the time with my parents."

"I've never been."

"You're from California and you've never been to Yosemite?"

"That's what I said," I told him, biting into my s'more.

The truth is, I was in awe of how much of California you had seen. Our home state is so big and beautiful, but growing up I never got to explore much of it. We didn't have that kind of money, which meant my version of the state was much smaller and more intimate. Sitting there listening to you, I drank in every description.

"What's it like?"

"The redwoods are amazing, Daniel—like, these ancient trees are as tall as a thirty-something-story building. So tall you can't see the top when you're staring straight up from the bottom of the trunk."

"I'd love to stand under a sequoia one day."

"We can go together. I'll take you to the coast as well and we can surf."

"I don't want to get eaten by a shark."

"I promise you won't, but honestly, Daniel, there is something so awe inspiring about riding a wave before it crashes back into the ocean. It is like the closest you'll ever get to walking on water."

"I just have so much of this country to see. I really hope I get to someday. I mean, look at the sky right now, all these stars. I've never been anywhere like here."

"Do you know any of the constellations?"

"Aside from the Big and Little Dippers, I'm clueless," I admitted.

"I'll teach you. Let's start with Orion, he's best for finding others. Do you see that one up there . . . it looks a bit like an hourglass?"

"Hourglass, hourglass, okay, yes, I see him. It kind of looks like some funny little dress."

"Sometimes you can see him holding an arch, depending on the light."

"Orion, the huntsman. I remember him from the *Odyssey* in tenth-grade English."

And you continued to name others for me: Aquarius, the water bearer; Hercules, the mighty hero; Aquila, the eagle, which I told you was similar in Spanish (el águila). This naming intrigued you: the origins of words, how they could be mapped to ancient civilizations, used as evidence of different cultures colliding throughout time. You then showed me Pegasus and, as you explained its myth,

I dreamt of flying on horseback into the autumn night. I imagined myself flying far away, stopping off to check on my family in California, before going somewhere even further just to see how my body would feel. You'd just pointed out Delphinus, the dolphin, when I asked you where you learned all these names for stars.

"Fifth-grade summer camp."

"Where was it? In ancient Greece?"

"Very funny. I'll have you know, Daniel, that growing up I wasn't always cool."

"Samuel Morris not cool?"

"Actually, for a lot of my life I was kind of a giant dork with bad acne."

I couldn't imagine you as anything but the person before me. You always walked in a certain way, taking up space with such ease. How you interacted with strangers on campus, or staff in the dining hall, came naturally. You knew how to talk to people. How to make others feel seen. But I did not say any of these things to you at the time because I was afraid that knowing how I saw you might scare you. Or worse, that it would cause our friendship to fade to black.

"And what were you like in high school?"

"Umm, a chubby dork with bad acne?!"

You smiled at me. "But, like, what were you into?"

"Hmm . . . books and writing. I was pretty precocious. Like, senior year I was both the editor for our school paper and president of the speech and debate team."

"Did you always know you wanted to be a writer?" you asked, between sips of tepid lager.

"I think from a very young age, yes. Whenever we had library time in elementary school, I just loved exploring the shelves and reading all the different names on the spines. I'd search for names like mine, or at least names that sounded different, not white. Something about the library felt like a possibility."

"It's incredible you've known what you want for so long."

"It's one thing to want something, it's another thing for it to happen."

"Well, I have high hopes for you."

I took another sip of my beer, wrestling with these ambitions of mine, both for the future and for the man in front of me. I wanted us to stay in this moment for as long as possible, in the safety of the trees surrounding us.

"What were your parents like growing up?"

This question caught me off guard.

"Umm . . . well, they were both incredibly loving and supportive. They have always wanted me to be happy, like they never forced me to do anything I did not want to do. They always left it for me to decide. Does that make sense?"

You nodded, inviting me to share more. "I think they left México wanting a bit of a do-over, and part of that meant raising a son who could do whatever he wanted."

"What do you mean?"

"Well, I was named after my uncle, my mom's older brother, but he died when he was like our age, I think. So, for them, they just wanted to raise a Daniel who was able to live a long and happy life."

"What is it like to be named after someone you never met?"

"Honestly, so weird. I mean no one talked much about him, but I know I look a lot like him, which is strange, almost like some kind of predestined fate. But I also know his death really broke my family and so I've always felt as if, between our shared likeness and name, I am a kind of . . . how do I even say this . . . a reminder of sadness?"

"Fuck, man, that's really heavy."

Your face was so kind, and I could tell you were speaking with care and sympathy. The truth was that it was heavy all throughout my childhood, because at the back of my mind, I felt like it was my responsibility to bring my mom and grandparents happiness and peace. To give them a version of Daniel who wouldn't bring about pain.

"Growing up, no one talked about him, but I know Tío Daniel was smart. My abuela always told me that: 'Eres muy listo, Daniel, como tu tío.' Maybe me coming here to Cayuga was some form of familial redemption, or, I dunno, maybe it was just because my parents have always celebrated my goals and never pushed me into things. So my love of learning came naturally and was not forced on me, which seems a novel approach to parenting, like, especially for immigrants, you know?"

"I am glad you found your way to Cayuga, or else we'd never have met." Raising your beer, you made the first of many toasts that took place that evening. "Go you for being so naturally smart!"

I stood up and took a bow as you clapped proudly. You then shook your bottle of beer, then mine. Both were empty. The whole time I had been counting the empty ones at your feet. Part of me was afraid that the less sober I was around you, the less I'd be able to control my feelings. That I'd slip and say something I couldn't easily take back.

"Let's open the tequila," you declared, a bit too loudly. "To celebrate your academic prowess and raise a toast to your namesake."

Against my better judgment, I agreed. I wanted nothing more than to make you happy. As you poured the tequila, I cut the limes using your knife. The sharp blade felt dangerous in my hands, and I forced myself to concentrate so as not to dismember my own thumb. You asked for the instructions because you wanted to do what was culturally appropriate. So I guided you: lick the salt, shoot the shot, bite the lime. "¡Arriba, abajo, al centro, pa' dentro!"

White-silvery agave pulsed through my veins and burned behind my eyes. We bit the lime. You poured another, and night began to stretch further into morning. After the fourth shot, I cut us off. My head was spinning in all directions and stomach bile was slowly creeping its way toward my mouth. I stepped away from the fire to get some fresh air. It was cold away from the flames' warmth, but majestic. As I looked up, I wondered whether my parents were watching the same moon as me, three time zones away from us. I longed to know what shade of dark their sky was, if it was shining romantic for them. I wanted to ask if they missed me, if they could explain what it was like to fall in love? All these questions felt important in that moment. All of it felt as unknowable as where words came from, why stars were given their names, how two friends could learn to be more.

Suddenly I had to pee but was too afraid to walk in the dark to the communal toilets. I scurried over behind a tree just out of the fire's reach and released a steady stream. The entire time, you continued rambling some nonsense about wanting to be a wolf. You tried explaining how you liked the idea of spending your whole life with a single mate, working together to hunt for food, protecting your pack. The beer was clouding my brain and I could not be certain whether you were trying to tell me something deep or just talking shit. By the time I returned, the temperature had dropped dramatically, and you saw me shivering so you took off your hoodie. I tried protesting, but you kept shaking it at me.

"You'll freeze, you idiot," I said.

"No, man, I have that nice booze blanket now," you insisted.

"Are you sure?"

You nodded as you opened your last beer of the night. I once again counted all the discarded bottles at your feet, but you chose to ignore me as my eyes darted between them. Your hoodie was too big for me, so when I wrapped myself in it, I was enveloped in extra fabric. Your scent coupled with the campfire sank into my skin, and I allowed myself to envisage you holding me instead of the cotton. We opened a packet of pretzels and began to wolf them down in an attempt to soak up all the booze.

"That's a funny phrase, isn't it?" I asked.

"What is?"

"To 'wolf down' food."

"Hey, I want to be a wolf," you said, sweetly, but clearly very drunk.

"I know, idiot, that's why I'm bringing it up!"

"Did I tell you that?"

"Yes, Sam."

"Fuck, I think I'm drunk."

"A drunk wolf."

We laughed uncontrollably as we both struggled to say the word "wolf." The laughter made my stomach hurt and I spit pretzels all over the place. You were laughing so much you started crying. You asked me to stop making you laugh, afraid you'd piss yourself, but I wasn't doing anything but laughing, so you got dangerously close. Everything sounded a stupid type of funny and I began to have trouble breathing. From out of nowhere, we swore we heard a howl calling back to us. But then we wondered whether we'd just heard ourselves. You got up and poured another round of shots, begging me to help mark the night's end: one more to celebrate our first trip together. Another to commemorate our friendship. All these requests you made with such urgent sincerity, and I obliged even though I knew it was a bad idea because, again, I wanted nothing more than to make you happy.

"¡Arriba, abajo, al centro, pa' dentro!"

"¡Arriba, abajo, al centro, pa' dentro!"

"¡Arriba, abajo, al centro, pa' dentro!"

I let it go on too long, unable to say "Enough, Sam" in either of my languages, and felt the agave burn my mouth, a form of penance, while we awaited the morning sun as the fire burned out in front of us. Slowly, everything began to grow hazy and black. When we awoke the next morning, you were stripped down to your boxers and a T-shirt. It was freezing cold, and you had pressed up against me, your long arms wrapped around my smaller frame. We had not managed to get into our separate sleeping bags. I turned to greet you, but you were completely passed out, and it was then that I noticed your massive morning wood piercing my ass. That's when the dread kicked in. I didn't remember how we'd ended up as big and little spoon. I couldn't recall what I'd said after all those shots, all your loving toasts, but I knew I liked the feeling of you hard against me, even if I was scared shitless I had done something to lead you on.

Nothing happened, I kept telling myself, running through our movements when we'd fallen into the tent, heavily inebriated, at three in the morning. My head was pounding, and I felt a lurch in my stomach, so I got up as quickly as possible to run to the restrooms. I forced a stall door open just in time, expelling the last twenty-four hours into the toilet. It took three flushes to get everything down. I waited a minute, then slowly shuffled to the sink and doused my head in ice-cold water. In the mirror, I took a hard look at myself. I looked like shit and I felt like shit and all around me the restrooms smelled of shit. All this shit was a perfect manifestation of the chaos I felt swooping in, unsure whether I'd done something to encourage this bacchanalian ending.

I arrived back at our camp area to find coffee on the stove. You had a small pot going for what would be instant oatmeal "pimped out" with fresh apples, raisins, and peanut butter. You assured me it would help with the hangover as you poured me a cup of coffee and greeted me good morning. Nothing about your mannerisms made it seem like you were plagued by the same fear I was.

"Did you sleep well?" I asked, trying to tease out any clues as to how you were feeling.

"I was out like a fucking log. Those pillows weren't half bad, were they?"

"Worked like a charm. Who doesn't love a pillow suspiciously doubling as a towel and/or clothing item?"

I was stunned by your lack of acknowledgment of the spoon-ing, the morning wood, the copious amount of alcohol running through our systems. Were you unaware of what had happened? Or were you instead trying to protect me—us—from dealing with it? All I could think about was your arm wrapped around me, your erect dick pressed against me, how big it felt, how I wanted to feel it even more inside my hand, my mouth, inside me. In my mind, everything was muddled confusion and self-doubt, and I knew I was getting way ahead of myself. I talked myself down from these lustful thoughts by saying you hadn't meant to fall asleep like that. You hadn't been coming on to me. But even as I thought these things, I couldn't quite be sure.

The pot started bubbling over and you saved the oatmeal just in time. I savored my first mouthful, and it was everything my stomach needed. I was more cautious with the coffee, afraid the caffeine would not agree with me. You asked me what I wanted to do with the day. You had done some research, you said, and Watkins Glen was supposed to be a nice little town to explore. I agreed, not having the brain space to think of an alternative, and within a half hour we were dressed and ready to go.

In the car, we kept the talking to a minimum and instead put some country station on low. Neither of us was quite recovered enough for loud music, and thankfully the drive was short. The streets were eerily quiet so early on a Thursday morning. Seneca Lake in the distance was placid under the almost-cloudless blue sky.

We got out of the car and walked to the harbor to get some fresh air. Dotted along the pier were pristinely white speedboats and sailboats gleaming under the morning sun. The boats bobbed in the gentle, undulating waves of the lake, and as we drew closer to them we were greeted by several old men, each polishing their respective boats' steel and glass. They wore outlet Brooks Brothers polos, JCPenney boat shoes, and looked like they could be sec-ond cousins of your dad's. You made small talk with them before we wandered further along the banks of Seneca Lake, eventually settling on a bench to take in the never-ending horizon. All the while I studied you for any signs of what had happened the night before. I was hoping, I think, that I'd catch the moment things registered for you, the moment you fully remembered, the moment you would take on some of the crippling fear I was holding on to. The moment I'd stop feeling so alone.

Your face only looked tired.

"We'll have to come back when it's warmer and go swimming," you said.

"That'd be nice."

"It looks like it would be so fucking cold."

As you spoke, I was thinking of you holding me like you were the big spoon. But instead of that cramped tent, I pictured a warm bed, both of our bodies naked. In this version, I would hear your breath against my ear, feel your heart beating against my bony spine. I tried to imagine a moment when I might be brave enough to turn my body around and say to you all I held within. But all I could manage to suggest was that we keep walking along the lakefront, and so we did.

We spent the next hour or so walking up and down the bank of the lake. We then treated ourselves to a second breakfast of Dunkin' Donuts. Over iced coffees and breakfast sandwiches, we came to a mutual agreement not to drink as much that night. But even as we made those promises, we knew deep down we would not keep them. Instead, around a second fire, on an even chillier night, we already knew that we would finish the tequila. We would then sleep poorly before deciding to return back to campus a day early, having run out of things to do. Driving home without speaking, again listening to that country radio station on low, we would not address how, for a second night in a row, you'd slept with your arms wrapped around me tightly, your breath a lullaby underscoring the night. All the questions I was too afraid to ask would be left behind until I was ready to face them. One day, I knew, we'd have to confront what had started around the fire, acknowledge how we first learned what burning desire felt like. We'd have to reckon with a flame that would eventually consume us, bringing with it all the light and pain to follow.

But on that day, we would simply continue walking toward a future we didn't understand.

NOVEMBER

It is getting colder, which means the year is almost at its end. Winter is drawing near, and this desert city will begin to frost over, thus ending my ability to walk alone for miles on end (at least for a little while). After Christmas, I won't have much left of school and I've no idea what's next. What am I doing with my life? What do I want to do? I feel I should know these answers, but I don't. It's pathetic not to feel called to anything. All I know is I want to be free. Freedom equals happiness. So I guess, more than anything, I want to be happy wherever happiness might thrive.

—D.M.

Early yesterday morning, I was looking at a small red album your mom gave me, full of photos of you throughout your life. It's amazing to see you at different ages, photos from places and times that precede our friendship. You were right: you were an awkward, gangly teenager. But even then, I know I would have found you beautiful, would have happily basked in your company given the chance. As I flicked through each page, I couldn't help but wish

I'd met you earlier, so our story together might have been just a little bit longer.

Your mom wrote a short letter that she tucked behind the front cover, wishing me well and telling me to keep in touch. She ended the letter by asking where I think your soul will go to pass the time as you wait for us. The question stunned me when I read it, and I have been thinking about it ever since.

In the final weeks of our first semester, I was uncertain of how to deal with what had taken place in that forest. I dreamt of you almost every night after our trip, as you yourself slept not far from me. I imagined your arms wrapped around me, the hardness of you digging into the soft of my back. Everything had felt too intimate to be unintentional, and yet I was left to wonder if it had even happened.

I was committed, at that time, to not falling into my usual bad habits of retreating or ignoring my feelings, so I dug deep into myself and made it my mission to get us back out of our dorm again. In my head, I thought that being in public spaces together would make it easier to understand how you and I worked. There was also the fact that having outside witnesses to our dynamic would allow me to seek their opinions. Really, I just wanted someone to tell me: "Daniel, you're totally right about Sam," or "You are deluded. He's simply a nice guy. Please move on now!"

Time was against me. Thanksgiving break wasn't far off, during which you'd be going home to California while Rob and I would be the third and fourth wheels at Mona's family holiday. I knew I needed to do something, but I was clueless about where to start. Thankfully, I'd soon meet someone who would point me in the right direction.

I had been invited by Mona to a party downtown, hosted by a grad student she was dating on and off. On the night of the party, I planned to attend with Rob, his boyfriend Shane, and Shane's best friend, Jeannette. Shane and Jeannette were going in a joint costume no one was allowed to know anything about, and so they got ready together at her place. Rob had made it clear to everyone he thought costumes were stupid, but Shane had pushed us to at least dress up as something, and we'd settled on hippies. It was while getting ready at Rob's that I began to share a bit more about you. We were raiding Rob's closet, searching for anything that might save us from having to spend money on actual costumes. Thankfully, he had lots of vintage clothes to choose from.

"So," Rob asked, taking off one shirt for another, "how was your staycation? Did you do the one hundred and one things Mona texted you?"

"Oh, it was really, really good. I ended up going away."

"What? Where to and why didn't you tell me?"

He stood there half-dressed, mouth agape, his happy trail an invite I was trying to ignore.

"Put a shirt on, weirdo, and I'll explain," I said, rifling through bandannas and silk scarves.

Trying desperately not to sneak glances at Rob (why did all my guy friends have impossibly toned stomachs?), I focused on the paisley pattern of a golden scarf. Once dressed, he began to mix us drinks as I explained what had taken place over fall break: Sam's canceled trip to Boston, the last-minute decision to go camping, our hike along Rainbow Falls, and the nightly spooning. As I spoke, I suddenly had the feeling that Rob was my priest, and this was my Lenten confession.

"Well." Rob paused. "How do you feel about it all?"

"I know part of me liked it, but I also don't know if it was all accidental." I took a sip of the drink Rob had given me, a whiskey and Coke. "I mean, we drank a lot of alcohol, and it was also cold, you know?"

Rob took a long sip of his own whiskey and Coke before responding. "I don't know, Daniel. It's one thing to happen, like, once, but the fact that it happened two nights in a row seems pretty fucking purposeful. I mean, it was Sam who was doing the spooning, right?"

"What do you mean?" I was unsure why it mattered.

"Was he holding you or were you holding him?"

"He was holding me . . . but I mean, he could have been cold, or thought I was a pillow, or just liked feeling safe."

"Daniel de La Luna . . . my sweet, naïve little cherub. You still have so much to learn about the ways of men."

I sipped at my drink, then paused so Rob could adjust the details of my costume. As he fixed my hair into a part and tied a bandanna around my head, he explained to me all the reasons why what had happened must've been you trying to open the door to us becoming something more. I sat there listening to him recount the different ways in which he'd tried to make moves on guy friends in the early days of navigating his sexuality. Again, my inexperience was so evident. In the end, I decided, although his stories did sound similar to what had taken place between us, it felt like I was being led down a dangerous path of hope and naïve speculation in allowing them to convince me that your actions had been intentional. Of course, it was exciting to hear Rob's theories, but I needed something more concrete before even beginning to think about confronting you or admitting my feelings. Somehow, I'd need to find a way to ask you about what had happened, and about the few weeks since. But I still didn't know what that looked like, and I didn't know how it might alter our friendship for better or worse.

Once finished with our drinks, we made our way to Shane's dorm, where we met him and Jeannette. I was surprised to find them dressed up as Jessie and James from Team Rocket of Pokémon fame, but with gender-swapped roles. Shane was stunning in his black thigh-high boots and silver-sequined costume. Rob looked delighted to have such sexy arm candy to walk into the party with, while I felt really lame seeing them, frustrated by the lack of effort we had made with our costumes. In all honesty, I looked like one half of a Dollar General version of Cheech & Chong. And more deeply, seeing Shane so easily subvert gender roles and stride in his costume began to unsettle part of me. I felt boring, straight-edged, obviously uncomfortable with my sexuality. Our first semester was slipping through my fingers. I still hadn't made much of a dent in my mission to discover myself, to embrace my new position in life as a student at one of the best colleges in the country. What if I'd never be exciting, edgy, or accomplished? What if this Daniel was the only version I'd ever be? These depressing thoughts hung over me on the long walk off campus to Mona's party.

"If you'd told me about your costume, I'd have offered to dress up as Meowth," Rob said.

"Thanks, babe, but this is a two-person kind of thing," Shane said. He planted a kiss on Rob's cheek. "Do you like it, though?"

"It's very sexy. I never thought I'd be into Jessie. Always had a crush on Brock back in the day."

"What about you, Daniel? Who were you into?" Shane asked me.

"Professor Oak," I said, trying to be wittier than I was.

"Silver daddies—I like your style."

We arrived at the most beautiful house I'd been inside since coming to Ithaca. Mona answered the door eagerly before ushering us into the foyer, and as we hung up our coats, I began to realize how rising in the ranks of academia meant having more space, nicer living arrangements. The artwork lining the hallway looked expensive, not like the stupid posters one buys at a back-to-school fair. We could smell freshly baked snickerdoodles wafting toward us, and hear the sound of excited voices gathered in deep intellectual conversation. Mona took us into the living room, where she introduced us to Kelis, her lover and one of the house's four occupants. We were the only undergraduates in attendance, but most of the guests had at least dressed up. When I say "dressed up," I should point out that it was a party full of master's and doctoral students from the philosophy department, so many of the costumes were lost on me. I went with Mona to grab drinks for everyone and was introduced to a Nietzsche, a Sigmund Freud, and none other than Judith Butler. I was unsure who Kelis was supposed to be, but luckily Jeannette asked her to explain her costume for the less learned among us.

"Frantz Fanon. I'm doing my dissertation on him."

"He was a political philosopher from the French West Indies," Mona added. "Kelis had us read part of *The Wretched of the Earth* in her seminar 'The Philosophy of Activism.'"

Kelis smiled before continuing, "You should all read him sometime if you haven't. It's important we begin to amplify BIPOC voices in the curriculum here. Enough with the classics being so male, stale, and pale."

"Preach, honey," Shane said, snapping his shellacked nails.

"So, you're like, Mona's teacher, and you're dating?" asked Rob.

I elbowed him immediately, mortified by his crassness.

"Seminar instructor, more like," Kelis responded with cold calmness.

"That must make things so interesting."

"We're very good about not distracting from the educational environment, right, Mona?"

"Yes. When Kelis is in teaching mode, I'm simply another student."

"How mature of our Mona. We are so happy to hear."

"Thanks, Robert. It really is great, isn't it?"

The conversation sort of petered out naturally after that. Rob was quite pleased with himself, but I felt awkward. I stood there munching on pretzels, unsure what to do, but fortunately someone called Kelis over. We let her and Mona return to the fold of their fellow philosophers as Rob and I moved toward one of the couches. We left Shane and Jeannette, who were discussing queer theory with some Italian postdoc student as part of a lengthy explanation of their costume. I nursed my beer while Rob went on trying to identify the other philosophy cosplayers, who were all beyond my point of reference. Suddenly, a man dressed in a white tunic and outlandish hat sat down next to us.

"Sister Bertrille, so very nice to meet you gentlemen."

"Sorry, who are you?" I asked, unsure whether I'd heard correctly.

"Sister Bertrille of the Convent San Tanco of San Juan, Puerto Rico."

I did not know if this person was being funny or microaggressive. Did they think I was Puerto Rican? I turned to Rob for help, but he looked equally confused.

"Do either of you follow the ways of Our Lord Jesus Christ?"

"Sorry, bud, but are you fucking with us or something?" Rob asked, a bit too much machismo in his voice. "Because we're just trying to enjoy ourselves, all right?"

"Jesus, and here I thought I had two Marys to jibe with. Millennials, am I right?"

I watched on with continued confusion, unsure whether I was drunk, having a stroke, or something else entirely. Why was there an escaped nun at this party?

"You've never heard of *The Flying Nun*? Only one of Sally Field's most beloved television roles. Ringing any bells? No! Girls . . . girls, please tell me you will go home immediately and watch it. You must."

"Oh, is that who you are dressed up as?" I asked, trying to be friendly.

"Yes, cutie." The nun smiled. "My name is Bernie, but my friends call me Bernice. Are you students at Cayuga?"

"We are. I am Rob and this is Daniel. We just started."

"Dear Madonna, *The Immaculate Collection*, and all her homosexual apostles! You're babies. Don't tell me you're fucking freshmen?" Bernie-Bernice asked this question way too loudly. "Ladies and gentlequeers, who said fresh meat was allowed?"

We nodded nervously, which only further encouraged Bernie-Bernice. He decided to take Rob and me under his little wings, and before I could fully understand what was happening I found myself being swept into a group of queer elders (now, when I say "elders," I mean people who were only five to ten years our senior). Bernie-Bernice introduced us as "Timid Daniel" and "Manly Masc Rob," which made me laugh but rubbed Rob the wrong way. He asked if Rob and I were dating and we both fumbled our replies, too anxious to properly explain. Luckily, Shane slinked his way over just then and draped himself on top of Rob, planting a very theatrical kiss on Rob's cheek.

"Interesting," Bernie-Bernice tutted, to which his band of merry queers agreed.

"What's interesting?" I asked.

"I just thought you two were an item. If not, then whom, my little chickadee?"

"Well, Bernie-Bernice, if you must know, I haven't formally come out."

Bernie-Bernice pulled me close to his bosom and began stroking my head like some lost lamb of Christ. Shane was obviously not enjoying the attention I was receiving, nor the insinuation that Rob and I looked like we belonged together, so he dragged Rob outside for a cigarette—but not before calling Bernie-Bernice's costume "basic." The nun slyly flipped off the young twink before returning to the matter at hand: the "whom" in my life. I explained who you were, how I felt, and what had taken place only a few weeks prior. It felt safe, telling this costumed stranger the inner workings of my heart. I knew that he had no clue who you were, and therefore wouldn't be able to share with you how I was feeling. I was also desperate to get advice from an older gay man. Bernie-Bernice listened attentively, and I could tell he was doing his best to really understand the situation. Like Rob, it turned out, he didn't believe in accidents or coincidence. But he was also very influenced by his understanding of sexual fluidity, and so didn't want to get caught up in labels.

"My little baby queer, it does not matter if this boy is gay, bi, or just curious. You said yourself you're not 'out-out.' My advice would be to create an opportunity in which you can talk about sexuality with him without pushing an agenda. Get my drift?"

"Not really . . ."

"Take this Sam somewhere where you'll be among other friends of Dorothy and ask him his thoughts."

"Like a gay bar?"

"That might be a step too far—and you're, like, eighteen—but maybe some place where the queers will be at. Do you understand?"

I nodded enthusiastically. It had finally dawned on me what must be done to create the opportunity we needed.

I spent the rest of the evening speaking with Bernie-Bernice and his merry band of older gays. As I listened to their conversations about the trials and tribulations of dating, I felt a sense of calm, as if this group of men were proof of what awaited me if only I could cross the threshold from understanding my sexuality to actually living it. I was mesmerized by their intimate stories of dating apps, hookups, monogamy, and open relationships. At that tender age of eighteen, all I wanted was a first kiss. Of course, I was a hot-blooded male and also longed for much more, but I knew the first kiss was the catalyst that would lead to all those other things. It was clear to me now that if I wanted to get there, I would need to create my inroad, need to heed Bernie-Bernice's advice. I needed us to actually talk!

This is how, a few weeks later, we ended up at Shane's cabaret night with Rob and Mona. In some small way, it was actually you who pushed for our attendance. You see, it was the week prior to Thanksgiving break and you wanted to hang out before we parted ways. I told you I had been invited to Shane's gig and you asked if you could come along. I was very clear about what the evening would entail and still you were keen to attend; you said you wanted to finally meet my elusive group of friends. I did reiterate that the event included a fundraiser for Planned Parenthood and that it had been described to me as queer, intersectional, and feminist.

You simply said, "Sounds cool. Can't wait to see some *radical* spoken word."

To my mind, this would be an opportunity to see you interact with people who were not into sports, NCAA division rankings, or keeping fit at the gym. It would also be a test of how comfortable I was sharing you with the wider world, but even more so an opportunity to gauge what my friends thought of you. Were you a worthy paramour? Or someone who I was stupidly pining after?

We headed out on a Saturday night after a dinner of delivery pizza, your treat. "Word of warning," I said. "I have no idea what kind of stuff people will be performing tonight."

"No worries, man. I'm just glad to be doing something that doesn't involve babysitting my teammates around a keg. My parents will no doubt appreciate me doing something cultured for once."

"Well, just so you know, we are going equally into the unknown."

"It's cool, Daniel. I'm not some caveman, okay? I can do all sorts of things beyond hanging with frat bros."

"Sorry, I wasn't insinuating anything . . ."

"Don't worry about it," you said curtly. "You're not the first person to box me in like that."

"Honestly, I didn't mean to . . ."

"I'm only kidding, dude. Come on!"

I was afraid I had really upset you, but you simply brushed it off in your jokey manner and pointed out that we had arrived at Frost Hall, so I let it go and entered the venue. You paid the donation entry at the door and made small talk with the volunteers, who were visibly perplexed by your presence. Everywhere you went, you captured people's attention. I felt proud being in your company, walking beside you. We made our way to Rob and Mona, who'd saved us seats near the front. I introduced you all to each other and Mona stood up to give you a hug. She was being overly familiar, and I feared she might let slip how much I spoke about you. Rob played it cool with a manly handshake, but you went in for the handshake/bro-hug combo, and Rob took the moment with you out of view to mouth how hot you were. Mona nodded in enthusiastic agreement. I was over the moon, even though you were just my roommate and friend. But it was true: you were brutally attractive, and I loved that my friends thought so too. I loved that you were mine and not theirs, and that I was right there beside you, out in the open.

During the fifteen minutes or so before the curtain went up, Mona asked you a million and one questions about your degree: Did you know where you wanted to go for medical school? What you'd specialize in there? And what about after that? She then started discussing an older cousin of hers who'd volunteered with Doctors Without Borders before she segued into white saviorism. You were polite and nodded along as she continually talked over you. Meanwhile, Rob and I went to grab drinks from the snack bar. As we waited in line, he asked me if I'd had a chance to confront you about our trip. I told him I hadn't because I was afraid of crossing a line, although I didn't totally understand what crossing said line would involve. It was true that I couldn't stop thinking about what it had been like to have you pressed up against me. That I wanted it to happen again, but soberly, in the quiet safety of our dorm room. But it was also true that I was afraid of ruining our friendship by wanting too much—and, trust me, I wanted so much more.

Just then the house lights dimmed as we were bathed in an electric azure from the lights on the stage. Rob and I quickly returned with our sodas. That sea of blue made it look like we, the audience, were also part of the performance, which only heightened the already excited mood. We were eagerly waiting for the proceedings to start when the clickety-clack of heels announced

Shane's arrival. He looked incredible, made for the spotlight, dressed in a smart business suit paired with black patent-leather stilettos. His makeup was an homage to the emcee in *Cabaret*, and on his lapel he wore a giant badge that read *F*ck Misogyny!* The audience erupted in applause before he uttered a single word.

In my periphery, I watched you and Rob take in Shane in all his glory. I saw before me someone who so confidently moved in his own body, unafraid of leaning into his femininity and unwilling to let society snuff out his colorful flame. I then looked to Rob, who knew he liked men, who unabashedly enjoyed sex and would never compromise his desire, his hunger for the male body. Then there was you, this person who unknowingly held so much of my affection, who was too beautiful for me, too gregarious, too perfect. Finally, there was me, Daniel—someone so stuck in his head, so afraid of the world; a man who had made a laundry list of promises to be better, live more boldly, but had never done a fucking thing to keep those promises.

Suddenly, out of nowhere, I felt the air escape me, slowly suffocating my body. I couldn't explain what was happening, but it felt bad. You just kept smiling and grinning at what Shane was saying: "Okay, ladies, boys, and gentlepeople, are you ready for a night of some sexy, tongue-in-cheek political art? Are you ready to help raise vital funds for our local Planned Parenthood and shout back at backward bigots trying to make life harder for those who need services like reproductive health screenings and access to judgment-free abortions? I can't hear you . . . Are you ready?" As my chest tightened, my mind melted into a vortex of calendar pages, ticking clocks, and deadlines, all reminding me that time was passing me by and reinforcing the ways in which my passivity was robbing me of real joy. At eighteen, what had I really experienced? I'd never kissed anyone. Never had a boyfriend. I felt like at this rate, I'd never get around to sharing my feelings with you. I was convinced everyone else around me was so much more confident, experienced, and free in their lives. I felt dizzy and sick, and tried to concentrate on the stage. Shane continued his introduction, walking seductively and powerfully around the stage, feeding off the audience's laughter.

The crowd, including you, hollered back loudly as Shane welcomed the first act. We sat there listening to spoken word, followed by comedy and more spoken word. I shifted uncomfortably in my seat, unsettled by the real fear that it was me—the bottleneck in my own growth—that was the issue. My breathing grew heavy, and you turned to me to ask if I was all right. You placed your hand on my leg, waiting for me to respond as I stared dumbly at you. My neck began to sweat and I felt blood rushing down near your touch, which appeared to be reawakening something in me even as I was shutting down. I tried to say something, but I was overwhelmed. Do you remember how I began coughing loudly? I tried desperately to muffle the noise, but the coughing became worse. The poet onstage stopped midway through her piece to ask if I needed help. I went red with shame and tried to signal that I was fine before getting up and rushing out of the venue. The sound of people shuffling and whispering with concern followed me as I flung open the doors. But after a few seconds passed, I heard the poet inside return to her set. In the cold November night, I spluttered until, eventually, I regained control of my breathing and turned to find you there watching me.

"Dude, what the heck?"

I smiled sheepishly. You looked concerned, but your voice sounded frustrated.

"Are you all right? I noticed you looking really uncomfortable in there, like you couldn't breathe or something."

"Sorry, I don't know what happened. I'll be fine though . . ."

"No, we aren't doing that . . ." you said, coming closer to me. "Something is up, Daniel. I'm not letting you do that thing you do where you just downplay shit."

I was stunned by the tone of your voice, its seriousness. People passed us, trying to get a glimpse of whatever was taking place: a fight, drunken drama, lovers' quarrel.

"I don't know what happened, honestly. It was like I just couldn't breathe, like I wasn't physically there for a moment. I couldn't ask for help even though I was physically next to you. Does that make sense?"

"Like a panic attack?"

"I don't know what that feels like."

"It's like you can't breathe all of a sudden. Your heart begins racing a mile a minute, almost like a heart attack. It might feel like the world is slowly closing in on you."

I stood there watching the yellows of a streetlight color you in golden, buttery hues, fixed between shadow and half-light and wanting to open up fully. I longed to step toward the light, but in my head, something was telling me to retreat into the shadows. Something was warning me this was dangerous, being so candid. It is impossible to say whether the silence between us lasted seconds or many minutes, but you stood there the whole time, feet planted to the ground, not letting whatever was happening go to bed. It was obvious you were waiting for me to respond to your definition, which in truth was an invitation to say what was really going on.

I remember feeling quite dizzy with nerves, but I pushed past them to speak. "How do you know what it feels like?"

I needed to know how you were so wise, how you had language to broach these types of things. I needed to understand how you, Rob, Mona, Shane even, were all so street smart. It was like everyone my age had already had all these life experiences, and I was playing catch-up. I longed for the right words.

"My dad used to get panic attacks after he opened his own practice. The stress of it started to affect him. It scared me as a kid, but over time he got a hold of his anxiety, and I grew up and better understood what was happening to him back then. We're an open family, fortunately, so my parents never bullshitted me about it."

I let a long breath out. "Sorry if I scared you. I really don't know what set this off. I have never, honestly, had a panic attack before—if that is what this was. I'm still not so sure . . ."

"I just wanted to make sure you were all right."

I moved closer to you and could feel you studying my face, which was now equally bathed in golden light. Exposed to your watchful gaze, I was shy and unsure of myself. I remember playing with the buttons on my coat while trying to think of something to say, incapable of mustering any new words. My body was exhausted. My heart was heavy and my mind annoyed with myself. But you stood there before me smiling, a firm presence, a safety net for me, and I was grateful. I heard laughter coming from inside—no doubt the comedy portion of the evening—and was reminded my friends were still in there, watching the show.

"Do you want to go home?" you asked.

"No, oh no, or Rob and Mona will think something is up."

"Well, is it?"

"I'm not sure, but I'd rather just watch the rest of the show and then leave when the others do if that's fine."

"Your call, dude. I'm fine either way." Your statement relieved me, but then you stopped me midstride: "But you're going to tell me if something like this happens again, okay?"

"I promise I will."

We entered just as the tech crew were helping a band set up their kit. The audience was stacking the folding chairs to create a standing-room floor near the stage. We approached Rob and Mona at the front, and I realized they were speaking in fast whispers. Loudly, you announced our return so as to stop any possible gossiping about me. Mona turned to see us and was immediately wrought with concern, but you assured them I was fine. Once the band started, Mona was quickly enraptured by the front woman's smoky voice and heavy guitar playing. She began to sing along to their covers of Bikini Kill, Liz Phair, and Blondie with impressive precision. The audience shifted and shimmied about, turning the old university hall into a nightclub of sorts. In one corner, a group of punk girls attempted to get a mosh pit going, but the security guards were having none of that. A few songs in, Shane joined us. He looked even fiercer up close as he began writhing against Rob's body, their synergy sensuous and intoxicating. Rob had his hands on Shane's lithe waist in the same way I've seen men hold their girlfriends at concerts. The fact that it was two men before me was hypnotizing, and I couldn't break my stare. Their confidence was a puzzle I was convinced I'd never be able to solve.

Suddenly, your hand reached for me, luring me into some weird dance you were doing. You looked ridiculous, but I knew that was the point. I was wise to your attempts to make me smile, imploring me to be present. So I relented and let the percussion take over my body. We laughed loudly as we cut strange shapes, orbiting one another in a universe all our own. It did not matter what others were doing around us; the point was to keep dancing to the music. I prayed for the song to go on as long as humanly possible. I prayed for the front woman's vocal cords to hold out. I prayed we would not lose that energy between us. But eventually the music wound down and we were covered in slick sweat as Shane sashayed back onto the stage to close the festivities. Everyone helped to clean up so the volunteers could leave sooner, and you and I took turns sweeping the floor, pretending we were Olympic curlers. I felt happier for your company, thankful you'd pushed us to come out together. After everything was locked away, Mona said goodbye— she'd ended up being invited to join an afterparty with the band. "Women only. Hope you understand!"

So the four boys decided to go to the twenty-four-hour diner, a regular haunt for underage college students. It was a bit of a walk, but somehow Shane managed it in his heels, for which he had no alternatives. I think Rob was a bit nervous at the attention he might garner, but Shane just rolled his eyes. "Who gives a fuck what anyone thinks?"

Again, I could not help but envy that confidence. So many of my life choices had been made in an effort to not draw attention to myself. I couldn't imagine living the opposite way, bright and shiny and unafraid. I couldn't imagine being brave enough to wear nail polish, or be loud and irreverent, could never visualize myself moving with a fluidity opposite to how both my cultures thought a man should move.

We arrived at Ithaca Diner, its neon sign shining brightly in the black puddles lining the road. You opened the door, and a nostalgic bell announced our entrance. A waitress greeted us, then led the way to a booth not far from where we'd come in, next to a window clouded in condensation. We excitedly unpacked the show as we scanned the menus, praising Shane for his hosting skills. He obviously loved being showered with praise and was eager to know which acts had been your favorites.

"I liked the band. That cover of 'Maria' by Blondie was amazing. It's, like, one of my mom's favorite songs."

"A Debbie Harry fan—your mom sounds iconic. I die!" Shane said, sassy with a flair only he could pull off.

"What about you, Daniel? What was your favorite part?"

"The dancing. It felt joyous, and it was nice to realize Sam is a far worse dancer than I am."

You punched me in the arm playfully, and I loved how in that moment Rob and Shane bore witness to our peculiar type of friendship.

"You two made a good double act—equally inept, yes, but also you both looked like you were having the most fun out there."

"We were, I think," you said to Shane, while looking at me. "I can't say what dance we were attempting, but we were committed to our art all the same."

You spoke with ease, and I could tell Shane was captivated by your presence, trying to figure out how our friendship worked. I felt Rob's eyes studying us both intensely, and I wanted to see what he saw. Did I look as bright and peaceful next to you as I felt? Did you look like someone who might make sense sitting next to me?

"So, Sam, what do you do for fun? I mean besides getting dragged along to things with Daniel here?"

"Oh, well, soccer is kind of a big thing in my life."

"Yes, Rob was telling me you're like one of the only freshmen to not have been benched this season."

"Well, yes, as long as I can prove my worth."

"What role do you play? Or position, or whatever the hell you call it . . ."

I felt glad that Shane, like me, clearly knew nothing about your sport.

As we ate fries covered in gravy and cheese and drank thick malted milkshakes, you walked us through the different positions on the soccer field. Rob tried to jump in here and there with facts from his youth soccer days. You were patient and let him remind us he was also there. I had to suppress my laughter. It was pretty obvious Rob was peacocking, and even Shane tried to get him to shut up. But you gently listened whenever he added another non sequitur to the conversation. You might not have realized there was a sparring match taking place, or maybe you knew exactly what was happening but understood you had the upper hand. Either way, I wiggled into the conversation to ask Shane if he'd ever played any sports when he was younger, as I was growing tired of Rob cutting in.

Shane had us in a fit of laughter explaining the one winter his parents tried to get him into basketball. He was deadpan in his retelling of how hopeless he was running up and down the court, afraid to pass or catch the ball. Still, his team was not the worst in the league. Just as Shane began explaining how he'd once actually made a basket, a couple came in and were directed to a table just behind us. I could feel the man's eyes watching us, then watching Shane in particular. Something shifted in the air, and I knew it was bad. But Shane, who was used to unwanted attention, kept sharing more of his story without missing a beat. Under his breath, the man slung an audible "faggot" our way. I felt the air being punched out of me once again as they took their seats. Rob turned to Shane to ask what the man had said, even though we had all heard it perfectly clearly. Shane rolled his eyes and told Rob to leave it, but we could hear the man frantically telling his girlfriend that Ithaca was becoming a cesspool of "fucking faggots." He was mocking Shane's makeup as his girlfriend tried to tell him to shut up. Shane flushed with hurt and embarrassment but kept talking, as though he were afraid of letting the silence win. All of it was very triggering, and I couldn't help but think of the times I'd sped through the hallways of my high school as other guys yelled "faggot," "homo," and "cocksucker" at me. Guys I never did anything to. I began to remember why I was so hesitant to come out officially. That's when I heard the scraping of chair against floor and realized you had gotten up.

"Hey, dude, don't worry about him," Rob tried to tell you, but your face was angry, and we could tell there'd be no stopping you as you brushed past us.

"Hey asshole, I think you owe my friend an apology."

"No man, I don't need to apologize to no faggot. He should apologize to us walking around like some broke-ass transvestite. What the fuck kind of dude wears makeup and shit. He looks like some fucking freak to me."

Rob and Shane remained turned away from you, too afraid to watch beyond the reflection in the window, but I couldn't turn away. I was afraid for you and for us, so I kept my gaze directly on you, willing God to keep you safe.

"What did you say?" you asked, voice booming and eyes raw with anger.

"I said your friend is some gay freak, and me and my girl are just trying to enjoy our meal. So how about the four of you go home and do whatever it is faggots do this time of night and let us normal people live in peace."

I watched in horror. Every word in every language I knew had left my body. The tension cut through me like a knife, and I felt every other table holding one eye on the three of us and the other on you and that jackass. I felt shameful and couldn't totally comprehend why. You tutted and shook your head before asking the man once more to apologize to Shane and the rest of us. But he continued to tell you to fuck off or you'd be sorry. I heard the waitress call to the cooks in the kitchen to do something just as the man threatened to kick all of our asses if you did not step out of his way.

"I really don't like how you're speaking to me and my friends, who've done nothing to you."

"Okay, little rich boy, I'm sick of your shit. I said get the fuck out of my face." He took his glass of water and threw it right at you.

His girlfriend looked horrified, but not surprised. "Richie, what the fuck did you do that for?"

That's when something in you changed, and you grabbed the guy by the collar and slammed his head hard into the Formica table, demanding an apology. His girlfriend started screaming and hitting you with her bag, but you kept his head there until one of the line cooks came out to pull you off him and threatened to call the cops. In all fairness, the cook did say the guy deserved it and that their diner was an inclusive space, but he also said they would not tolerate fighting. The thug was threatening to kick your ass as the staff were holding him back. I felt conflicted. I wanted to have the man and his girlfriend thrown out, but I also wanted to leave immediately, the night robbed from us by a bigoted stranger. We left some money on the table and rushed outside into a flurry of snow. I hailed a cab and we all climbed in, making little talk with the driver beyond directions to our dorms. It was intensely quiet, with all of us a bit shell-shocked. I was sitting in the front, and in the rearview mirror I was watching you, Shane, and Rob. Shane was on the verge of tears but managed to whisper softly, "Thank you." You patted him on the knee and told him not to mention it.

I sensed the driver understood something bad had happened based on the color draining from our faces. She turned the radio low and told us we'd be home in no time. Besides the music, we drove the rest of the way in complete silence. We eventually arrived at Rob's dorm, and he got out with Shane and promised to text me later with an update on how they were doing. It was only a short drive from there to our place, but it felt infinite and somber, with neither of us sure what to say. It was not how I wanted to part with you so close to Thanksgiving break. It was not how any of us wanted the night to end, and yet there we were.

If I am honest with you, the night played out like my biggest fear, a manifestation of the very thing stopping me from living more openly. It wasn't that I assumed my parents would disown me, or my grandfather would stop loving me, or my friendships would crumble. I feared the unknown stranger, their angry judgment, the silence of a gaggle of witnesses. No one intervening when I was in danger for being something I could not help but be.

The taxi pulled up in front of our building and you offered to pay. I got out and waited for you, digging deep inside for the right words. When you came out you looked so tired, your face weary, and I knew it had taken so much courage for you to do what you did. You were not an angry, violent man. You were kind and gentle and the brightest light in a room. I needed you to know that. I needed you to not regress into some barbarian; into the kind of man I feared most.

"I'm sorry."

"For what?"

"That this happened. That you had to step in and that it all escalated so quickly."

"What he said wasn't right, Daniel. No one deserves to be humiliated like that."

"Thank you for not being like them," I said, getting closer to what I meant. Your face was unsure. "Thank you for not being an asshole, Sam. Thank you for not judging my friends or being like, like all the guys I went to high school with. I know it meant so much to Rob and Shane that you stood up for them."

I wanted to say more but I was so afraid I was going to start crying. You pulled me close to you. In your arms, the world felt safest, infinitely possible. In your arms was our world, but that did not mean the rest of the world did not exist, and this reality is what I needed to start coming to grips with. I couldn't hide from myself forever.

"Like I said, Daniel. No one deserves to be humiliated like that. We all deserve to be ourselves. Shane owes no one any explanations, nor do any of your other friends. You or me, we all deserve happiness. Do you understand?"

I wanted you to say more because I felt like we were getting so close to one of us saying something deeper, tipping us over the edge to where I longed to be. But then the buzzing began. You got text message after text message just then, the phone vibrating between us. We let go of each other and you quickly read the messages. You shared how you had been invited to a frat party. It was still early, at least early enough for college students on a Friday night. You were unsure if you should leave me, but I could tell you wanted to see your friends. I made a show of telling you to go, saying heartily that not everyone's Friday night needed to be ruined. You said I could come, but I knew you were being nice and also knew I would not enjoy myself. It was obvious you hungered to shake off the sour turn of the night, and so I told you to go. I said

I'd try calling my parents before heading to bed. I swallowed my feelings and sent you off into the night to join people who likely would never see you how I saw you. A group of people who didn't understand the lengths you'd go to protect me.

I clambered up the steps to our dorm slowly, my body aching from the highs and lows of the night. I closed the door and sank to the floor and began to cry, finally understanding the fear I carried. Realizing how a night out could so quickly change into something ugly and dangerous. Had you not been there, what would have happened? Who would have helped? Eventually I'd crawl into bed, and you wouldn't come home that night. Instead, you'd roll in just after ten in the morning, and I'd be full of dread envisaging all the ways you'd chosen to let loose. Imagining all the things you'd done to wash the sour hate from your body. Punishing myself with ideas of strange rituals you'd participated in to remind the world you were a strong, completely straight, unburdened man.

I wanted to know whose lips you might have kissed, if any. I wanted to know if you regretted coming out with me at all. I wanted to know if my friendship was proving too much for you. I wanted your company. I wanted your arms to hold me. I wanted you forever. I wanted to know if you loved me. But I was still too afraid to ask. So instead I let silence take over, allowing all those wants of mine to pile up, left to be dealt with at some later date.

DECEMBER

Today I helped Amá make tamales at her gran tamalada. Her sisters could not understand why a young man like myself would not be out "chasing skirts" or gallivanting with other boys doing unscrupulous things. But something told me that today I needed to be near my mother, and although she had to put up with her sisters' incessant questions, I knew my presence was a salve for her. Sonia was not interested in receiving the knowledge of making Amá's tamales, and so it fell to me, her son. Her small hands guided me as I spread the masa into the moistened husk. I added a spoonful of the red meat, dripping in ancho chile sauce. How proud I was when I was able to bite into a freshly steamed tamale of my own making. It made me think how boys are so often kept from these moments, and how girls are often trapped from seeing the outside world. What would happen if, for a day, we reversed expectation? What if, for a day, we let everyone be free? What if, for a day, my sister could go out into the world and find herself, and what if, for a day, I could simply be the young man I know is hiding inside me?

—D.M.

It goes without saying that I became extremely anxious and paranoid after the incident at Ithaca Diner. Each time you went out, I feared you might get jumped or pulled over by the cops, inventing scenarios in which the line cooks or waitress ratted you out as some no-good thug, and each day that passed with nothing said between us only added fuel to the dumpster fire of my worrisome heart. I was convinced you now saw me as a liability. As the days grew busier and the semester began to wind down, I imagined a world in which you would fade from me. I even had nightmares of you submitting a room change over Christmas break and abandoning me in the home we'd built together without even saying goodbye. You may be thinking, *Dear God, Daniel! You always were an overthinker*, and the thing is, Sam, yes.

It did not help that, days after the incident, we parted ways for Thanksgiving break. You went off to the bright coastline of our home state and I joined Rob at Mona's family farm in the verdant countryside of Connecticut. Do you remember that we texted every day during the break? You even called me briefly on Thanksgiving with your parents on speakerphone to wish me well. So yes, I was overthinking this entire time, but also aching to know we were fine, because the thing is that not knowing hurt me. You'd seen the world read me as gay even though I hadn't confirmed it yet, and I wasn't sure what that experience had done to us. The other thing was, although you'd been defending me and my friends, I'd seen a change in you that scared me, and I didn't know what to do about it. Your anger, I'd learned, could cause you to lash out, to slam a man into a table. I didn't have that in my spirit. It felt like another example the world was using to tell me we were too different.

Every night, I would strike out the day on my wall calendar and with each pen mark feel like a chasm was erupting between us. Days were vanishing and life was passing us by, and I had nothing to show for it. But then, one Friday morning, you asked me to join you on a run. It had been snowing the past two days, and the flakes had built up into mounds of tightly packed powder. I was surprised by your invite, but I agreed to join you and cobbled together an outfit to keep me warm. You laughed at me when I came into the living room. I was wearing sweatpants over my shorts and a hoodie over my T-shirt. I looked like Forrest Gump when he runs across America.

"What is so funny?"

"You look like the Mexican Michelin Man. Don't you have proper running gear for the cold?"

"I didn't even know there was seasonally specific athletic wear."

You returned with running tights, a hat, and spare running gloves, and I went into the bathroom to change. It was strange to wear something of yours so close to my body, something you would wear after. Having the Lycra on was like wearing your skin over mine, and it thrilled me. I was unsure whether I should wear shorts over the tights or not, and opened the door to check what you had done. Your muscly legs were on full display. Your body looked beautiful, dangerously so.

"We should get going before it starts snowing again. You ready?"

I sucked up my self-doubt and exited the bathroom, marching out the door. The tight fabric clung to every curve of my lower body, putting my ass on full display. It was the closest you had ever been to seeing me naked. One part of me wanted you to see me from all angles, and the other was telling me to pull down my hoodie as low as possible. I felt at war. I had never had sex with anyone, had never kissed anyone, guy or girl. But I knew a body could be desirous because your body, your soul, your mind were things I desired. And yet I did not know who or what you desired. I did not know if you had a type, guy or girl, or a history with someone. We'd never talked about dating or sex. Most nights you'd come straight home from a party, and so I had no reason to believe you were sleeping with anyone. But as your friend and roommate, I had no right to care either way. And also, I mean, come on, Sam, you were so beautiful and popular, and a varsity athlete. Surely you had girls throwing themselves at you all the time at parties. At least that's what I thought.

"Let's hit the road."

"Not going to lie. I feel like we're going to freeze our balls off."

"It'll be good for us, don't be a baby."

I adored running. It was the only form of exercise I had done since puberty. As long as I had a decent pair of shoes, I could run far and wide. It was how I got to see so much of the city during our first year in Ithaca. But I would only ever run alone; running with you was an altogether different experience. I was swallowed up between your long strides—for every step you made, I was managing two and a half. You had never invited me to a game, so I had never seen you on the field, but I imagined you were lightning fast. A bolt ready to strike at any moment.

You led us to Cayuga Gardens, where we ran along the creek feeding into Cayuga Lake. The paths were covered in snow and ice, which made things a bit tricky. The crunching snow announced our presence and caused small sparrows and robins to flee the sanctuary of their ice-covered bushes. Their movement created an echoing crescendo that spooked me, but I knew I was safe with you. As we ran through the trees, you pointed to glass icicles forming on their branches. They were beautiful but could easily impale us if a gust of wind came on too quickly.

You told me you wanted to go a little further and then we could stop. You said there was something you wanted to show me, so we sprinted the last few hundred feet. When we reached your secret spot, we both had to take time to recover our breath. We stood there bent forward, bracing our knees as we tried to steady our heart rates. I remember that the mixture of cold air entering my body and warm air leaving made me feel like my chest was on fire. Our lungs produced a frosty vapor of carbon dioxide that came out in big puffs. The curlicues of warm air meeting the cold atmosphere were mesmerizing. For a few seconds, our breath existed together in the world, little clouds fading into the blinding white around us. Sometimes I imagine we are still floating together somewhere along that creek, and I only have to return to it to find you.

Eventually you shared the name of your secret destination: Flat Rock. True to its name, the creek spread far and wide over a shallow expanse of rock before returning to the steady stream we had already run past. It was covered in huge sheets of ice and thick snow. I followed you to the footbridge connecting the gardens to the other half of our never-ending campus. You told me the bridge was as old as our university. I was always amazed at what you knew about the place we lived. The bridge was a gorgeous feat of engineering, wood and steel cable working together to connect two places. We walked together across it, careful not to slip on any hidden ice. From the middle of the bridge, you could see for miles. Everything was stark white, quiet, and completely still. It was just you and me there, and we stood taking it all in. There were few leaves hanging on the trees; mostly it was just bare branches covered in lichen. The dark wood stood out like bristles of a comb against the clear gray sky and paper-white snow. It was close to freezing, but the running had warmed up my body. I was content standing there, looking at everything in front of me; content having you beside me.

"I think I owe you an apology," you said from nowhere.

I didn't know what to make of that. For the past three weeks I'd been eaten up with dread, thinking you were avoiding me. Each night, I would pray silently before bed that something might change to give me peace. I prayed for you to show me, somehow, that we were all right. Overwhelmed by it all, I studied a small island of snow before me where a little wren was keeping watch. It felt like everything hung on your next words.

"I've been avoiding you and I feel like an asshole."

I took in a deep breath and turned to you. "Did I do something wrong?"

"No, dude. It was me. I've been so embarrassed about what happened at the diner."

"Embarrassed?"

"Yeah, embarrassed. I overreacted and I put you all in danger. I am so sorry."

"You were defending my friends, Sam. You don't have to apologize for that."

"I wasn't."

"What do you mean?"

Just then, a second wren descended from the sky to join the first wren on the small, snow-covered islet. Slowly, they shifted, turning their bodies toward us. It was as if we were now being watched, studied by these natural wonders.

"It was you I was worried about."

"Me?" I turned away from the watchful wrens to look at you directly. We both knew that the guy had been harassing poor Shane more than anyone else, that I was just a secondary casualty in his line of fire.

"I didn't want anything bad to happen to you. You're like my best friend, Daniel."

It was the first time you had ever called me that. It was not the B-word I lusted after, but it was the more meaningful word at this point in our lives. It took me awhile to respond.

"I didn't mean for you to get caught up in anything," I said. "But I'm grateful you were there. I wouldn't have known what to do if the guy did anything stupid."

"Can I ask you a question?"

The wrens kept watching us, and I was staring at you but keeping them in my sight line, preparing for whatever it was you were about to ask. I was unsure if the question would be a footbridge connecting our two islands or a river creating a valley between us, but I thought it was best, just in case, to prepare for the worst.

"Do people say shit like that around you a lot?"

"Are you asking if I'm gay?"

"No. I'm not. Not that it matters to me."

"I'm a quiet, nerdy, short, brown Mexican, Sam, whose best friend is a jock, and whose other best friends are a lesbian wannabe-revolutionary and a gay hipster with a boyfriend unafraid to wear glittery eye shadow in public. I'm always going to have a target on my back, but I'm a big boy. I'm fine, if this is what you're getting at. You don't have to worry about me."

We stood there in the quietude, neither one of us talking, our breathing light. Without any distractions I could hear the soft babble of water, the creek feeding into the lake somewhere beneath us. Somehow that little sliver of water managed to keep on going, able to fight off the harsh grip of cold air that had frozen over nearly everything in sight. I listened closely to the sound of it shifting and shaping itself over rock and pebble, through the debris of fallen branches and trees. How amazing, I thought, that despite all the obstacles presented by Mother Nature, water still finds a means of moving itself forward to where it truly belongs.

"I just need you to know, if you ever feel unsafe or, like, in danger, you can always call me. Even if I'm hanging out with my teammates or whatnot, I will be there in a flash. I mean it."

"Thank you, Sam."

You pulled me to your side in a fraternal chokehold. Although we'd skirted around some bigger topics, I felt closer to you, not just physically, but as if I understood you more. It was not easy for me to matter to people. Hearing you talk about why you'd done what you'd done made sense. I was your best friend and you were mine, and you'd feared I was in danger. Maybe I was? But I was tired of running. I couldn't hide anymore from who I was, and knew I had to come face-to-face with reality. My body, the person

I loved, the people I was friends with, might not always be welcomed by strangers. But—I promised myself then—I would no longer remain in the shadows like a white hare blending into his surroundings. I needed to be present. I needed to stand tall and proud in a flowing river. I was hungry to be seen.

Just as we were gearing up to head home, the two wrens took off in flight. Their warbles echoed against the stark silence, their brown feathers fluttered bright against the snow, but it was something else that kept me looking at them as we made our way back down the footbridge: the way they were flying side by side, the tips of their wings just touching. It was as if they were holding hands in the air, searching together, trying to find their place in that city on the hill.

PART II

JANUARY

This morning I woke up and my shoes were filled with candy bars and money. The Three Kings had visited me. I laughed at the sight. Why the three Magi would visit a man who was not far from turning twenty is beyond me. But Amá and Apá insist their majesties work in mysterious ways. Part of me hurts knowing how desperately I want to leave all this comfort behind. How, like those Three Kings, I have an urge, a calling to follow a star to get me where I am meant to be. How these childhood walls, even my parents' great love, none of it is enough anymore. How I don't deserve all the love they have to give. How, more and more, I need to give my love to someone else, a someone my parents dare not even imagine. But I know I need this year to bring change. I'm tired of having only written words to speak my truth. I need to live loudly.

—D.M.

I returned from Christmas break a few days before you. Everything in Ithaca was coated white, like marshmallow whip spread generously from the jar atop the grassy lawns and winding roads of our city. Our dorm was mostly empty and the campus all but dead, but I leaned into the solitude, soaking up that quiet period before the rush, knowing now how quickly the first semester had passed me by. I took long walks up and down Fall Creek, familiar with it now thanks to you, and allowed myself to be amid the deafening silence, a quietness that only happens in winter, when half of nature is hibernating and the other half carefully chooses when to venture out into the frost. Two months into winter and I had not yet grown tired of ice crunching under my feet, adding company to my otherwise solitary ventures. On the last day before you arrived back, I left just as the sun had come out in all her glory. I wanted to have as much light to walk under as possible, keen to see how far I could make it on my own.

I decided to go further than we had on our run back in December, and headed for the equine center. Across a footbridge and through a forested border was an expanse of field separating the creek from the veterinary campus. It made me think of your dad, walking over that bridge and through that field many times over when he was our age, just to get to class. How wonderful it must have been for you to share a connection to this place with him, to understand the environment that shaped the man he is. I wished to know my own dad like that. But those were thoughts for another day, and so I continued walking through snow and over ice with the sun as my only companion. The thing was, I wasn't alone. I carried you everywhere that year, and still do now. Each little thing I saw was something I wanted to share with you. Each sound, smell—all were cues that made me think, *If only Sam were here.*

When I made it to the top of the slope, I had views of both Cayuga Heights and our campus. Everything was glorious in the light of that January morning. I filled my lungs with the frosty air and took off my beanie. Steam rose from my sweaty hair, creating smoke signals. I decided to take a photo of the view. It came out grainy on my ancient phone, but I was grateful all the same to have something to remind me of that day. You were the only person I wanted to send it to. So I did, unsure how much it would cost me, unsure if I had great signal. But I stood there with one hand held high to the heavens, like a whirling dervish, until I heard the ding of your response.

SAM: *It looks beautiful. Wish I was there.*

ME: *Me too. Soon enough.*

SAM: *Be safe and save some adventures for me.*

I put my phone away and continued walking, and my socks began to grow damp from the melting ice. The sun was now directly above me and uninterrupted by the clouds. I'd always imagined the cold would be gray and soulless, but some of the brightest blues I've seen were during my first winter in Ithaca. It didn't matter that it was cold or that the trees were bare, because to me everything still felt so full of life.

On the walk home, I received a photo you sent me of the beach with two hands in the frame, clinking bottles of beer. Your father had skipped work on your last day home and surprised you with a trip to the beach. On one side of the country, I remember thinking, you were bathed in salt spray, and on the other my lungs were filled with icy air, but both of us were basking under the same sun.

Do you remember how you arrived the morning after that massive cold front hit the East Coast? Everything was dusted with even more snow than the day before. It was up to my calves, but fortunately the roads had been cleared during the night. You texted me when you were not far from our dorm. I was so eager to see you, I didn't even think to wait for you inside. I needed to see you with my own eyes as soon as possible, so I descended the stairs two steps at a time. You almost slipped coming out of your taxi. Luckily, I caught you before you face-planted into the sidewalk. We held each other for only a few seconds, but after a month of not seeing you, I remember it felt like a lifetime. You let go but were still smiling at me when you shared how happy you were to be home again.

We walked up to our dorm room, each of us carrying one of your heavy suitcases. I made fun of you for how much stuff you'd lugged back after being gone only a month. You told me you had presents for me, and if I was going to make fun of you then I wouldn't get any. I stuck my tongue out at you and you jostled my hair like a big brother before asking if I had anything for you. I told you my present to you was breakfast, which was all set out when we opened the door. Over coffee and blueberry bagels you told me about your flight. You were beginning to detail the scary turbulence from the storm you'd passed through when it started to snow, and we became distracted. We stared outside the giant window of our living room in awe, like little boys learning the magic of weather patterns for the first time. All of it was so glorious and new.

"It's like a snow globe," you said.

"Something straight out of a Christmas movie."

"I can't remember the last time I saw so much snow."

"You should have seen Fall Creek yesterday. It was incredible."

"I wish I had been there with you."

This is when you suggested we take the bus down to Cayuga Lake to see the ice-covered expanse. I thought you might be tired after your red-eye, but you insisted the coffee had woken you up and the fresh air would be good for you. Knowing it meant I'd have more of your company, I was happy to oblige. We finished our food and cleared away the dishes before putting on layers upon layers of warm clothes. We talked excitedly on our walk to the bus stop about all the winter activities we might get up to over the coming weeks.

As we waited for the bus, I began to remember my promise from the day before. I told myself I was going to find a way to share my feelings with you. This felt like the prime time to do so, but all of a sudden, I was incapable of keeping my word. It came on fast, like an illness. No matter the excitement I felt and promises I'd made before your arrival, my resolve began to disappear as soon as you sat down next to me. Not because anything had changed; quite the opposite. I think I began to realize then just how strong my feelings were for you. What I so desperately wanted to tell you would most likely create a seismic shift that I wouldn't be able to fix, and yet I felt like I had no other option. I couldn't contain all those feelings and never share them with you. But, dear God, I mean, how do you tell someone you are in love with them when you believe they don't love you back? At least not in that way. How do you do it in a way that won't ruin a friendship? This was the mammoth task I had to contend with during our journey to the lakeshore.

If I could turn back time, I would have said more. I wouldn't have wasted minutes in your company in which I could have heard your voice. I would have found a way, even if it was awkward, into conversation. Looking back now, I'm so angry with myself for doing things like letting whole bus rides happen in silence. Because if I could, I would do anything in the world to speak to you again. But on that bus ride, back then, I could not find an inroad to talking and so I sat next to you without uttering a word, wallowing in my own anxiety as you stared out the window. Thankfully, you always found a way to get me to open up.

"Did you enjoy being home with your family?" you asked.

"Yeah, it was good. I missed my grandfather more than I'd realized. Spent lots of time with him going on walks around my local park, which was nice for us. I think he has been a bit sad without me there and with my parents working all the time."

"Dude, you're so lucky to have grandparents who are still alive. I'd give anything to have one more day with mine," you said soberly. "I'm glad you two are close."

"Yeah, I love him so much. He was like my third parent for most of my life and I just hope he doesn't feel lonely without me. I didn't want him to think I was leaving him behind when I came here, but I sometimes worry he does."

Before I could continue the conversation, the driver announced our stop and we clambered off, trying not to slip on the wet stairs. The light was bouncing off all the white surfaces and was so blinding it took a good minute for our eyes to adjust. But then we both saw the giant lake, completely covered in snow, a sheet of arctic-blue ice, and we smiled great big smiles.

A few families sat on nearby benches, mostly parents whose kids were running about, plopping down to make snow angels. Even in the depths of winter, vibrant euphoria could be found everywhere. We walked further out onto the beach. It had stopped snowing by then, but the polished rocks were still slippery with the mixture of ice and snow, and we had to take turns balancing on each other. At the edge of the lake, we stopped for a moment and stood. The frozen, snow-covered water spilled out over the horizon, playing tricks on my mind, as if snow and sheet ice existed for infinity. We both agreed it was too dangerous to try walking on the surface, so I walked a little further along the beach to where a small bit of land jutted out. I stood there debating how to say something meaningful to you. Something that would articulate my intense feelings. While I was deep in my rabbit hole of overthinking, you had snuck up behind me, tapping me on the shoulder, and I shrieked before I realized it was you. You pulled me close, hugging me tight like a bear: your little brother, your best friend. Pulling me back into the present.

"Daniel, do you ever just think, my God, I am lucky to be alive?"

I shielded my face from the sun to take you in, basking in your omniscient question still echoing around us. I studied your beautiful eyes, the same color as the sky. I made a note of your tall frame with those long arms that could so easily encircle all of me.

"Yes," I said quietly.

"I mean look at it, Daniel. Really look at all of this in front of us."

"I'm looking," I insisted.

"Like, here we are. These two guys from Cali and we get to have all of this."

You let go of me and walked a few steps ahead before turning around, extending your arms as wide as humanly possible. You were showing me all that was ours to have: the hills, the frozen lake, the dormant trees, the horizon extending for miles before us.

"It's ours. Like, together, it's ours to share," you repeated.

My heart was once again stuck in my throat. I wanted to say something more. I wanted to say all the right things in this perfectly right moment. I wanted to get to the center of my feelings. The ones I could no longer shake, totally aware now of just how real and deep they ran. You stood there looking toward me, your back to the lake, and for a moment your blue eyes and the sky and the water all melded together into a whirlpool of my longing.

"Thanks for coming here with me," you said.

"I wouldn't have missed this for the world."

There was a small snack bar open selling old-fashioned doughnuts, hot dogs, coffee, and other warm drinks. I remember we ordered a hot chocolate each and some of those oily apple doughnuts, and sat down to enjoy them on a bench under a bare elm tree. There was steam rolling out of our mouths, the drinks equally hot, sending smoke to the heavens. I felt so alive, as if we were the kids playing in the snow. Our second semester would soon be starting, and our lives would become consumed by studying, extracurricular activities, and hanging out with our other friends. But just then, and for a few more hours, I had you all to myself, and I was so grateful.

"What do you want to accomplish this semester?" I asked, way too formally.

"Hmm . . . I just want to enjoy life."

"Good answer."

You took a sip of your hot chocolate and leaned back, stretching out like a gazelle. You looked like some off-duty sports star in your navy parka, those gray Nike sweatpants, and your favorite pair of Timberlands, and I thought, I have no idea why this guy, but I'm grateful it's him I'm falling for. Truly, there was no one else I'd rather have had those feelings for. You were a gift, and I am only now understanding what a rare gift you were.

"And you, good sir?" you asked, breaking the silence.

"What about me?"

"Your turn. What do you want, Daniel?"

Again, it was like your mind always knew what I needed to hear, understood what I longed to be asked. I looked out onto the lake with majestic birds guarding the edge of the frozen banks, trying to formulate my answer. What did I want as I sat there listening to the wind rustling over the surface, shifting loose snow until it began dancing around like monks in a deep trance? So many thoughts were running through my head in that single moment, but these were the things I wanted: more time, you, to be happy. If you asked me that same question today, I'd say the same, but this is how I answered then:

"This. I want to enjoy this."

I answered while looking straight out at Cayuga Lake at all that bright snow, the landscape of ice and trees that would be full of green leaves in a few short months. But that wasn't what I saw in my mind; no, what I saw was you and me sitting there on the bench. The world stretching out before us, a spring of possibilities to come.

MARCH

Today at school I kissed a boy, and he kissed me back. Then we kissed together, and we didn't die. The sun was shining, and the birds were singing, and we had kissed, and I was happy. Today, I kissed a boy and finally understood what it means when you can 100 percent, without a doubt, say, "I am free."

—D.M.

February's four short weeks passed by quickly enough. Between snowstorms and late-night sessions in the library, we somehow blinked and it was March. We laughed about not having anyone to celebrate Valentine's with, but there was no time for dating or romance. Not in those first few weeks of spring semester, at least. It was an incredibly stressful time for me, if you can remember. Naomi was pushing me hard to get as high a GPA as possible so I'd be able to keep my scholarship for the coming academic year. In those weeks I became a bit of a recluse, especially in the lead-up to midterms, and didn't really see anyone. I mean, I did go out for lunch with Rob and Mona and tried to maintain my few evening meals with you, but I spent most of February studying like a maniac. You joked that I had temporarily moved into the library for most of winter, and it was sort of true. Though I think I'd have been lonely otherwise, because you were gone quite a bit with training and the gym. These peaks and troughs of spending every waking hour with each other and then having weeks when we'd hardly come into contact were becoming a bit of a habit of ours.

Again, I missed your company, but what could I do about any of it when we had so many other things going on? Then, one morning while eating a hurried breakfast between classes, you ran into me in the dining hall and invited me to your soccer game later that afternoon, a friendly between Cayuga and a nearby school. I was surprised because, until now, you'd compartmentalized your soccer life from your Daniel life, but I still said I'd go. I even asked if I could bring Rob and Mona along because I didn't want to sit alone awkwardly in the stands.

"Of course, dude. You do know anyone can come to the games, right?"

"Great. Well, we'll be cheering you on from the bleachers."

"Cool. We need all the support we can get."

I smiled at you, and you stood there looking into my eyes. It was a look I couldn't make heads or tails of, and I was afraid I might have had milk on my chin or something, or a really big pimple. I was usually the one who got stuck staring at you for uncomfortably long periods of time, and was not used to switching roles like that.

"Anything else?"

My question woke you from your daze or whatever deep thoughts you were processing. You smiled before saying something.

"I've missed you, dude. It's been ages since we've been home at the same time. We've got to fix this whole not-hanging-out thing, okay? Like, it's already March."

"I'm sorry. You're right."

"Hey, it takes two to tango. Sorry if I've let training take over my life as of late."

When we said our goodbyes, I immediately texted Rob and Mona to invite them to your game. They wrote back to say it sounded fun and that they'd meet me at the stadium just before the start. I felt happy at the fact that I was leading the planning this time around, although really it was a plan you'd initiated. But it felt good to invite my friends to something. We had been blessed with a glorious March afternoon, and the promise of sun shining down as we sat in the stands was enough to lure both of them out of the comfort of their dorms and hipster anarchy.

I headed to class radiating joyous energy. I think it was the fact that you'd acknowledged you missed me, which meant something far deeper to me than you could've realized. Why did I not think I was important enough to be missed? But hearing you say it, being asked to rectify the absent presence of my being, I just felt electric with happiness. It carried me buoyantly to my last class of the day, during which all I could think of was you. As my professor read different passages from Shakespeare's *As You Like It*, I was lost in my own world. Like Orlando, I wanted nothing more than to nail love letters to every tree of our campus and declare to the world how much you meant to me.

When the bell rang, my class quickly spilled out into the main quad, which was washed in a spring perfume of crocuses and snow-drops. All over the grassy lawn groups of students sat in human puddles, basking in the sunshine, and there was a buzz in the air, pure exhilaration from the feeling of warm heat on skin. I decided to treat myself to an afternoon of doing nothing until it was time to head to your game. I found an empty bench and let myself sit in peace for the first time in a while. I often hurried around to and from classes with immense guilt at being so privileged. I studied so much because being at Cayuga felt like a luxury, and not giving 110 percent to my studies would have felt like a slap in my parents' faces. But that afternoon, I allowed myself to root into the green grass and simply be a flower. At this point in time, everything felt wonderfully hopeful. Looking back, I think I was operating with this sense that we had all the time in the world. It's always been a problem of mine, inaction, or maybe this is just what it is to be young. We really did believe the city was ours to explore over the course of four years. Remember when you said that to me on the lakeshore? "It's ours. Like, together, it's ours to share."

As I sat there basking in the sun, I must've looked euphoric and high. In truth, I was still buzzing from your invitation. You'd even bothered to send me a text to confirm the kickoff time. You really wanted me to be there, and for my part, I felt like I was being given the last piece of the puzzle of who you were. You had always been so open with me, but your sports life was unfamiliar beyond the stories you shared on occasion when you returned muddy and sweaty from practice.

Later that afternoon, when I met Rob and Mona outside the soccer stadium, I was still full of enthusiasm. It was tangible, and the pair of them poked fun at me, this different Daniel, full of school pep, but really full of an overflowing desire for you, my best friend, my first crush. You'd have thought I was Cayuga's biggest sports fan. We entered what I kept referring to as a stadium but soon realized was where our school's track-and-field team held practices. In total honesty, the soccer team was not as loved by our school as, say, the football and basketball teams, both of which were highly funded and much lauded, with some players even making it to the NFL or NBA. All the same, when you ran onto the field in your crisp red-and-white uniform and shiny cleats, I was mesmerized. You looked every bit the professional athlete, and I couldn't help but think, *Wow, that's my friend, my best friend in the entire world.* When you lined up with the opposing team before the game began, we whooped and hollered like we were teenage girls at a Justin Bieber concert. It felt silly, but you seemed to appreciate the fervor pouring down from the bleachers. Your captain was called to the half line with the opposing team's captain, and the referee flipped a coin in the air. Heads or tails, I don't know which, but whatever he called, your team was happy with the result.

"Some of these guys are really fucking hot," Rob offered to no one in particular.

"Umm, aren't you in a committed relationship, Rob?" Mona asked—quite judgmentally, I thought, for a queen of ever-changing paramours.

"Didn't I tell you and Daniel? Shane and I are taking an extended break this semester."

"Sorry to hear that. I honestly adored Shane and his politics, and, on a less intellectual level, you both looked really good together. Such a shame."

"Geez, Mona, we're still hanging out, and he, well, you know, still comes over from time to time to fuck. So please, don't mourn the end of our formal relationship. We're grown-ups."

Mona just shook her head and turned her attention to me. "What about you, Daniel? Anyone in your life?"

"Me, dating? Ha! I'm too busy with my crippling self-doubt and mountain of essay assignments to meet anyone."

"Well, I think the one you should be getting busy with is about to score a goal," Rob said, pointing to you midway down the field.

Watching you move out there was like watching a dancer make full use of his stage. You were balletic in how your feet moved in coordination with the rest of your frame. The power in your long body was mesmerizing. Around us fans were screaming and jumping frantically as you passed the ball back and forth with another player. But all I could do was study the way in which your tendons worked in harmony with your core to deliver a pass that sailed yards upon yards. I was in awe of the discipline with which you'd trained your body to do extraordinary things. You confused the opposition with quick movements; you looked like you were going to go right but at the last minute you passed the ball left, to a teammate I hadn't even noticed. One, two, three—and, like magic, you made the perfect play. When your teammate shot the goal that sailed past the goalie, you all swarmed at him like a flock of sparrows, swiftly darting across the green.

I saw how you hugged them, and I realized that hug was the definition of fraternity. You grabbed with vigor and rigidity. It was not how you held me, which was always with gentle kindness, soft and enveloping. Although you were clearly happy and celebrating with these other men our own age, as I stood there I could not help but realize that I must've been something different to you. What exactly that difference meant, I did not quite know at the time. But it was revealing itself more and more.

The next twenty minutes were full of continuous excitement. My heart could barely take it, and I had to grip the cold metal bench the whole time to stop myself from freaking out. You made one final goal before halftime was called. It was magnificent. Your teammate was in a dicey situation with two players coming right at him, and so, in a moment of panic or sheer genius, he walloped the ball high enough for you to head it straight into the goal. Mona and Rob exchanged high fives with a group of spectators near us. My friends were jubilant and full of school spirit, a spirit that hadn't existed in them prior to this game. Their new friends were toasting with what was obviously a Nalgene bottle full of Malibu Rum. They offered us all a drink and we took it, despite not knowing who these people were beyond fellow students at Cayuga. We passed the time between the first and second half that way, sipping rum and discussing our opinions on how the rest of the game might go.

When you came out of the locker room to start the second half, you searched for me in the stands. We caught each other's attention and you waved with your long arms, smiling and calling my name, and I felt so important as strangers looked up to see who the star player was speaking to. I felt like I was part of your world more than I'd ever been.

Cayuga ended up winning 3–1 that day. There may have only been around a hundred people watching, but it could well have been a stadium full of thirty thousand people and I don't think they'd have been able to cheer any louder than those of us who were there. After the final whistle and exchanging handshakes with the visiting team, you ran over to the stands to talk to me. Dozens of people wanted to congratulate you, to have just a minute of your time, but you were focused on me and my friends. I couldn't hear you over the chanting. I think you were asking what I thought of the game, or you might have said you were so glad we came. I kept struggling until Rob and Mona grew impatient and poked me in the side, telling me to go and actually talk to you. I was being stupidly shy, coy even, but something about you made me nervous. It might've been the thrill of crossing the threshold into that final sacred space of yours. I knew how much you loved soccer, and to be in attendance, to see your magic, to see you so eager to come talk to me—it was all too much. I congratulated you on your win and you thanked me for bringing Rob and Mona, who were now busy exchanging numbers with their fellow fans. The way you and I talked then was so strange upon reflection, as if we were neither friends nor roommates. We spoke as if we had not known each other as long as we had, like this was our first meeting. You asked if I was up to anything that evening, and I told you I didn't have plans, again being far too coy, and you mentioned there was a party being hosted by both the men's and women's soccer teams. I didn't know if it was an invitation or if you were telling me you wouldn't be home later that evening.

"I want you to come, but only if you want to. I'm not forcing you," you said.

I felt your eyes on me, your brow heavy with sweat, your face shining from the stadium lights just turned on. I felt the presence of people hovering behind me wanting to speak to you as if you were a celebrity and I was some plebeian hogging the meet-and-greet time.

"I know you won't know anyone. But I think you'd have a good time, and I promise I won't ditch you."

I wanted to be with you, but I didn't want to be with all those other people. I didn't think I'd fit in. I didn't want to seem aloof and small to you, and I was afraid I wouldn't know how to shine brightly enough to justify your invitation.

"I hope you'll at least think about coming," you told me before being called over by your coach. "Let me know, okay?"

Rob and Mona finally came down to me so we could leave.

"So what did he say?"

"He wants me to come to a party with him."

"Daniel, that's, like, really great. Are you gonna go?" Mona asked, poking me in the side for an answer.

"I don't think it will be my kind of crowd."

"That's kind of judgy of you," Rob said, chastising me. "I mean, Sam has hung out with your crowd, which isn't really his crowd. You know?"

I rolled my eyes at him. "Do you think I should go?"

"Yes, you idiot," they both said emphatically.

I texted you to say I was going to grab pizza with Rob and Mona before heading back to our dorm, and you wrote back quite fast to ask if I was gonna join you after—suspiciously fast. Only now do I understand just how much you wanted my company.

Sure, let me know where to meet, I wrote back.

Woo-hoo, I'll meet you at home. Be ready at 10.

When I arrived back to our dorm, I immediately went to shower. I wanted to make an effort for you. It felt important to do that, at least. I turned the tap on extra hot, squirted bodywash onto a loofah, and scrubbed my body hard to wash away my lingering doubts. I couldn't deny that your actions were saying you wanted to hang with me, that you missed me. I thought of my semester goal: to enjoy Ithaca, life, you. Whatever was to come of the night, at least I wouldn't be hiding in a corner of the library behind a stack of books. At least I'd be with you, young and present in my ever-shifting life.

When I came out of the bathroom, you were standing at the kitchen sink having a glass of water. I hadn't expected you to be home just then and so was walking around in nothing but a towel. You turned to me and smiled, drinking me in as if I were the glass of water in your hand. I didn't know what to do or what to say, so I stood there awkwardly, on show.

"Thanks for coming to my game."

"You were awesome. I can't believe how good you are."

"Thanks. I was probably showing off because you were there."

My heart was beating a mile a minute. I felt all the blood rushing down my neck through my torso, straight into the rest of my body. Why was it that being nearly naked in front of you felt so liberating? I was afraid you'd notice my growing erection, so I shifted my stance and tightened the towel around my waist.

"Are you excited about your first proper party?" you asked.

A palpable heat hung in the air, wrapping both of us in a thick warmth. Was it the steam from the shower? Was it the humid air outside? I couldn't tell, but something was changing. Perhaps, I thought, desire was creeping into the space between us?

"I know it might get raucous, but I promise you everyone is really nice."

Although you were there with me, I felt like I was slipping into another plane. The attraction I had for you was spilling out before me and I was afraid I could no longer contain it.

"What was that . . .?"

"Dude, are you even listening to me?" You waved a hand in front of my face.

"Sorry, sort of spaced out for a second. I wasn't ignoring you."

"I'll try not to be offended."

"I should go change."

"No worries, dude. I should get showered anyway, but let's have a beer before we go."

You patted me on the shoulder, gripping my skin for just a fraction of a second before stripping off your hoodie and shirt and waltzing into the bathroom. When I heard the door click shut, I let out the biggest sigh. Your touch, your gaze, all these things were having such a visceral effect on my body, and I didn't know what to do about it.

As soon as I heard the water running, I went to my room to get ready. You took awhile in the shower, and I felt nervous being left alone with my thoughts for so long. I was afraid I'd convince myself not to go to the party, afraid I'd think of all the reasons I might become uncomfortable or bored. I tried distracting myself by watching music videos on YouTube while you got ready, and was listening to Broken Social Scene when you joined me in the living room with two beers in hand. As we drank our first beer of the night, you began explaining to me how the party was actually a fundraiser for the women's soccer team to buy new uniforms. The men's team was sponsoring it by buying all the booze, but you said it was all really driven by guilt, because the women's team was more talented but the men's got more money from the school. I drank quickly, trying to drown out my budding anxiety; I wanted to have fun with you in your element.

"You look good, man."

I was wearing a vintage guayabera and jeans. I looked at myself and for once felt like I had earned the compliment.

"You're not so bad yourself, Samuel Morris."

"Muchas gracias, Señor de La Luna."

Whenever you spoke Spanish, I fell for you even harder. I loved hearing the way your tongue rolled the *r*'s of "burrito," or how you knew *ñ* makes an "n-y" sound like in "montaña" or "mañana." Sometimes, in those moments, I'd imagine you speaking fluently to my grandfather over beers, eating food made by my mother. I would dream up these scenarios in which all our worlds would so easily come together, free of any prejudice or hardship. Thinking back on it now, I see that I only ever wanted the most ideal version of love with you. I didn't want a difficult life. I didn't think I had it in me to fight more battles.

"Let's get going."

"Okay, sounds good."

Off we headed into the night, passing dozens of couples en route to parties, dates, bars; couples about to do all the things I could only dream of doing with a boyfriend one day. While walking next to you, I couldn't help but think, *Fuck, Daniel, you're crushing on someone who isn't even gay. You're pining after your best friend, wasting time on a pipe dream.* I wanted to wake myself up, throw cold water on my face. But then, part of me was holding out for a sign, because it also felt like maybe you were trying to tell me something by opening up your world to me. First the soccer game and now this party. I mean, you weren't hiding me away in a corner of your life. You wanted to share so much of yourself with me. Why was I taking so long to see that? Even now, I'm searching through memories, trying to make heads or tails of things, while you were saying *I'm here Daniel, right in front of you.*

"You're always thinking, Daniel."

You were standing there waving at me, calling out as I looked up to find you a whole three yards ahead, speaking more loudly than was necessary as if making a joke about how behind I had fallen.

"You always have some deep expression on your face."

"Sorry for being weird and zoning out again!"

I had to sort of jog to you to catch up, and as I did you cheered me on, as if I were a marathon runner and you my spectator, my audience of one. When I reached you, I was victorious, and you draped your arms around me in a celebratory hug. As if your hug was my medal, the prize for having closed the gap that had opened between us. Somehow you were able to force a smile out of me just by the feeling of your body against mine. I think even then you understood the power your touch had on me.

"Is it lame to be an overthinker?" I asked as we broke away.

"Not at all. Just know it's okay to not overthink everything all the time."

"I'm trying, honestly."

At that moment we were at the top of a street stretching all the way downtown to the center of Ithaca. You gave me a look and I knew exactly what you wanted to do. On the count of three, we raced each other down that steep hill. Fighting gravity, trying not to trip and eat shit or send ourselves to the hospital, we galloped at dozens of miles an hour. For a few moments I was free, my body fueled by adrenaline and my mind quelled by watery beer. Although you beat me by an arm's length, I said we should call it a draw since you were almost a foot taller than me. You happily accepted this ruling as we continued on, covered in a light sweat.

By the time we arrived at the party, it was just past eleven and things were in full swing. I instantly felt like I was in the wrong place, somewhere I did not belong. All I could see were guys and girls who looked like athletes, muscular and sun-kissed. I was lost in a sea of people who did not come from my world, or the worlds I operated in at Cayuga. But I felt your hand on my wrist the whole time, keeping hold of me as we moved through the dense crowd of people. I didn't know where we were going, but I was happy to have you there to guide me as we pushed forward. I thought of Rob and Mona. I told myself to be open-minded and to try and have fun.

It was dark and hard to see, with the only light coming from a sporadic strobe in the corner, and we were soon separated by two drunk guys play-fighting in the middle of the dance floor. A crowd started to grow around them, people calling out the name of whichever one they thought would end up the victor. We were both unsure what to do, where to move; the energy was chaotic and debaucherously over the top. I saw a group of your friends and pointed them out to you.

"Go and say hi if you want, I'll be fine." I wanted to be fun, an easygoing me, and so I was letting you go.

"Are you sure?"

I wanted you to be free, and I also wanted a bit of breathing room. All of it was starting to be a bit too much. My instinct to flee was pulsing within me.

"Yeah, come find me in a bit if you want."

You nodded and left me to it. People were squashed up against every available space, treating the smallest of surface areas as their private bedrooms. Hands were cupping breasts and rubbing the outlines of indiscriminate erections. It was a free-for-all of hormones and heteronormativity—way too early in the night, I thought, to be this horny and unhinged. Sober and alone, I went searching for the drinks table, hoping alcohol might calm my nerves, but the loud music and writhing bodies made it nearly impossible. I spent what felt like an hour trying to move through that massive house.

Out of the corner of my eye, I spotted an empty staircase leading to the second floor, so I headed to the top of the stairs to see if I could find you in the crowd. All around me was a sea of straightness, people our age giving in to their desires, however temporary, exploring bodies they might not remember the following morning. Nowhere around me could I see anything that resembled me or my group of friends. There were no queers or punk feminists, or men dressed up as 1960s comedy heroines. This was your average college party with your average group of straight people, and I was desperate to find a way out as soon as possible. But among all that carnage, I could not see the one person I wanted. Just as I was about to give up, I felt a tug on my shirt and looked down to see your hand resting on my forearm once again. Your presence immediately calmed me.

"Finally, I found you," you said. Over the loud music, you mouthed, *I'm glad you're here.*

"Me too," I said, hoping you'd sense the sincerity in my voice.

You mouthed the word "drink" and signaled a cup with your hands just to get the point across. We made our way to the bar, which was, in fact, a dining room table with a plastic tablecloth thrown over it. The selections on offer, according to a poorly handwritten sign, included vodka or rum with Coke, Hawaiian Punch, or beer from a keg. Everything at this point in the night was room temperature except the beer, so we filled our cups and you poured four shots of vodka, which we downed.

With beer in hand, we navigated our way toward the living room. Someone's laptop was playing the role of DJ. While we were trying to find somewhere to sit, a remix of Katy Perry's "Teenage Dream" came on and every girl in the house descended upon the living room floor. I watched them, so free with their bodies and each other, dancing beautifully, stupidly, without inhibition, and I longed for just some of that freedom. I longed to join them and jump, turn, shake my ass with every fiber of joy possible. As I turned to look back at you, I thought I caught your eyes wandering to some pretty redhead from the women's soccer team. She was sensuously dancing closer and closer to another girl, and then, to my great surprise, they began to kiss. Some of the boys watching cheered loudly and made gross hand gestures to imply fingering and fucking. The girls flipped them off while continuing to focus on each other. You looked to me and then indicated the group of guys and mouthed the word "assholes" before taking a sip of beer. At least you were not like them, I thought. At least you were different from other guys.

It wasn't long before some of your teammates saw you and called you over. I could tell you were worried about me, and the promise you had made to not abandon me, but I insisted for a second time that I was fine. You conceded and joined them, all hooting and hollering from your earlier victory on the soccer field. In that moment, cast in the shadow of a moody dance floor, I was just grateful for your kindness, your gentle type of friendship. For now (or then) it felt like enough, and so I downed my beer and went to get more from the keg before heading out onto the porch. It was surprisingly warm under the stars. I remember a deep humidity hanging over the nearby gorges. Mosquitoes swarmed around the porch light, and the quietness of that outside space was a nice reprieve.

"It's amazing, isn't it, how many bodies of water run through this town?"

I turned to see who was speaking to me and was surprised to find a towering goddess standing at my side.

"Sorry, didn't mean to scare you. Just came out for some fresh air."

"No worries. It's gorgeous . . . the lake and all those creeks. I'm Daniel, by the way."

"Adelia. Nice to meet you."

Adelia Flores needed no introduction for me. Everyone at our school knew of her. Heir to a Brazilian media company, model for *Vogue Brasil*, one of only a handful of Black students. She was more beautiful than her reputation made out. Somehow, even though we represented the small minority population at our school, I'd never run into her.

"So, Daniel, what is someone like you doing at a party like this?"

"What do you mean?"

"Come on, amigo, this really doesn't seem like your crowd. I mean, I play soccer with these girls and sometimes I can't even stand them."

"Oh, I see what you mean," I said. I studied the moon's reflection in the water. "Well, I came with my roommate, Sam . . . Sam Morris."

"You're Sam's roommate? No way! That's so cool. He's like a really fucking good soccer player."

This made me smile so brightly even though I had no claim to your athleticism. But I loved hearing people speak about you with the same fervor I had.

"Yeah, he's pretty great."

"I'm sure you're just as great, guapo."

"I'm not so sure, but thanks, Adelia."

She rubbed me on the shoulder and took a sip from her cup. "So Daniel, what do you do besides join your very talented roommate at gross wannabe frat parties?"

"Hmm . . . I'm an English major, and I write poetry, and, well . . . I'm still finding my footing. I haven't really found my thing yet."

"That's okay. When I got to Cayuga it took me awhile to figure out what I liked. I mean, there was always soccer, I'm Brazilian for Christ's sake, so of course I had to join the women's team, but it took awhile to learn other things about myself. Like, I'm not a fan of parties like these, or I want to study politics, or, like, I'm into women."

I turned to her, and she had a nonplussed look on her face, but I could detect the smallest start of a smile.

"Not many people know this about me. Not that I try to hide it . . . I guess I'm what they call a 'lipstick lesbian' in this country?"

"Oh, well that's . . . awesome. Not about being a lipstick lesbian, unless that's what you want to be called, I just mean figuring out who you are."

"Thanks, chico. I kind of felt you'd be a . . . what's the phrase?"

"Kindred spirit?"

"Yes. Kindred spirit. Someone I could share it with, anyway. And really . . ." Adelia paused. "What's college for if not this? To figure these things out . . . what we want . . . what we no longer want in life."

"Yeah, you're right I suppose."

"Yes, well, I think I should head inside and show face or else these girls will continue to think I'm some stuck-up snob, which

I am, but, like, hey, that's for me to say, not them." She gave me a kiss on the cheek. "It was nice to chat, Daniel. Hope to see you around town."

I was struck by how easily Adelia had shared such a significant part of herself with me, as though it were no big deal. If only I could view life in that way, allowing myself that kind of bravery. But I wasn't ready just then, so I remained in the quiet gloam of my thoughts until the temperature dropped, forcing me to return to the chaos inside. Electronic dance music was blaring loudly as soon as I entered (we were living at the height of David Guetta and Calvin Harris), and the floors were caked in beer and jungle juice, making it difficult to walk around. I tried pushing past the dancing crowds and almost tripped on a couple making out on the floor. Luckily, they were so deep in the throes of passion they didn't even notice me. I went on searching for you to no avail and began growing despondent. I made my way to the door, trying to be discreet, not wanting to draw attention to myself as Sam's lame roommate who ditched him at a party. I made a promise to myself that I would text you during the walk home. I felt I owed you that, at least, but was otherwise 100 percent ready to bail.

On my way to the exit, I saw you there sitting by yourself, sipping on a beer, mindlessly playing with your phone. It was movie magic the way the strobe lights caught you. Even away from the buzzing crowd, you were the most beautiful person in the room. I just stood there for a few seconds staring at you and dreaming of all the things I could do if I were a braver, more confident version of myself. You must have sensed my presence because you looked up with the greatest sense of relief. You stood and immediately pushed by people to get to me.

"I thought you left."

"Nope. I was just outside enjoying the views."

"Talk to anyone?"

"Yeah, I was speaking with Adelia Flores."

"Oh okay, Mr. Big Shot. You know she, like, doesn't speak to anyone."

"I think that's exactly why she spoke to me, because I'm no one at this party."

This made you laugh, and I was happy to see you brighten up. You then asked if we could leave and I did not hesitate to say with great confidence, "Fuck yes." Although I felt slightly guilty, I was also glad to see that you weren't having as much fun as I'd thought you would. To know we were more similar than we might appear on the outside meant so much to me. As we exited, a group of people were coming, their nights just starting. They tried to give you a hard time about leaving so early, but you took the punches and said you'd make it up to them later. Then you looked to me happily and said we should go.

It was mostly quiet away from the rows of party houses with people spilling out onto their lawns, that post-party rabble deciding on its next move. The sensible thing would have been for us to go the long way through campus, which was well lit, but we decided to take a shortcut through the gorges, which is something you should never do in the dark of night. I told myself I'd be safe in your company. I was also slightly buzzed, so responsible decisions no longer felt important at that time. Really, I just wanted to be with you in the dark. The wind picked up, causing the trees to sway and make eerie noises. Pointing this out only made it seem more sinister, but you assured me you'd fight any monsters on my behalf.

"Thank you, kind sir," I joked.

"Mucho de nada, señor."

At the apex of the gorge, we stopped for a moment to take in the vista. The moon crept through the leaves overhead, casting shadows along our path. The stars reflecting on the glassy plane of the creek below had captivated our attention; the sound of the water trickling over mossy stones, the rest of the city sleeping. Had

I not been so buzzed, I might have asked to take a picture with you, but I let us just be still in the silent dark of night.

"Honestly, Daniel, I am so glad you are my roommate," you said, out of nowhere.

"What makes you say that?"

"You just make me happy. To have someone who is a genuine friend but not in my classes, or on my soccer team, or just like, you know . . . I know I sound drunk but what I'm trying to say is . . . well . . . at the party I was thinking how it's nice to have a friend who is a friend because we actually get each other. You're not like other guys, not some self-centered asshole. You're . . . you are a really nice person, Daniel."

"I get what you mean."

"See that? We get each other."

"We do. It's special."

"Yes . . . special."

My cheeks were beginning to go red from all the nice things you were saying. So red, I was confident you noticed even in the dark of night, because you pulled me close to you, hugging me tightly. You were always hugging me tightly, and I was too dumb to understand why. But in my tipsy state, I allowed myself to bury my face into you, smelling the salt of your skin, the citrus of your cologne. I breathed you in, like really breathed you in; I did not even try to be subtle about it. Then I felt your hand on my chin. You pulled my head up so we were face-to-face and you kissed me. Just like that. You kept kissing me, and something took over me because I leapt onto you, wrapping my legs around your waist, and you grabbed my ass, hoisting me up. I didn't know if we were kissing or making out, because I had never done either, but after a minute your legs gave out, sending us tumbling down the hill. At the bottom, we stopped rolling forward and started laughing maniacally. It all happened so fast, the staring and the kissing, the falling and the tumbling.

"Are you okay?"

"Yeah, just bumped my head," I said, trying to wipe dirt off my clothes. "But that was umm . . . nice."

"Yeah. Sorry about that. I don't know what came over me."

"No problem. I didn't mind."

You went to say something but stopped yourself. I waited for whatever it was, but nothing came out. It grew quiet between us; even the animals had gone to sleep. The sound of the creek was the only noise to mark what was a magical, messy moment. Your hand rested atop mine and I tried hard not to freak out, to let it just take place, whatever was taking place. But that was it, just a hand. No more kisses. Above us were hundreds upon hundreds of stars, some of them part of the constellations you'd given me language for back in the fall. I wanted to tell you that, but I didn't. So we lay on our backs watching them until we both fell asleep. The ground was cold, and the temperature was dropping quickly. By some miracle I woke up shivering, only to realize just thirty minutes had passed. I was so tired and wanted to get home, afraid sleeping in the damp frost might kill us.

"Hey, wake up, Sam. We need to get going."

You slowly got up as it dawned on you where we were.

"Fuck, did I really fall asleep in the dirt?"

"Yeah, you did."

"Sorry about that. I must have had more than I planned on."

"Yeah, me too," I said, unsure if you were already on the defensive, unsure if you remembered what had taken place not long before.

We stood slowly and with much pain before beginning our journey back to the dorm. The shortcut, at this point, didn't feel so short in the early hours of what was now Saturday morning. We were trying to be as quiet as possible while walking up the stairs, but in that way in which drunk people are more chaotic than they think they're being. As we crept down the hall, someone told us to shut the fuck up from behind their door, and you shouted apologies, which made us laugh loudly. After considerable effort, we overcame our struggle to open the door, then said good night and retired to our own beds. My body was so exhausted, so sore, and yet so alive; I was covered in cuts and bruises, but I felt euphoric. It took only seconds for me to fall asleep once in bed, but that night (or morning) I kept dreaming of your eyes, the taste of your lips, the way your hand had held my body close.

I awoke hours later to find you not in our dorm and, within seconds, I was hit with a pang of sadness, caused most likely by depressants from the alcohol and my intrusive thoughts about our kiss. Had you initiated it or had I? Did it even matter if, in the end, we both kept kissing? Then I remembered how, after our fall, you'd been about to say something to me before giving up and just staring at the stars. What had you wanted to tell me? What were you going to ask? I sat in bed but couldn't think of what the answers might be, so I rose in search of a glass of water. I was thirsty and miserable and confused. I thought about texting you but was unsure of what to even say. It was while filling a cup that I noticed your small note next to the coffee maker. You must have made a fresh pot right before leaving that morning. The note at least brought me some comfort, seeing this kindness, a love language of yours. I read it slowly:

HEY DANIEL,

I totally forgot I promised to meet my project group at the library this morning. I had to run out and grab a bite to eat before then. Worst hangover ever! Anyway, I had so much fun last night. Thank you for helping celebrate our win and coming along with me to the party. Let's do it all again soon.

SEE YOU LATER!
SAM

I freaked out as I read and then reread the note. What did you mean by "having fun" and "wanting to do it all again soon"? My mind was swirling with a million thoughts, my brain thumping with the pain of a hangover, my stomach churning with alcohol and regret. My phone began to buzz, and I was praying it was you so we could address all this right away, but it was my mom calling to catch up. I ignored the call and returned to my bed, hoping when I woke up later, I'd have a better sense of how to move forward with things. I knew we would have to deal with what had happened, but that morning would not be the time when we did so. Nor, it turns out, would the next. Or the one after that. We were about to enter a chapter that would fundamentally change the entire course of our friendship. But in that moment, I needed all the rest I could get, because at least when I was sleeping, I could dream of you. At least when I was dreaming, you would be there with me. We could be ourselves freely, and I could say all the things running through my mind.

APRIL

I went to confession today in preparation for Easter. I must confess I don't believe in confession. I don't believe one needs a priest's "chismoso" ear to ask the Lord for forgiveness, nor do I believe, in such moments, that their ears are a direct line to God. I only went because I wanted to make Amá and mis abuelos happy. In their minds, to truly celebrate the end of our Lenten journey, we must confess our sins. So as I sat in the confessional booth, I thought about all the things I would not absolve myself of. I decided I would not absolve myself of the way I stare at the laborers who line this city with brick and mortar, their dark copper muscles glistening in the sun, their jet-black hair wet with salt. I would not absolve myself of my dreams in which these men take me into the shadows of a street corner, then take turns, each one filling me with all of himself, my body a whirlpool of their frenzied ejaculation. I will never seek forgiveness for my desire to be coveted by these men. I will never ask forgiveness for the things that make me who I am. As I sat in the booth, with the priest offering to lend his ear, inviting me to share what "weighed heavily on my heart," I thought of everything I'd never apologize for and was all the lighter for it.

—D.M.

In the days after our first kiss, I could think of nothing but your lips. Despite the dizzying rush of the night, I could still recall with perfect clarity the shape of your philtrum, the saltiness of your saliva, how your mouth fit perfectly around mine. But in those following days, I was also facing the very real possibility that I might never know any of it again. I was wrestling with guilt and regret and fear, all things we could've resolved if only we'd spoken about what had happened. But, as usual, we didn't. We allowed friends, classes, and the rest of our lives to fill in the silences, dancing around each other in a neat choreography of training, cramming for tests, and quotidian routine. And though we did come together for our weekly meals and our laundry, we allowed eating and the hum of the dryers to take the place of any meaningful conversation.

But this avoiding, as you know, could only last for so long. Eventually it ran its course. Finally, something had to be done, and it was me, for once, who led the charge.

One day I woke up and decided to go for a run along Six Mile Creek. I needed to be away from textbooks, from campus, from you and all the burning questions I had. I was determined to move toward positive action—a change, I felt, that should begin with actual movement. So I ran through thick morning heat as the city was just waking up. The trail was empty except for a few people out walking their dogs, and I was surrounded by tall oak and elm trees. I breathed in moss and birchwood. It felt calm in the woods, the solitude something I had chosen. On that path, I wasn't Daniel, or a college freshman, or a son, or a friend. I wasn't in love with you. I was just a body in motion. One leg after the other, negotiating stone and decaying branches broken by April storms. I was at peace for the first time in weeks, and so I decided to go further simply because I could. I didn't want peace to leave me, and feared being confronted by all I was trying to break from. I dug deeper; each step, each breath, a tiny gift to myself.

I reached a natural stopping point, a quiet clearing at the edge of a gorge, where I was able to see the city as it looked from South Hill. From this direction, I could see our campus over on the east side. I had never seen it like this, and it struck me as strange how distant our campus was from the rest of the city. It was like the founders had created a fortress to keep out the townsfolk, trying to protect privileged students from the reality of what their privilege meant in relation to the rest of the world—the world I grew up in, a world in which people didn't get to while away their days in libraries of leather-bound books. As I stood there dripping with sweat, gnats swarming me, I felt a sense of clarity. This— Cayuga—wasn't real life. None if it mattered at the end of the day. It was transient, all of it, and I wouldn't give it the power to destroy me. I would survive this semester and the subsequent three years and, after, there would be new experiences. I'd be free again. With all that natural beauty around me, it felt like God was showing me how life was made of seasons and each season had the power to teach me something about myself.

I sat down on a small boulder and closed my eyes, the sound of birdcall keeping me company. Each bird's voice was many octaves high; some were shrill, some melodic, most were soothing. I tried to differentiate one from another, wanting to understand them all. What were those birds saying? What did they know of the world? If only we could speak to one another, perhaps they could offer advice that would help me figure out what to do about you and me.

When I opened my eyes, I was stunned to see a swarm of sparrows flying above a lake not far to the west of me. They moved through the air with such ease. How brilliant it would be to fly among their flock, I thought. I took out my phone and snapped a photo. Without allowing myself too much time to think, I sent it to you along with a request to talk. I then put the phone away and made my long way back to campus, along the creek, through downtown, and up East Hill. I let my breath and feet lead the way, running without thinking, just one step, another step, breath. It wasn't till I was in front of our dorm that I saw your response.

Hey, yeah. I'm home now. Think it'd be good to talk.

I let out a heavy sigh and looked up to our floor. It was now or never, and I knew we couldn't hide any longer from all the things slipping through the cracks of our once-platonic friendship. The seams were at their bursting point, the dam overflowing—whatever metaphor you used to look at it, it was time. I could run and run and run, but I couldn't outrun this.

I felt another buzz at my thigh: *Nice photo by the way. Wish I had been there.*

I wrote back to you: *Coming up now.*

My heart was beating at a dangerous speed as I walked up the two flights of stairs and down the hall to where you were waiting. I didn't know what I was going to say, but I was the one who had initiated this confrontation and I was the one who needed to make sure it happened. As I worked up the courage to open our door, I had all this fear bubbling within me. I would finally get answers to the questions consuming me, but I might not like those answers. You could very well tell me something I did not want to hear. My hand gripped the doorknob, I turned it, and there you were on the couch, waiting for me like you said you'd be. You may have looked somber, afraid even, but at least you were there.

You nodded toward me and said, "Hey."

You were always the talker, the one who could fill the room with your voice, but it was just one single word you offered me, a tiny greeting that held so much in it: fear of the unknown, acknowledgment of the dangerous territory we were now entering. Both of us were so full of desire, and yet so afraid of the possibility of hurt, rejection even. I see that now. I see how we were battling the same things but felt so alone even when together. It's ridiculous, but even now, as I revisit it, my own heart is thudding and I am back in that room, watching it all unfold.

You scooted over to let me sit down next to you. What was usually an electric heat of desire I felt radiating off your body had become a quiet sadness. It was as if you were awaiting punishment, when really all I wanted was to give you the freedom of honesty. I allowed myself time to gather my thoughts, to center myself. I was safe in our room. You were my best friend. We did not want to hurt each other, nor did we have to let things change if we did not want them to. If it was going to be too much, if it could destroy our friendship, then I'd learn to quell my desire. All this to say, I was desperate not to lose you.

"What was it you wanted to talk about?"

The air escaped me as I took in your question. It was finally happening. We were so close to the truth. The stage was set, we had taken our places, now all we had to do was speak. But the room suddenly felt even smaller, somehow, too small to hold all I'd held on to since August. As I summoned the courage to answer you, you watched me in your periphery. Your fingers were nervously picking at the coffee table, trying to remove some dried-up pizza sauce. Six foot one, all muscle, and yet you looked so small. Not the Sam I knew.

"I feel like you know."

"Yeah, I figured as much," you said.

Still neither of us could quite say it. It felt Olympian to actually confront what had happened with words because, if we did, the reality was that we would no longer be just best friends. We would be best friends who had kissed, who had kissed hard and passionately and with abandon. The truth is, we would never be able to go backward, only forward to whatever lay ahead for us.

"Did you mean to do it?"

"The kiss?"

"Yes, the kiss."

You weighed it all up in your mind before speaking. Were you replaying the events in your head? Were you remembering the taste of my lips on yours? Because it looked like you were giving your answer the most serious consideration. I sat there waiting, scared, unsure of what I was about to hear.

"Probably."

Again, you gave me one word, which contained so much. I took a few seconds to process it, and you sat there, unflinching.

"What does that mean?"

"It means I probably meant to, yes."

Your tone. It hurt me. Did you realize that at the time? I felt inconsequential to you in a moment when you were my entire world.

"I don't understand."

"We were drunk, Daniel."

"So you didn't mean it, then?"

"That's not what I'm saying. I'm saying we were drunk, and I kissed you."

"It is really shitty of you to say it like that, and you know it."

I could feel tears starting to form. In spite of myself, I was beginning to tap into a well of anger and confusion that had long consumed me.

"Please, don't be like that," you said.

I felt so angry with you. You were like a petulant child who knew what he was doing, shirking any responsibility, blaming the kiss on watery beer from a keg, downed at a shitty party you'd dragged me to. Do you remember, Sam? You made the plans. You brought me further into your world. You kissed me. Yes, I was really, really fucking angry with you.

"Do you even know how much I like you?"

"What do you mean, you like me?"

"No, no more of this bullshit. No more of this playing naïve crap. I mean come on, Sam, you must have known for a while now."

"Maybe, but does it even matter if I did?"

"Of course it matters. What a fucking stupid question."

"Hey, don't blow up at me, Daniel. It takes two to tango."

I was dumbfounded. It was going completely the wrong way, and it felt like you were being cruel. Somehow we had become something else altogether, no longer in sync with each other. Our dynamic, our free-natured friendship, all of it felt like a ruse. There was no going back from here, and I knew it. But I wouldn't run anymore; I would stand firm.

"Do you like me? I don't mean as a friend. I mean, are you attracted to me at all?"

There. Somehow, after nearly nine months, I'd done it, straight up asked you the million-dollar question. I'd thought I'd die if I ever did, but I didn't, and although I wanted to crawl into myself as I waited those long seconds for a response, I didn't. I stayed present. I stood my ground and waited.

"I'm not ready to do this, Daniel. I'm sorry," you said. You stood up.

"Not ready for what?" I asked, blocking you from leaving.

"I'm not ready for this whole 'saying I'm gay' shit, if that is what you're after."

Again, your reaction threw me. Were you deflecting me? Insinuating, somehow, that I was forcing you to do something besides answer one single question. I couldn't even look at you, I was so hurt. I remember pacing around the room, trying to formulate a sentence that didn't contain all the expletives pumping through my mind. The room had continued to shrink, and it could no longer contain all we were thinking. We were at a breaking point. My body was hot with a fiery anger so new to me. I was learning how someone I loved could disappoint me, how disappointment could be a form of hurt.

"You're a fucking coward, you know that? I mean, I can't even begin to explain my anger. How are you putting all this on me? 'If that's what you're after.' All I'm asking is that you tell me whether you like me or not, I'm not inviting you to a fucking pride parade."

You sat down, wincing, in silence, just staring at me. You had never seen me like this. I could see you formulating the words, but each time you went to say something you stopped yourself. What were you so afraid of? What stopped you from wanting to be open with me? I wish I could ask you, but I'm still not quite sure what you'd say. I can't pretend to know what was stopping you from being your normal, assured self.

"I've spent too long hiding from myself and what I want. I'm not doing that anymore. You want to know the truth? Well, I like you, Sam, okay. I like you and I have for a really fucking long time. You want to know something else—I'm glad we kissed . . . I mean, I loved it. I'd do it all again if I could. But, fuck, all I'm asking you now is what do you think about it all? Because if it was a mistake, if you want to take it back, then we can do that. I'll act like it never happened because you mean that much to me. Your friendship is that important. I'll let it all go if that's what you want. I just need you to talk to me."

If before you were struggling to speak, you were now paralyzed by choice. I had given you the chance to either sail away from truth or let down the drawbridge, so I might cross the threshold and move deeper into your world.

"Why do we have to complicate things?"

"I don't know what that means."

I stood there visibly shaking, waiting for more from you, tired and tearful. It was as if love was the most difficult human language, honesty the most painful human act.

"I'm not ready, Daniel."

"Again, I don't know what you mean by that."

For eight months, I had let so much go unsaid, failed to address things head-on. Although your face was saying a lot, I refused to read into it. I needed you to speak clearly to me, so I just stood there. You on the couch, our giant window behind you. I turned from you and looked at the view before me, trying to calm myself.

The trees were full of their big green leaves, the hills covered in grass and flowers, and our room went from bright light to deep shadow as the clouds blew by. The weeks were winding down, and this view would soon be a distant memory. So much had happened here, and yet it felt like we were just on the cusp of things.

"Yes, I meant to kiss you. Yes, I'm glad I did. Yes, I had wanted to do it for a long time now. But I don't think I can be what you need."

"What do I need?"

"I mean deserve. I can't be what you deserve."

"What do I deserve?"

"Openness. Someone who isn't ashamed. Someone like Rob."

"Fuck Rob, what about what I want? What about what I think?"

"What, then?"

"You, idiot, I want you," I said, tears streaming down my face.

Saying it did something unexpected to me. I felt both freed and completely broken, vulnerable and laid bare. I could not stop the tears. The very thing I had held on to, the very thing that had kept me awake for so many nights and filled me with such dread, was now out in the open. It was before us, alone and scared, wanting someone to acknowledge it so it would not be alone any longer.

"I like you too, Daniel. I swear to you, I do, but I'm not ready to come out and say I'm gay or have a boyfriend."

"I'm not forcing you to be anything. I just need to hear you say it again," I mumbled between crying and heavy breathing, my nose filled with snot. "I just need to hear it."

"I like you, Daniel. I have for a long time now."

There. You said it with conviction, and I believed you. It stirred something in me, hearing those words, and so I rushed to you and took your face in my hands, and I kissed you. This time it was me who initiated, and you kissed me back. Your lips were a freedom, a home for me, a vortex into infinite time, a place just for us.

When I finally pulled back, I could see that the weather outside had changed. It was now all gray clouds and spring showers, but I didn't see any of those things as bad omens. To me, they were the start of something new. The water that would nourish and feed what we had sown, what was now ready to grow.

"I didn't know if we'd ever do that again," you said.

You then pulled me onto your lap, your hand combing through the dark black locks of my hair. The gesture was so full of kindness, but there was also a new emotion pulling us closer: wanting. I let myself be held against your longing. The way you cradled my head, I had nowhere to look but directly into your eyes, so blue and expansive, utterly magnetic. I can see them now, even without you here.

As I sat there, I could feel us both getting hard, your erection pressing into the back of my thigh. My heart was pounding inside, an animal rattling its cage. You kissed me once more, this time while sliding your hand up the opening of my shirt. My back, sweaty from my run, felt small in your hands. I looked down and my erection was on full show. I was both excited and genuinely frightened because all of it was so new to me. I didn't fully understand how men were meant to be intimate, but I understood I was enjoying your touch, something I had longed for since the day we'd met, prayed for even. Now it was happening.

"I like feeling your hands against my skin."

"Me too. I've wanted to hold you like this for a while, but I was never certain what you wanted."

"Really?" I asked, genuinely surprised.

"Sometimes it's hard to read you."

I'd always thought I was an open book, always thought you could understand my desires even if I struggled to share them. My desire was so obvious to me, but I'd been more guarded than I had realized. I wrapped my arms around your neck, resting my head against yours. I breathed in deeply, inhaling your scent.

"I've been scared. I always felt I was misreading things or projecting my feelings onto you. I mean, come on, Sam, you don't really come off as the kind of guy who likes guys."

You laughed at this. I laughed because it felt easier than unpacking what I meant by that. I was still afraid because I did not know what any of this was, what you wanted, how you saw us. If you saw yourself as someone far removed from a person like Rob or Mona or even me.

"It's raining," you whispered into my ear.

"It was nice when I was out this morning, but it looks pretty gross now."

"I guess we're stuck inside."

I could feel your erection pulsating against me, but I did not know if I was misreading the moment. Our bodies were warm with a carnal heat, your voice thick with longing, and I needed more than just to be held by you. I wanted all of you.

"What will we do then?"

"I think I have an idea," you said before laying me down against the couch.

You began to kiss the soft of my neck and then behind my ears. The stubble of your face against my skin was electrifying. We had not totally dealt with things, had not articulated what we wanted or where we were going, but at least we were allowing our bodies this. Two bodies, two men, together in the safety of their home. I was ready for all you might give me through touch. I would deal with the repercussions later. For now, I just needed more.

You sat up and removed your hoodie. Your body was beautiful. I had seen so much of it before through quick, stolen glances, but now you were in front of me, purposefully. You were allowing me to see all of you, to stare openly, to drink up the water of your soul. My body was yours to consume, and I wanted you to know you could have your fill of me. I was ready. You helped me to take off my running top, and you began to kiss my shoulders and then my chest. You called me beautiful, and I realized I'd never been called beautiful by anyone outside my family. It thrilled me. This was what wanting was. We continued to kiss, grabbed handfuls of skin. You asked if I wanted to do more, to get fully undressed. I said yes, please. You helped strip me of my briefs and shorts. I feared I was smelly from the run, but you breathed me in hungrily. You told me you loved how I smelled like a man. You then asked me to help you, so I stripped you of your sweats and underwear. There we were. Two men completely naked, ravenous for each other's bodies. But we were also two best friends about to cross a threshold, and we did.

I remember you as respectful, always courteous. Asking me if you could do this or if I wanted that. You kissed me between my thighs, kissed the skin stretching from thigh to pelvic bone. Your tongue traced a line from my belly button to my cock, and then you wrapped your hands around it, took me into your mouth. Your tongue was warm, and as you licked and sucked, I was taken to another plane, a whole new universe. I gasped for air, gripped the cushions tightly. My body was not prepared for the rushing sensations of your touch, your heat. I asked you to slow down because I didn't trust myself not to explode all over you. You pulled yourself up to kiss me on the mouth and it was as if I were tasting myself.

"I could do that for you, if you want," I offered shyly.

"Only if you're comfortable."

You were so tall you had to sit upright on the couch, and I moved to the floor on my knees. You were much bigger than me, and my hand looked small holding your shaft. I began to stroke you softly, telling myself you were a man, and I was a man, and I understood what men wanted. You moaned with pleasure. I enjoyed this power I had. With you in my hand, both of us naked, I was no longer aloof and cerebral. I was sexy and beautiful, the very thing you longed for. I took you in my mouth, a struggle at first, but I got the hang of it. I studied your groans, altered the rhythm accordingly. I took you right to the edge, then stopped. You laughed in ecstasy. I pulled myself up onto the couch, nestled into your arms.

"What else do you want?"

"Hmm . . . I could think of some other things, but I think we should save them for later," you said.

"Okay . . ." I said, a slight hurt in my voice.

"I don't want to rush anything, Daniel. But please know I want to sleep with you, like so badly, but we have all the time in the world. So let's take our time."

This made me smile. I was safe with you, and, the thing is, we really did believe we had all the time in the world. So I agreed. We spent the rest of the afternoon kissing and grabbing each other until, finally, we could not contain what had been percolating away for too long. But we did not go all the way that first day. We allowed ourselves to wade in fresh waters, but out there in the distance the tide was shifting, and soon a bigger wave would come, bringing with it both growth and destruction.

In the days that followed, we fell into a pattern of allowing ourselves to swim in those new waters. We maintained our usual schedule of seeing friends and studying; you had your soccer games and I was getting more involved with various clubs on campus, trying to expand my friendship circle. I had my Hispanic Heritage Club, and Rob and I were regularly joining Mona at Young Democrats of America, who were really pushing the legalization of same-sex marriage in many states across the country. When it was just the two of us at home, we were manic in our bodily exploration. But full-on sex was still waiting out there in the distance, some island we had to build up stamina in order to swim out to.

Though I thought about telling Rob and Mona what was happening, I felt afraid to discuss it with them because I didn't know what we were. I didn't want to invite their questions if I didn't have clear ways of explaining the dynamic between us, and even now, I don't know how to define our relationship at that time. You weren't my boyfriend, but you weren't solely my friend. Lover? Amante? No. You were my Sam, a different Sam from the person you gave the rest of the world. And with you, I was a different Daniel. I was becoming more forthright, more self-assured; better able to articulate my deepest desires, and now fully aware of how to use desire to bring about pleasure. I was a new man because of you.

I remember the exact day we did go further and finally had sex. It was a warm Thursday. I had just finished my class with Naomi. I was wandering around the quad and happened to pass the gym as you were exiting. You had been frequenting the gym on your own in addition to your workouts with your team, calling them double sessions. You told me at the time that you wanted to add on more muscle. *More muscle*, I thought, *where?* My body was so underdeveloped compared to yours, but still you pushed yourself harder, further, and I was able to reap the benefits every time we undressed. If I was beautiful to you, you were heavenly to me, a sculpture, a Greek god.

You were putting your headphones in your bag when you saw me: "Hey, fancy meeting you here."

"Yeah, just walking home now. That's me, done for the day."

"I can't believe how early your classes start."

"It's not bad when you get the whole of the afternoon to enjoy."

"Do you have many plans today, Señor de La Luna?"

"Are you coming on to me, Mr. Morris?"

You looked around to see if anyone was near us, then leaned close. "You are looking quite sexy in those jeans."

I looked down and noticed how snug my jeans were. I was still growing into my manhood, filling out in different places, my ass in particular. I joked that the Mexican in me was starting to show.

"Lucky me," you said, which instantly made me hard.

"It's not fair that you're turning me on in public."

"Well, how about we go home and do something about that?"

This was all new for us. We had found a different cadence to speaking, new language. What might've been allusion or innuendo in the past, misreading or misunderstanding, was now fully direct, open, desirous speech. We were no longer afraid of sharing with each other our most intimate wishes.

As we walked back, far from the company of others, you began telling me all the things you wanted to do to me. It was like a game you were playing, so I joined you. I began to tell you what I wanted to do to your body. You were laughing and had to adjust yourself because your hard-on was fully visible in your loose gym shorts. We rushed through the door to our building and up the stairs. We took the steps two at a time, then slowed down as we walked along the hall in case anyone else was home. I was nervous and blushing as I attempted to open our door, my hands sweaty from trying to work the key.

Once inside, I dropped my backpack and you let go of your gym bag. You lifted me into your arms, then carried me to your bedroom, where you tossed me onto your bed and climbed on top of me. Shock waves shuddered through my body as I felt your hand slide down past the elastic band of my underwear, tangling your fingers through my thick black pubic hair. You reached hungrily for my erection. I remember letting out a moan so uninhibited and loud, you described it as sexy. This time, you explored all my crevices and folds with studied care, and I wanted nothing more than to be yours forever. As I lay there, I couldn't believe that it was actually happening, that I would know what it would be to go all the way, to have all of you, and you me.

You kissed me softly while unbuttoning my jeans one-handed, managing to take off my underwear with deft expertise. You were a magician ripping off the tablecloth without breaking the dinnerware or candlesticks. At some point in all of the foreplay, you had taken off your gym shorts and boxers, and your body was glorious: golden tan and a down of ocher hair, the cut of your flank, parts of you still stark white. I suppressed all the voices telling me, *Daniel, your body looks nothing like his, what are you offering this gorgeous man?* I stayed present. All your actions, your hunger, all of it, said I was enough. I was more than enough.

You flipped me so I was on my side, so we were face-to-face, and continued to kiss me. This time with such clear, sober intent. You then laid me on my back and climbed on top of me, my legs spread open for you, your muscular frame hovering above me. You took out a condom and lube from your dresser drawer, rolled the condom on. The lube felt cold against my skin as you slipped your fingers into me. I still couldn't quite believe it, but here it was, happening. We were finally going all the way. This time, what we were doing was born not from anger or tears or drunken frivolity, but from a steadily built understanding of each of our desires and wants. On a quiet morning, you had found an opportunity to show me how two bodies fit together.

As you pushed deeper inside me, I gripped your shoulders tightly and muffled my pain by breathing hard against your skin. You asked if I wanted you to stop, if I was okay, but I said to keep going. I said it was fine, and it was, eventually. Something about the pain was electrifying because it meant I was now connected to you. As you thrust gently, I could feel each of your muscles contracting, your brow filling with sweat. I grabbed hold of your ass cheeks, so firm, so beautiful, wrapping my legs around you. I felt so alive. Nothing will ever take that feeling from me. I asked you to go deeper, harder. I was learning the language of sex, what my body wanted. I was learning how pain could be pleasurable and turn into beauty. For so long, I had hidden from myself, tried to quell what I saw as badness, as something that made me unworthy of love and compassion. But with you, I was my full self.

"You're so fucking beautiful, Daniel," you told me, your voice low and sultry.

"You too, Sam. You are the most beautiful man I've ever met."

I remember this made you laugh, and you kissed me, and then told me how close you were to finishing and I said go for it, I was ready, and together we crossed another threshold. You pulled out of me, ripped off the condom, and together we came before you collapsed onto me, our bodies slick with sweat, salty and sweet, covered in each other's cum. But it was not gross; it was beautiful. It was what bodies did. There was nothing to be ashamed of, nothing to feel sick about. This was how we learned to express our love.

"That was amazing, Daniel," you whispered, softly kissing my shoulders.

"It wasn't what I was expecting to happen when I left for class today."

"I know, but the moment felt right."

I shook my head in agreement and nuzzled into you. You wrapped your arms around me tight. You held me how I always wanted to be held by you, like you never wanted to let me go, like I was the one person you wanted to have beside you, naked and free, alive and strong.

"Just so you know, that was my first time," you said, offering me a gift.

I was unsure if you meant with a guy, or your first time having sex in general. You were handsome, funny, charismatic—the archetype of the beautiful American male—and I'd assumed this meant that you'd spent your high school days being chased by girls, and must've at least tried to sleep with a woman. But then I reflected on all the messages you had tried to send me throughout the year, the special way you treated me relative to other friends, and I realized you were telling me that I really was your first.

I then thought about my own high school self, the boy who kept his head down low, deep in books. The one who dreamt of escaping his small town, his home state, fleeing to the other side of the country. I thought about all the secrets he kept inside, his desires, his longing. What would he think of me now? Could he ever believe one day he'd be lying naked next to someone who looked like you? The most beautiful man in the world. Could he ever understand that this was how he'd learn to fall in love?

"You're not falling asleep, are you?" you asked.

"Nope, just thinking."

"You mean about what we just did?"

I didn't respond immediately, but smiled to let you know I had no regrets from having lost my virginity to you. In the moment, words were not necessary. Younger me might never have believed our story, but it didn't matter because it was real, all of it, each and every word, and it was mine and yours to have, for as long as the world would let us.

We continued lying together as you played with the tufts of my pubic hair. I was strumming my fingers on your hard chest, working up the courage to say something I had been holding on to since a few days prior, since the first time we'd held each other naked like this.

"Can I ask you a question?"

"Go for it," you said, cupping my ass in your hands, cradling me.

"When did you start liking me?"

"Like, as 'more than friends'?"

"Yes, as in 'more than friends.'"

You turned on your stomach to face me directly, your smile wide and pure. "Like, honestly?"

"Yes, that's preferable to dishonestly," I said, laughing but afraid.

"Remember when we were with my dad in the food court at the shopping center?"

"So, day one?"

"Yes, day one. It started the moment you stepped out of your room and my heart dropped when I saw you. I'd never felt anything like that for a guy before, or at least not as strongly, not enough to believe I might be attracted to guys. I couldn't stop thinking about you the whole car ride even though you were next to me. Is that weird?"

I lay there listening, not saying anything.

"I remember being desperate for the shopping to be done with because I wanted to see you again just to make sure I was feeling what I was feeling. Then when you joined Dad and me in the food court, I sat there trying not to look at you too much, but it was happening all over again."

"What did it for you? Was it that sexy way I wolfed down my pretzel?"

"No, it was how awkward you were."

"What the hell? Please explain immediately," I asked, sitting up.

"You were making small talk with my dad, and I could just tell how nervous you were, which was like a type of kindness you were offering him and me. Like, I don't know how to explain it, but you were doing your best to be in the moment, to push through what made you uncomfortable about chatting with a stranger, and I thought, *Man, that takes a lot of courage.* Here you were on practically your first day, alone, and me with my parents helping me. But you were the braver one, even if you were kind of cute and awkward. Does that make sense?"

I turned away while nodding. My heart was in my throat, and I was desperate not to cry again in front of you, especially in this moment, naked with both of our bodily fluids covering us. I was oscillating between the various ways humans can be intimate with one another. Sometimes through touch, sometimes through words, sometimes with just the slightest of looks in which we are not necessarily looking at each other but into each other, deep into our souls.

"Honestly, Sam, that's one of the nicest observations anyone has ever made about me."

"For a while, though, I couldn't figure out if you liked me or not or, like, just saw me as your roommate, and of course I was scared because I hadn't ever thought I could like a guy, and, still, I don't understand everything that's happening right now. I hope that is clear even though I know it's not."

"Okay, I have one more question."

"Here we go again . . ." you said, in your joking way.

"Was the spooning intentional?"

"What do you think?"

"Were you trying to tell me all along?"

"I think I was just cold . . ."

"You think you're so funny, don't you."

I grabbed a pillow and pretended to smother you. You kept muttering how you were joking. You told me you'd meant to spoon me just like you'd meant to kiss me. I asked you to say it louder, to prove what you meant. Then you pushed me off of you and flipped me onto the bed, pinning me down with your long body. We stayed fixed there, looking deep into each other's eyes, and it was like we were seeing each other for the first time. Not as Daniel and Sam who had been roomies since August, but Daniel and Sam who together were learning to be something much more. You kissed me, and I kissed you, and we went on kissing with all the desire that had built up since we'd first met. We let go of words for the rest of the morning, allowing touch to say all that we had left unsaid for too long.

MAY

I woke up today and thought of my Abuela Soledad. How when I was scared, she'd hold me close to her, the smell of rose oil on her dark, thick hair. During our famous tumultuous summer storms, she'd try valiantly to distract us grandchildren with stories. As the thunder cracked loudly outside her house, she'd tell us of the generations of family who'd worked the land around us, how our family have long reared cattle in an unforgiving landscape and how we learned to make abundant these arid plains. Her stories somehow turned the rainstorms friendly, made the land come alive, and in her company, I was no longer afraid. As I get older, I find myself wondering: Who will be the one to calm me with such stories? Who will teach me how darkness is not to be feared, but embraced for all that it might contain, for all the light that will come flooding forth?

—D.M.

I have spent these past few days back in Ithaca, waking up each morning and going for long runs along the paths you first showed me. It's good to be physically present in these places, ones I've shared with you. In the serenity of dawn, I will often find a rock to sit on and allow my body to be in a place you once were. I allow myself to remember, to laugh and to cry. I allow myself to feel you. Everywhere you were, I think, is somewhere I can return to. Everywhere you were is somewhere I can choose to hold on to until I'm ready to let go. Our year may be drawing to a close in my telling, but I can still return to all of it. I can still show you all that is left of us. I can find my way back to you.

When we woke up the following morning, it was May, and just like that we were only three weeks away from saying goodbye to each other. You had an away game and had to leave early on a bus to Philadelphia, and so I had the weekend to myself. Knowing you'd be gone all weekend drove us further that last day of April. We hadn't been satisfied with sleeping together just the once, no, not now that we knew each other's bodies in that way. So morning bled into afternoon and on into evening, and we wrung ourselves dry of our mutual desire. We tried to hold out as long as possible until you needed to catch the bus. But even in the final hour together, we were hungry for company, so I joined you for a shower in our small en suite, where we kissed and scrubbed each other clean with soap and shared what little time we had left. I kissed you goodbye and you kissed me back with greed and affection, and then you were off. Now I needed to find a way of passing the time until you came home late on Sunday, until we once more could claw and grab at each other in the heat of passion.

Mona had invited me to join her and some of her Young Democrats of America pals at one of the gorges to go swimming, but I said I had to run some errands and would see her Sunday night at the meeting. I took myself downtown with the hope that I could enjoy solitude in public. As I walked through Ithaca's bustling main plaza, I wondered if I was somehow different. If my gait, or scent, or general aura had been altered now that you and I had gone all the way. It was one thing to have fooled around the past few weeks, but to have fucked was much more serious (at least to me). My mind at the time was a swirling mixture of serotonin, dread, euphoria, and deep fear. There was no going back, but time was also running out, and I didn't know where we were headed. I kept jumping to the future. How would our actions impact us next year? Would everything that had happened destroy our friendship? Could you ever love me enough to come out? Was it even my right to want you to come out, when I myself was not out to anyone besides my small group of friends and you?

I was overthinking, but I couldn't help it. I wandered through gridded streets before happening upon a small bookshop in Dewitt Mall. It sold mostly secondhand books, lots of textbooks, and piles of magazines like *National Geographic*. I browsed the fiction section and found some books by Gabriel García Márquez. I hadn't ever read many books by Latin American or Hispanic writers, so I picked it up and went to pay. The bookshop owner was an older man in his sixties, handsome and well dressed. He asked if I had ever read Márquez and I said no, but my family was originally from México, and I was keen to read more Latin American writers. I told him I knew Márquez was Colombian, but I had to start somewhere. This made him chuckle, and then he told me to wait a second before disappearing to the back. He returned with a copy of Sandra Cisneros's *The House on Mango Street*, which he said he'd just gotten in the other day. He charged me only for the Márquez book and said he hoped my literary explorations went well. I thanked him and continued my downtown wanderings.

Across the street, I could see the local Planned Parenthood. Part of me wanted to go in and get tested for HIV even though both of us had been each other's first and you had worn condoms each time we had sex, but there was a guilt eating at me. Was it shame or fear, a kind of vergüenza? I could not quite decide, but then I remembered how the campus health center emphasized the need for regular testing, especially among men who slept with other men. How quickly would you know if you had an STD? My mind was running in a million directions, but instead of doing anything productive I walked right past the clinic, and as I did, I bumped into none other than Bernie-Bernice.

"Dearest Daniel, my sweet baby gay, what a pleasure seeing you here. What are you up to?"

"Oh, I was just looking at a bookshop in the mall."

"The secondhand shop? Love that place. I go often during my lunch break for a small peruse. Gary, the owner, has a great selection of queer classics."

"Where do you work?"

"Right here. I volunteer twice a week at the Planned Parenthood."

"That's great, really great."

"It is. So is everything good with you? Ever manage to deal with that troublesome tryst from the fall?"

"Oh, Sam, you mean? Well, yes, umm, you see, we are together."

"Daniel, that is so fucking awesome to hear."

"Well, not together, more like just 'enjoying the moment.'"

"Oh, okay. Well, hey, that is something."

I nodded, unsure what else to say as Bernie-Bernice studied my face.

"And does this make you happy?"

Again, I nodded, unable to decide now whether it did. It was early days. You and I had not had a chance to talk at length, but in describing our situation aloud to Bernie-Bernice, it didn't sound romantic in the least.

"Well, I don't have all the tea, Daniel, and I don't purport to know what it is you want. But my unsolicited advice would be to really think hard about what that is. Sex can be great, but if whatever is happening between you and . . . Sam, was it?"

I nodded again, still unsure what to say, but desperate for whatever advice I might get from Bernie-Bernice.

"If whatever is happening is not what you want, or you want something more, it's important to make that clear. Don't get trapped in silences, okay? It won't be a good and true start if you hide your feelings."

"Thanks, Bernie-Bernice. I appreciate that."

"Well, I'm off to grab lunch, but it was really great seeing you, Daniel. Don't be a stranger."

I hugged Bernie-Bernice goodbye and made my way to the bus stop. I could see my bus arriving and made a dash for it, trying not to drop my books. Quickly, I climbed aboard and took a seat near the window. The plaza was now full of people grabbing lunch in between classes or work. In that moment, I was struck by how all of us were there, seemingly fine as we went about our days, but surely, like me, everyone was dealing with their own issues, their own joys or hardships. None of them could have known how my life was changing so dramatically, how I had just slept with the man of my dreams, a man who was bound to break my heart. What, I wondered, might I not know about them?

As the bus neared campus, I got a call from my parents, which was surprising as it was Friday and we usually caught up over the weekend. I answered, hoping it would be a nice distraction from everything happening around me, a momentary break from my thoughts about us and Bernie-Bernice's lingering questions.

"Hola, Daniel," my mom said over the phone.

There was something different in her voice, something I could not quite pinpoint. I held the phone close to my ear, trying to listen for any clues.

"Hi Mom, I'm just on the bus right now, on my way back to campus."

"Oh, okay, how are your finals coming along?"

"Good, thanks for asking. How are you?"

It went silent on the other end, and I checked to see if my signal had dropped. I thought I could hear the radio playing softly and cars zooming by, which again was weird because my parents would normally have been at work.

"Daniel, are you good to speak now?"

"Yeah. Mom, is everything all right?"

"It's your grandfather, Daniel."

"Oh my God, what happened?"

"Well, mijo, it's nothing too bad . . ." she said, not giving much away.

"What do you mean?" My voice rose an octave, too loud for the bus. People turned and began shaking their heads.

"Your grandfather has been down lately . . . 'depressed,' he has been saying." Her voice was far away in thought.

I was unsure what she was getting at. Was he dead? Was he in the hospital? I waited for her to say more, but she kept silent.

"Okay, well, do you think it's about Abuela? I know her anniversary is coming up."

"Oh, I think it is so many things. Since you left after Christmas, he has not been himself. He is so quiet and keeps mostly to his room. I struggle to get him to talk to me. Honestly, it's like a stranger has taken over his body."

Hearing this, I felt stunned. It was like someone was throwing me another heavy bag to carry on top of everything else. You might remember how close I was to my grandfather—he was like my third parent. Hearing my mother's words made me feel like I had let him down, like I'd failed at not keeping in touch as much as I should have during the past few months.

"I'm sorry to hear that. Can I speak to him now?"

"Mijo, that is the thing I'm calling about. Your grandfather is in Chihuahua now."

"What do you mean, he is in Chihuahua?" My voice was turning angry with frustration. "Do you mean he up and left you guys?"

By that point, I didn't give a shit about the other passengers and their desire for a quiet ride. I needed to know what was happening at home. My mom began telling me how my grandfather had spoken to them a week before about wanting to go back to México for the summer. He had been feeling sadder and sadder, and he needed to see his siblings because he had not been back for nearly seven years. He had been thinking lately, he told them, of all he'd lost since leaving México, my grandmother and also my uncle, whose death was the reason my family left in the first place. My parents were stunned because this announcement felt as if it had come out of nowhere. But I thought the signs had long been there, especially that sadness I'd started noticing when I'd been home for Christmas. From the way my mom described the conversation, my grandfather wasn't asking for permission. Apparently he had savings, and so he bought himself a ticket with the help of a friend's son. I couldn't believe it. It wasn't in his character to be bold like this, or to hide the fact that he had been saving money. Although I was impressed by his determination, I was also angry at the worry he was causing my parents.

"We did not want to stress you, mijo, but we're driving back now from the airport. I wanted you to know before you came back, so you weren't in shock."

"It's honestly a little shocking, but what about you? How do you feel about it?"

"I'm nervous, Daniel. I don't like thinking my father is depressed, but also, I don't like him being away from me. I'm all that is left for him now that your grandmother is gone. I don't know what his plan is or if he wants to come back. I'm just so hurt he has been hiding all this from me . . ."

As my mother cried, I felt utterly helpless. It was strange to have to comfort my own mother at a time I wanted—no, needed—comforting, but I parked my own concerns momentarily and told my mother it would all be fine.

"I'll be home later this month, and I'm sure it's only a short visit, that he'll be back renewed, and happier."

"I just don't understand why he couldn't open up to me?"

"Maybe because of how much he loves you, Mom. He probably was afraid his sadness might make you sad. I'm sure he thought he was protecting you. I'm sure he was doing what he thought was best."

"Oh, mijo. When did you become so wise? I'm supposed to be the parent."

I listened to more of her concerns, let her voice carry me further up the road to campus. She was angry, she was frustrated, she was sad, she missed her father, and I could sympathize with all of it. I understood the need to get away, but also the ache of homesickness. I understood what it was like to love someone so much they could make you cry angry, hot tears. I understood how absence makes the heart grow madder, burn more fiercely.

"Everyone deserves happiness. Everyone deserves to feel at peace," I told her.

"You're right, mijo. I know you're right."

"I love you, Mom, and I know everything will be fine. I'll call you later tonight."

"God bless, mijo."

"God bless, Mom. Talk soon."

I got off the bus in Collegetown and decided to walk the rest of the way. Longing for fresh air and some time to think, I chose a longer route, but was no more than a minute into my walk when I received a text from Rob, whom I hadn't spoken to in a while: *I think I just saw you pass on the bus. I'm sitting on a bench near the Iris Café. Come meet me.*

The idea of sitting in the sun with Rob was enough to stop me from making up an excuse to just head home. This afternoon was becoming overwhelming, and I didn't want to be left alone. I found him on a bench reading the *New Yorker*, which made me laugh, as it was such a Rob thing to be doing on a Friday afternoon. I tried to make a joke about it, but when he looked up, his face was stony and cold.

"Hey, are you okay?"

"Daniel Manuel de La Luna, where the fuck have you been, man? Are you avoiding us? Mona and I have been fucking worried about you. I haven't seen you in two weeks!"

"No, I'm not avoiding you, honestly, just been caught up with things."

"Well, friends shouldn't randomly go AWOL on friends. It's kind of shitty."

"I know, I know. I am sorry, honestly. Mona invited me to go swimming with her friends today, but I needed to be alone."

"Are you all right?"

I couldn't hide things anymore, so I sat down and told Rob everything about you and me. About what had happened after our confrontation, after the kiss, which I'd never gotten around to sharing with him and Mona. As I was saying it, it felt like I was trying to justify things. The sex, the not needing to be out in the open, how I had willfully hidden these developments from my two closest friends. We sat there in the sunshine, and I opened up to Rob about how I was unsure of what the future held for you and me, how we had not moved beyond the physical and were running out of time. We didn't show affection in the romantic way I knew I wanted. Rob told me it was obvious I was carrying a lot of emotional baggage. But I felt relieved having laid it all out on the table, even if I didn't totally like what was staring back at me. You and I weren't going to have our storybook ending. I felt that much was obvious, having updated Bernie-Bernice and now Rob. I could no longer lie to myself.

Rob hugged me and told me I'd be fine, and I believed him despite my doubts. He even offered to treat me to bubble tea to make me feel better, so we wandered to a little tea shop not far from Collegetown.

"Are you happy, Daniel?"

"Loaded question there, Rob, but I'd be lying if I said, with total confidence, yes. I have gotten part of what I wanted, but I'm not so sure it was for the best."

"Would you be okay with just a physical relationship?"

"I don't think so," I said, and there was the truth.

We sat outside the tea shop on a shaky wooden bench and enjoyed our drinks under May sunshine. The tapioca balls were delightfully squishy, and the mixture of juice and green tea, tart and sickly sweet, reminded me of the Mexican candy I grew up on. I had never had bubble tea before. I had never had sex until twenty-four hours ago, I had never been naked with another man until a week ago, I had never kissed another man until a month ago. So many life-changing things had happened within such a short time frame, and it was utterly overwhelming, and now my family back home was falling apart.

"Did I ever tell you my great-grandfather immigrated from Taiwan in the 1930s as a little boy?"

"What? No—oh my God, Rob, you are one of my closest friends and I never knew you were anything other than white."

"Surprise!"

I almost spit out my drink. It was classic Rob to be so non-plussed about things—his clothing style, his sexual freedom, his thoughts on whether someone was being a shitty friend, and now this part of his identity, which was new to me. Every day, it seemed, I was being confronted with the reality of how not in tune with the world I was. I had been so caught up in my own story all freshman year, I felt I had not given back what my friends had given me, hadn't even bothered to learn important things about them.

"So have you ever been to Taiwan?"

"Yeah, I have been, quite a few times. I still have some family there. My cousins introduced me to boba. They have, like, a thousand more flavors there, things you could never even dream of."

"I have always wanted to travel to Asia. Japan is on my bucket list, but maybe I could travel to Taiwan too."

"Maybe I could take you one day . . ." he said, in his classic flirtatious tone.

"Do you think I'm chasing someone who will never give me what I want?" I asked, turning serious again.

"I think, Daniel, the body wants what it wants, but not everything happens how we might expect it to. Look at you and me—I adore our friendship, but honestly, I'd have thought we would have slept together by now."

I nearly choked on my tapioca.

"Rob, my God, I'm going through an emotional crisis and now you're telling me you want to sleep with me."

He smiled as he sipped his tea. He was handsome and easy to be around, and available, but I couldn't think about anyone else but you, as fruitless as it was. In the deepest part of me, I knew things would not go how I wanted them to, but I needed to at least see them through. I needed us to finish what we had started.

"Will you tell Mona for me? I don't think I can face her right now."

"Sure, for you, I will take one for the team."

"Thanks, Rob, I really appreciate you."

"No problem. Will I be seeing you at the last Young Democrats meeting on Sunday? Mona says it will be super-duper fun. There might even be some dry-ass gluten-free pizza."

"I'll see how I feel. Sam comes home from his away tournament that day, and I think I need to be by myself until then."

"Well, I am always here, Daniel, if you need to talk about this more. Just don't be a little bitch and go AWOL again, okay?"

"Yes, Rob. I promise."

We got up and kissed each other goodbye, and I walked home in the sunshine. I drew up an action plan to get through the rest of the weekend. I would call my mom and then I would call my grandfather and hear his side of the story. I would spend the remaining time reading and running and trying to soak up the atmosphere of our city on the hill. I would not allow myself to wallow.

When I woke up on Monday and looked at the clock it was 5:45 AM. You'd arrived back later than planned and had an essay to work on, but of course that was not all you got up to upon your return. You and I had spent the night working on finals, having more sex, and avoiding talking about our relationship status. So, during those early hours, I was thinking about—but not doing anything to broach—the question of what we were. I studied the gray clouds hanging above the tree line just beyond the view out your window. We had only two more weeks left of living together, or so said your wall calendar. Next year you'd be joining the fraternity your father was in—information I had just learned upon your return. I guess while you were in Philly, one of your teammates asked you to pledge, and you agreed to do it. There was nothing in your voice when you told me, which made it seem like you hadn't considered my feelings, had no interest in whether I wanted to be roommates again. I knew when you were telling me this that I was already losing you. But I couldn't bring myself to confront you about it. Something told me to hold back, so I added the question of next year's situation to the growing list of questions weighing on my mind, slowly suffocating me. I felt then that I'd allowed our hunger for the body to eclipse the heart's need for truth.

I remember how the light from the window caught the remnants of you still on me, your sweat, your cum and mine, flaking on my stomach. I didn't find it gross. I was learning to accept pleasure as a right, not something to be ashamed of, and I remember just lying there, staring at your beautiful body. Your butt, which was both sexy and cute, cast in an orange light by your lamp, which made the fuzz on your ass cheek shine golden. The shadow highlighted the musculature of your glutes, your thick hamstrings, all that hard work you had been putting in at the gym. Your legs were many shades of deep caramel and bright white. I then looked to the floor, covered in bottles of Gatorade, in condoms wrapped discreetly in tissues, and saw a kind of chaos mirroring what was going on in my mind. There were some beer cans, two glasses of water, your dirty laundry piled up in the corner. Although I was there in bed with you, I was alone with my thoughts, and I didn't have it in me to open up to you.

Again, I thought then that I had all the time in the world to deal with things, to work out my questions with you at your pace. In the quiet limbo of your room, I began to draw up a list of everything we'd have to do to get our place in order before moving out. It was easier to be proactive about these kinds of tasks, those unrelated to what was happening between you and me. As you slept heavily, I took stock: we'd need to dust the shelves of our bedrooms, scrub and bleach the bathroom, vacuum up the crumbs and detritus . . . but even this list soon became overwhelming, so I decided to get up and go on a run. I put on my running clothes and headed out into the early morning. All of those tasks could wait a bit longer.

The campus was completely quiet; some students had even left already for summer at this point. I put my iPod on shuffle and ran past Schubert Hall, then up the long campus avenues, out toward a part of Ithaca I had yet to see. It was amazing to have been there nearly ten months and realize there was still so much I hadn't yet experienced or explored. I knew I would have the next three years to make the most of Ithaca, but still I ran faster, wanting to see as much as I could that morning. My feet took over from my mind while I ran, and I allowed myself to take in everything around me. The smells, the noises lingering just outside my headphones, the way my knees felt as each step hit the pavement. I willed myself to be present, and I kept going as far as I could. In that moment, running was the only thing I had control over.

The reality, Sam, was that time was winding down faster than either of us was able to measure. I knew in my heart of hearts that we'd never confront each other about you choosing to join a frat, or about whatever was happening between us, if there was indeed something more to us than just sex. I knew I didn't have the courage to ask for something more, that to be in an actual relationship required a bravery I didn't yet possess. So I kept running that morning in the hope that, if I could go fast enough, I might just outrun my feelings for you. But the thing about emotion is that, as humans, we carry it. So as fast as I might go, I knew my feelings would go equally fast to wherever in the world I took them. One day there would have to be a reckoning. One day I'd need to face those feelings head-on and deal with what I'd helped create. I would have to make right the chaos we were both implicated in. One day I'd need to cease being a voyeur and instead be an active participant in my own life.

But until then I would keep running toward the horizon as fast as I could, in the hope that the braver me was already there, waiting to tell me what to do next.

PART III

LAYOVER

The school year has ended and I am free, at least for a few months. One more year and a set of exams and then this chapter of my life is over. Apá says I need to get a job for the summer, that I can't just sloth around the house. Amá says I am young still and I have many years to find a job. But I like the idea of finding something to pass the time. I think I might try to get something at Mercado Ocho. Luis has a cousin who works there stacking shelves and it seems all right. I can walk there until I'm able to save up for my own car. Either way, I want to get out and do stuff this summer, and I need money to do that. I need money to get out of this boring little neighborhood and see the city. Somewhere in all those streets there has to be someone else like me, someone who wants what I want. He might even be writing down the same thoughts, wishing for the same things. Wherever he is, surely he is dreaming of somewhere else.

—D.M.

You might have gathered by now that I wasn't home for more than a few days before once again boarding a plane. With my grandfather migrating south for the summer, my parents felt it was best for me to join him. I think the real reason was to have me keep watch over Abuelo—but I also think they understood, as I'd just turned nineteen, that I'd be bored at home. I had seen too much of the world now, had too much hunger in me to be content with a quiet life. They figured the big city of Chihuahua and family reunions would do me some good after so long away from the motherland. I was not keen on this idea at first, feeling like I'd be a third wheel to my grandfather's adventures. But the more I thought about it, the more it made sense. At my parents', with nothing but free time, I knew all I'd do to pass each day would be to think of you and our abrupt ending. In this sense, going away might not be the worst idea. I also had no other option.

"We think it will be good for you."

"But what about Abuelo? Won't he be annoyed you're sending me as some kind of watchdog?"

"Ay mijo, no. He will be thrilled. He is thrilled, actually," my mom insisted.

"You already spoke to him?"

"Yes, we asked him before you left Ithaca if it'd be all right for you to join him for the summer."

"Okay . . . but wasn't he wanting time on his own to catch up with family?"

"You are his family!" my mother said, trying to counterargue.

"I think this will be good for both of you, mijo," said my dad. "You will cherish this time together when you're older. Trust me."

So that is how I ended up on a layover at an airport in Dallas only a week after returning to California. So much was going through my head at the time. I felt unmoored, unsettled, and utterly liminal, in a state of flux. I didn't even have time to really process things before packing up my life to return to a country that was so very much a part of me and yet also so utterly foreign. In the manic rush of getting things organized, I also didn't have much time to think about you or how things had ended between us. All of this was put on pause until I arrived at DFW for my final flight. I'd embarked on the trip thinking I could keep you on one side of the border, but of course, life never works out as planned. Somehow you managed to come crashing back into my life when I least expected it.

I was in between flights, staring at my ticket and then up at the screen announcing departures and arrivals, trying to match the information from the ticket to the screen. A series of flight codes, airlines, midway points, and final destinations stared back at me. I was tired and bored, but also, by that point, excited. Having resigned myself to the fact of the trip, I was now feeling ready for a change. Freshman year had felt like a decade, and you had left me confused by the way you'd shut me out of your life. Those rapidly changing final weeks at Ithaca had left me marked and bruised, and I was looking forward to a summer of convalescence, a summer sans Sam.

I had also given so much of myself to my studies in the previous months, and although I passed freshman year with good grades, I was burned out. I had spent too much time questioning and rarely doing, and there was a fear inside me: if I didn't stop this behavior, I might miss out on so many beautiful things in life. I wanted to reclaim what I gave and how I gave to others. I wanted to use summer as a season for change. But I didn't foresee the change about to come my way.

It was while I was looking for a coffee shop that my phone buzzed, and I checked to see who was contacting me. I assumed it was my parents. Knowing I'd reached my layover destination, they no doubt wanted to make sure all was going well for my next and final flight. I took my phone from my pocket, ready to speak to them, when on the screen I saw not an incoming call but an email from, of all people, you.

[Sam Morris . . .]

It was you reaching out after not speaking to me for weeks. After leaving our dorm and not saying goodbye. After not offering me any closure, after making me feel like it was my fault for opening up the Pandora's box of our desire, the very thing we'd both tried to keep in for so long. In the seconds it took to read your name, I was sucked back into our story. How we'd gone from friends to a kiss, to me giving you all of myself and you giving me everything I ever wanted—or thought I wanted. Do you remember all that? Did you think about it as you sent me that email? Did you recount our year together as you composed these words I'm about to share with you?

I clicked on the home screen and read the subject line once more. I couldn't quite believe what was happening. There you were staring back at me in the form of words at a time when I wanted nothing to do with you.

[Sam Morris: It's been a while . . .]

I remember thinking, *Fuck!* Of all the days to get in touch after not speaking with me, you had to pick that one. You must have known I was leaving because I'd posted a photo online of an eight-year-old me with something along the lines of *Back to the motherland for the summer.* I don't know why I did it—maybe for clout? So our fellow classmates might think I, too, led an exciting life? But either way, you had to have seen. We were still Facebook friends. We hadn't totally cut each other out. All the same, my stomach was in knots as I debated reading your email then and there. I didn't want to ruin my trip, but I also couldn't board my next plane without knowing what you wanted from me.

I closed the screen. I opened the screen. I closed the screen once more. Then I opened it and just looked at the notification staring back at me. All twenty-two letters.

[Sam Morris: It's been a while . . .]

Was this your apology? Was this an olive branch you were finally willing to extend? Had you seen the error of your ways? I needed to know. I was missing you so much, more than I wanted to admit. I needed to believe we still had a chance. So I opened your email and took a seat near a random departure gate free of witnesses. As people pulled little suitcases up and down the terminal, as they laughed and smiled, rushing past me, I prepared myself for whatever I was about to read.

DANIEL,

I've been writing and rewriting this email for over a week now. I don't know where to begin but I will start with an apology. I am sorry, Daniel. Truly. How the last few weeks of freshman year played out was not something I planned, and I can't say I was prepared for any of it. I know I shared how I had feelings for you from the first day I met you, and although true, I never thought I'd ever do anything about it. Never thought I'd have the courage to kiss you, let alone have sex, and as much as I wanted it all, I know I can't give anything else to you. It's so hard to write out, but I must be honest with both of us.

I've tried to draft and redraft this next part a hundred times, but I don't think we should stay in touch after this email. I'm sorry for how cruel and harsh it sounds. In total honesty, the world I come from is not ready for me to be gay and I'm not ready to prove everyone in it wrong. I know you love my parents, but this would be something else for them. And all my teammates, my high school friends, all these people who see me in a way totally opposite to what you see . . . how could I explain all this to them?

You are incredible, Daniel. You don't deserve to be made to wait. Especially on someone who doesn't know what he feels about himself, or who he might be. You're too kind, thoughtful, funny, considerate, handsome. Too good of a guy to be made to wait. You deserve to find someone who can be open with you. That's not me, and staying friends will only confuse and hurt us both. It will only cause us to fall into bad habits, however much pleasure they might bring us at first (I can't trust myself around you, I'm weak like that).

One day I hope you realize it's me losing out on something special here, and not me pushing you away. I hope you have a blast in México with your grandpa and family . . . I saw your Facebook post. I hope you enjoy your summer. I really mean that.

For what it's worth, you gave me an amazing first year at Cayuga and for that I'll always be indebted. You'll always hold an important place in my heart and my life.

YOURS, SAM

P.S. Please know I'm forever grateful you came into my life. You're my compadre, always.

I closed the email and put my phone in my pocket. My heart felt like a Boeing 747 had crashed right into it, blowing my life to smithereens. I kept telling myself not to cry, but it didn't work, I'm afraid. You had hurt me in a way I'd never thought possible, hurt me far more than you had in those final few weeks, which already felt so huge, so unwieldy. To make it worse, I was surrounded by people who were oblivious to this upset, unaware of the havoc your email had just brought upon my life.

The world was closing in on me and I felt dizzy and panicky. I ended up sprinting to the toilets, pushing my way into a stall as the tears began to erupt. There. It was finally happening, what I had long expected to happen, because I knew we had started something we could not finish. But, fuck, I wanted the agency to make the call myself, or at least make it with you, but you didn't even offer me the opportunity. I once again had waited too long. Spent too much time overthinking and not doing. I'd missed my chance to confront you, and now you had written me out of your life completely.

As I sat on that toilet seat crying, I thought: *Why hadn't I been the one to act first? Why hadn't I been brave enough to send my own ultimatum?* Now here I was in a dirty bathroom stall next to someone taking a massive shit, temporarily trapped in a major airport in a city full of millions of people I didn't know, en route to a country that wasn't even really mine. I wrestled with a myriad of questions: *What do I do? Do I respond, or do I just say this chapter of my life is now closed? Do I simply delete the email and move on?* I felt like I had no cards left to play in this game that was destroying my life.

In telling you this, Sam, I'm not trying to make you feel bad. I promise. I'm just sharing with you what happened because it's important that we don't forget the way our stories intertwine. Even when you are not physically with someone, you can still very much be part of their story, and you were very much a part of mine. You still are, Sam. I carry you now as I share all these memories with you. I won't lie, rehashing this episode still brings back a lot of upset. On what was meant to be a happy day, a day of fresh starts, you had pulled the rug right out from under me.

The tears erupted once again as I thought of your smell, your smile, the weight of your body on mine. How it felt to feel the rise and fall of your lungs when tucked into your frame while you held me. Big spoon and little spoon. I tried to calm down by reminding myself that you had written nice things too, and seemed genuinely torn over having sent the email.

I'm forever grateful you came into my life.

I'd always known, in some way, that you weren't going to be my forever, but rather a season. Even with that understanding, it still hurt.

You're my compadre, always.

Did you understand what that word meant? Would I really be your friend forever? How was that possible if you were asking me to part from you completely?

With no one to answer my questions, I had no choice but to exit the stall and find a quieter section of the airport where I sat down and tried to focus on a book. I kept reading the same line over and over again until I had to give up, unable to concentrate on anything but the crushing hurt and loneliness closing in on me. I went to check for updates on my next flight, then busied myself with trying to find any little task that might distract me until my connection began boarding: getting a coffee, sampling cologne at Duty Free—anything to stop myself from crying over you again.

As I awaited my flight, I tried to think through the next few days. What would they look like for me? I didn't know. When I arrived in Chihuahua, Abuelo would be waiting for me. My cousins and aunts and uncles would no doubt welcome me into the fold, do everything they could to make me feel at home, but I would be a stranger in that place. No matter how much my family tried, I would never be from there. I would always be a product of my parents' decision to leave México, their attempt at a fresh start in life. But somewhere on the other side of that border, another version of my life existed. A life I might have led, had my parents never left. I wanted to delve into that for a while. I needed to find out more about my family's history, more about the man whose name I have carried these nineteen years of my life. I also wanted to quell the pain building up in my heart. I wanted to find a way forward. I needed to move on from you, once and for all.

As I gathered my bags and headed down the jet bridge, I prayed God would grant me a summer free from any more heartache, and for a little while longer, I allowed myself to believe my prayers were being answered. As the cabin crew made the final checks for our departure, I prepared to cross the threshold between two countries while my heart was splintering in two. As time was winding down on us, where were you, Sam? Where had you gone?

EL PRIMER DÍA

JUNE 9, 1991

Today on my morning run, I passed the local tennis courts with their rust-tinged fence and bolt-cut corners. There were two men, a few years older than me, in the middle of a lively match. I paused to watch, drawn by how attractive both of their sweat-slicked bodies were. There was something about their energy that made me believe we might be kindred spirits. Something told me they wanted to be watched, admired even. I looked on as the shorter of the two men bounced the ball twice on the hot clay before throwing it in the air and driving down his racket. It sent the ball flying toward the right-hand side of his opponent. The shorter player (the more handsome one) dove for the ball, stretching his body long like a muscular gazelle. His mesh shorts rode up, revealing the strap of his jock underwear curving along his round ass cheek (a nice surprise). The shorter one was able to lob the ball back just in time but was met with a backhand, starting a lengthy rally. I watched the men go back and forth, back and forth, each one stretching, grunting, bouncing, sweaty. Eventually, the taller man won the match. As they took a break for water, they sensed my presence and looked up at me. We stood there. The three of us, smiling, sweaty, enraptured . . . on the cusp of . . . what? I did not know because I took off running. Pounding pavement the whole way, thinking of nothing other than the handsomer man's ass, a thought I wanted to finish in the safety of my bedroom.

—D.M.

I arrived in Chihuahua in the ungodly heat of a late June afternoon. Abuelo was waiting outside the arrivals hall, as he had promised, in a rusty green Chevy pickup. He'd left for México a little over a month before me, and already he looked like a new man in his sombrero and cowboy boots. He also looked the happiest he'd been in a long time, with a sparkle in his eyes that wasn't there the last time I'd seen him. I hugged him with all my strength, and the strength of my missing mother, saying without speaking that we loved him and only wanted him to be happy. When I finally let go of Abuelo, I saw the silent tears in his eyes. The past few months had been the longest stretch I'd ever gone without seeing him, and it hit me just how much he had missed me. I wiped his tears and kissed him on the cheek, inhaling the woody musk of his aftershave. The scent brought me back to childhood, to all these memories of wandering in his and my grandmother's room as they got ready. On that day of heartbreak, I found comfort in his presence. I wasn't alone. I was with someone who had known me all my life, who had loved me from day one and would go on loving me all his life.

"Te quiero mucho, mi niño hermoso."

"Te quiero mucho, Abuelo."

A traffic warden whistled at us, saying we couldn't stand there blocking the other vehicles. When I looked up, I noticed the bustle of taxis, cars, and trucks trying to drop off and pick up passengers. The road was full of mad dashes and extended hellos, happy reunions and exhausted returns. It felt so alive under the June sunshine in that desert city. We jumped in the truck at the behest of that power-hungry warden, and I rushed to the passenger side as she kept blowing her whistle at us and the other arrivals. In a panic, I almost sat on the small package left on the seat.

"Es para ti, mijo. Abrelo," my grandfather instructed me. "A belated birthday present."

I unwrapped the brown paper and carefully unstuck the Scotch tape. Inside was a leather journal with a silver plate sewn onto the cover. A repujado of Emiliano Zapata on horseback. I fingered the bumps and grooves of the metal design. It was the most beautiful gift he'd ever given me. When I leafed through the pages, I discovered an inscription that read, *Para recordar tu experiencia de tu patria.* To remember your experience of your homeland. When I looked up at the scorching road, part of me was hundreds of miles away, chasing your memory, but the other part was right where it belonged.

"Gracias, Abuelo. Me encanta."

"De nada, mijo. I hope by the end of summer its pages are filled with beautiful memories to look back on one day."

Maybe this was the point at which I began to think of writing not as a way of creating new worlds, but instead of preserving the present, honoring the past. Those pages, and these pages you're reading now—all of them hold such beautiful memories, and all of them I will look back on one day to truly understand all that was ours to experience together. Because that is what this has all been about, Sam: my attempt to make sense of loss, to halt our story from being lost to time, forgotten. But of course, on that day, I didn't have such clarity.

"Thank you, Abuelo. I am sure I'll find many things to write about."

He pulled out of the arrivals area onto a busy highway, taking us straight into downtown Chihuahua. As we entered the city, I studied the roads full of people on their way home. There was a kind of hustle that felt a world away from my life in Ithaca or my hometown in California.

"What are you thinking about, mijo?"

"Nothing, Abuelo, just taking it all in. I can't believe it's been so long since I've been back."

"Yes, I regret how much time your parents and I let come between us and this beautiful city."

"Me too . . . but I'm here now."

He put the car in park and turned to me. "Yes, mijo. We both are, so let's make the most of it. Okay?"

My aunt's house was strangely quiet when we arrived, but also buzzing with sounds from the past. As I walked along the long hallway, I recalled faint memories of screaming children at play, tiles clapping underfoot as we ran amok, the Charlie Brown mumble of adults chatting in the living room. I could hear my great-grandparents dancing along to some performance my cousins and I were giving. The further into the house I ventured, the more the memories seemed to come back. As I delved into the past, Abuelo must've been busy doing something in his room or letting my aunt and uncle know we had arrived. Whatever it was, I was by myself for a moment, alone with my thoughts. My brain was trying to process all these things at once: the past year, being there in Chihuahua without my mom and dad, memories of México, the uncertainty of what summer held for me.

I stopped at a painting of San Sebastián tied to a tree trunk, his muscular body oozing blood. I looked at the picture and, for a second, you were staring back at me and speaking. *You're my compadre, always.*

I opened and closed my eyes, blinking fast once more. You were there and then you weren't. We were friends and then we weren't. Even with a thousand miles between us, you were haunting me, and I was failing at my plan to not think about you.

One day I hope you realize it's me losing out on something special here, and not me pushing you away.

I brushed away these thoughts and continued toward the back of the house, unsure what I was looking for. At the end of the hall was my Tía Hela's—Abuelo's older sister's—former bedroom, untouched for a decade, everything carefully maintained as if she and my uncle were still alive and had just popped out to buy groceries. I turned to find my grandfather standing there smiling at me. He looked so much lighter, and I wanted to know what had been weighing his spirit down back home, what allowed him to now feel so free, but that's not what I asked.

"Do you ever wonder what life would've been like if you had stayed?"

"What do you mean, mijo?"

"Like, would you have led a different life had you remained in México?"

"Well, mijo, I think after your uncle passed away, there was not much worth staying for. I had already lost one child and I wasn't going to lose another one."

I remember his eyes looked somber. Immediately, I felt guilty for asking without thinking. But, in all honesty, no one ever spoke about my late uncle in any meaningful way. All I knew was that Tío Daniel had been two years older than my mom. He was smart, like really smart, and he had wanted to see the world—my grandmother always said that like it was a prayer. He died in a freak accident a few weeks after turning twenty-two, and his death was a catalyst for my parents choosing to leave México. Growing up, I'd always felt like I wasn't allowed to ask too many questions about how he died or what he was like, and just then, going through my own loss, I wondered if my mother feared misremembering or forgetting who he was. It had been over twenty years since his passing, since them starting over, and maybe it was too late to get answers. Maybe I'd never know who he was or what we had in common, but still I heard a calling from within me. An echo from the past, inviting me to push deeper, but I didn't know what to ask or when.

"I'm sorry, Abuelo. That was a stupid question."

"No such thing as a stupid question, but remember, today is not a day for sadness."

He patted my shoulder and once again told me how grateful he was to have his niño hermoso back in the homeland. Then we walked through the patio door out into the back garden, where, to my surprise, my extended family was waiting: cousins, great-cousins, great-aunts and great-uncles, baby cousins I'd never met. There were about a dozen people I didn't know, but who were likely distant relations. All of these people were there to welcome me back into the fold. All of them had come to celebrate my homecoming.

"Sorpresa," they shouted in unison.

I kept turning, trying to take it all in, as a mariachi band started playing "Volver, Volver" by Vicente Fernández. My mind was trying to process how I had gone from a quiet stroll down memory lane to a full-on party in a matter of minutes. In the middle of all the commotion was a taco stall for my now-obvious welcome party, and in the middle of the stall was the most handsome man, chopping a bunch of cilantro. His brown skin, almond eyes, and arms covered in tattoos were so distracting I could not help but stare. As he continued chopping, I could barely concentrate on the band or the dozens of conversations happening around me. I smiled and applauded while stealing glances at that man, his muscly arms, at the idea I wanted to finish.

Before I could think more about who the man might be, my cousin Marisol ushered me to a group of family members who'd traveled from out of town to meet me. They told me stories about my mom and grandparents and made note of how much I looked like my uncle, just as handsome with "those knowing brown eyes." In my periphery, I watched my grandfather as all these thoughts and memories were being shared, and he looked nothing but happy, nodding in full agreement. When he looked at me, did he see my uncle? And if so, did it hurt him? Was he able to appreciate me as my own person, a being totally separate from the son he had lost? I needed to know.

After about a half hour of conversation, my cousin Victoria gathered around all my young cousins and poured tequila. She made a toast welcoming me to Chihuahua.

"It's such a blessing to have our primito Daniel here for the summer in the land of his ancestors. We know how brilliant you are because when our prima Sonia calls, she is always updating us on your adventures, your brilliant accomplishments. We hope this summer is full of countless opportunities to remember all the beautiful things that make our country its unique self. To México and to Daniel."

I took in her words against the backdrop of a house full of so many childhood memories, all the smiling faces outside welcoming me. Although it felt both familiar and foreign, I took comfort in the thought that at least I wasn't alone.

We raised our shots and clinked glasses, and for a few hours, I did not think of you. I wondered whether the impending summer might indeed be the tonic I needed.

"¡Arriba, abajo, al centro, pa' dentro!"

The tequila swirled around in my head as I tried to maintain conversations with the excited relatives who rushed toward me. Thankfully, Victoria saw what was happening and rescued me from my great-aunts' well-meaning barrage of questions, which were moving dangerously toward my dating life.

"You must be starving."

"I haven't eaten since late this morning."

"Come, come. Let's get you some food."

So it was hunger that led me to introduce myself to the mystery man. His name was Diego. He was a few years older than me, I learned through rusty Spanish, scarfing down a plate of tacos del pastor he'd made for me. I remember how I found his voice husky and inviting. I liked how he made the *D* of my name turn into a soft *Th*, and how the middle of it sounded like *ñ*, as in "canyon" (cañón). I liked how my body felt around him, immediately comfortable.

Maybe it was the tequila, or maybe I was starting to understand how to read other bodies now that I knew more about my own.

"These tacos are the nicest thing I've eaten all day," I told him. "Well, truthfully, the only thing I've eaten. But still good."

That made him laugh, and his laugh turned into a smile he held for the longest time, until my grandfather called me over for photos. Diego handed me a roll of napkins to clean myself. I smiled for him, asking if anything was in my teeth. Again, his presence made me feel strangely comfortable, and I was doing things I'd never normally do. He told me I was good, and I lingered near him for too long, wanting to finish the idea stuck on the tip of my tongue. We smiled at each other like two fools, each caught in the other's orbit.

"You should go. Your grandfather wants you, and you should never ignore a grandparent."

"It was nice speaking with you."

"¡Felicidades, Daniel! I hope to see you around," he said, waving me off. "Welcome home, by the way."

I made my way to my grandfather, thinking about all the versions of "home" I knew: California, Ithaca, our dorm, my house, this city in the desert. That day so much had happened, and my mind had no time to rest between the music and the chatter. But standing there in the throng of so many of my relatives, I began to map the origins of myself to that homeland. My arched nose, thick eyebrows; my smile, more lip than teeth. I could see so much of myself in these people. A sense of peace washed over me as we hugged one another closer, trying to appease my grandfather in his desire for the perfect reunion photo.

"Okay, smile for me on three . . . uno, dos, tres!"

My grandfather was alive with joy as he archived this first day of mine. In that moment, I only wanted him to be happy. After so much of his own loss, he deserved to be happy, and like he said, that day there was no room for sadness.

"Okay, one more . . . everyone say, '¡Bienvenido, Daniel!'"

"¡Bienvenido, Daniel!"

Throughout the photo shoot, I kept thinking about my body, but in Spanish: mis ojos, labios, nariz. Words I never got around to teaching you. I thought about mis brazos, which held you; mi pecho, which your tongue would lick, your mouth would bite. Then I thought of your body, tu cuerpo. The golden fuzz on your nalgones and the dimples of your espalda. The stretch marks on your caderas from when you grew two feet in one summer; how your mom mentioned them in passing, not knowing I'd see her son's bare hips and so much more of his body. I thought of how I'd given you so much, and in spite of my efforts to keep my mind elsewhere, began to worry that you might already be forgetting me. After pressing send on your email, had you started deleting my memory? Were you remembering me at all that day, the way I was remembering you? As the thoughts swirled around in my mind, I told myself to focus again on the party around me, on the coming months and all the possibilities of a summer stretching out ahead.

At around ten o'clock the party began to wind down, which is to say my family had moved on to drunken slow-dancing while the kids ran around in the dark. My grandfather was sitting with his siblings, sharing a bottle of mezcal, illuminated by strings of lights. I liked watching my grandfather just like I liked watching my parents during childhood visits. As I observed his animated body, face grinning ear to ear, I began to get a deeper sense of why he'd returned. It wasn't a crime to miss people. It wasn't a crime to need a break from home. It wasn't a crime to want to be in multiple places at once. He could miss my mom and miss his siblings; these forms of longing were not mutually exclusive. I could be happy to be here with him and still feel a desire to be somewhere else—with someone else.

"Hello again!"

I turned to find Diego standing in front of me with two cold beers in hand. His arms were almost completely covered in tattoos: calaveras, Aztec warriors, the Virgin Mary, koi fish—but no names of women or naked ladies. *A good sign*, I thought.

"Are you enjoying your party?"

"Yes, and the food was great. Thanks for that."

"Anything to welcome a compadre home."

I asked how he knew my family and he explained that his father was the best friend of an older cousin of mine. No relation to me. *Another good sign*, I thought. He asked me about my life back home and I explained what I was studying, how I was on summer break. I didn't mention you, or the painful email I had received earlier that day. I didn't want to come off as desperate or broken. He then asked how often I came to México, and he was shocked to learn I hadn't been back since I was twelve, after my grandmother passed away. He turned somber and offered his condolences, which was strangely sweet even if seven years late. We finished our beers while listening to the music and chatter of the older folk. Then Marisol came by with some shots.

"Hey chicos, take these before the viejitos ask for any more."

"Okay, prima, but only if you have one with us," I told her.

"For you, mijo, I will—but only one. I have to get back home soon. Analyse is falling asleep over there on your Tía Carmen's lap."

I clinked shot glasses for the umpteenth time that night.

"¡Arriba, abajo, al centro, pa' dentro!"

The mezcal burned the back of my throat. It was far smokier than the cheap tequila we were used to at Ithaca parties. Diego and Marisol laughed at the faces I made. I'm sure my face read more American than Mexican, but I couldn't help myself. Marisol gave me a kiss goodbye and went to help finish cleaning up as my aunt rocked her daughter to sleep.

"You should come out with me and my friends tonight."

"Tonight? It's like ten PM. Where are you going at this hour?"

"Don't sound so old, Daniel. We're just off to a small bar down-town. It's a cool place, te lo juro."

"We just met. What if I'm, like, a boring person or something?"

"No. I think you're cool. I can just tell. ¡Venga, por favor!"

I wanted to say yes, but I was worried about leaving my grand-father. I didn't want him to think I was bored already, or desperate to find some form of entertainment beyond his company. But just as I was wrestling with my decision, Abuelo walked over to us. His cheeks were rosy with drink, and he had the funniest look on his face.

"Hola Diego, that was an excellent meal. Thank you for all your help."

"De nada, Señor Omar. It was my pleasure. I can tell your grandson is very loved."

"We are all so happy to have him in the homeland."

I watched on as they chatted. It was strange to watch my grandfather speaking to a man who I was beginning to develop an attraction to. It was the closest I'd ever been to being my whole self in one place—what I mean is, out in the open. It excited me and scared the shit out of me at the same time. My grandfather then stopped talking and just kept smiling. He looked at me and then at Diego and then back at me, not shifting the smile painted on his face. I then looked to him and then Diego and back to him. Diego just smiled and shrugged his shoulders.

"Are you all right, Abuelo?"

"Claro, mijo. I was just thinking you shouldn't be stuck here with us old folks."

"It's fine. I'm glad to be. Not stuck, I mean. I'm glad to be here."

"No, no. Diego, you should take my grandson out. The night is young. He has the whole of summer to be stuck by my side."

"Are you sure, Abuelo? I'm not bored if that's what you're wor-ried about."

"Please, Diego, show my grandson a good time. You only get one first night back home before everything starts to feel familiar."

"Okay, Abuelo, but I promise not to stay out late."

"No te preocupes, mi niño hermoso. Here is the key to the front door. Disfruten la noche, both of you."

I kissed my grandfather goodbye and my aunts and uncles. Each of them blessed my forehead and slipped money into my hands, as if it were my birthday or confirmation. It felt unfathomable and surreal to be going away with this handsome stranger, but I also felt I had nothing to lose. So that's how I ended up going out on my first night in Chihuahua.

After my cousins and I had helped Diego clean up his catering equipment and return it to his truck, he drove me about twenty minutes to the other side of the city. During our drive, I learned that he owned his own company and that his family had been in the restaurant business for quite a few generations. I tried to ask him where we were meeting his friends, but all he said was it was a place he knew I'd enjoy. We pulled up to a tired-looking bar. Except for the few people smoking outside, it looked dead. I remember the music was loud, audible as soon as I opened the passenger door. Then in the window the light hit a performer at just the right time, a woman who looked too tall and with hair too big to be anything other than a drag queen. My mind was going back and forth, but I was almost certain Diego had taken me to a gay bar.

We entered an eclectic interior full of lights and veladoras and loads of niche Mexican pop-culture memorabilia. There were more people inside than I'd expected and it took us a moment to find his group of friends, tucked in a corner near the bathroom: Yoli, Sebastián, and Emilia. We offered quick introductions and then Diego and Sebastián went to grab drinks, leaving me with Yoli and Emilia. I took a seat and tried to appear like I belonged.

Yoli turned to me quickly and began asking questions: "So, you just met Diego this evening, right?"

"Yes. He was catering my surprise party and then invited me out. It was very nice of him, or else I'd still be stuck at home with all my great-aunts and -uncles, doing nothing."

"Que interesante. You must be special, Daniel," she said excitedly before giving Emilia a look.

"How do you mean?"

Before she could answer, Emilia cut in to offer her thoughts. "Diego doesn't warm to people very easily, if that makes sense, so we were surprised when he texted us he was bringing a friend. You see, we all grew up together and so we kind of know all his friends. Understand? The mention of a 'new friend' was a bit of a surprise to us, that's all. No te preocupes. We're just being chismosas, you know what that means?"

"Of course."

I smiled at both of them. I had found Diego flirty during the party, and now I was being led to believe my assumptions might be right.

"Do you all come to this bar often?"

"Yeah, we try to support Diego as much as we can," Yoli replied.

"What do you mean?"

Emilia sort of laughed and then seemed to think carefully about how to word what she said next.

"Well, Diego owns Bar Gloria with his sister, along with his catering company."

"Oh, I didn't know that."

"Yeah, he doesn't like to talk about his money. But his family, los Salazar, are pretty well established in Chihuahua. His great-grandfather owned a well-known restaurant just off the Plaza de Armas. Diego has even catered weddings for the governor's family."

The men returned with the drinks before I could ask either Yoli or Emilia to unpack more about this mysterious Diego. We scooted over to let Sebastián and Diego take the two end seats. Diego passed around the drinks and made a toast to welcome me back "home." I took more shots of mezcal with my four new friends before moving on to beer, trying to stay lucid and not embarrass myself in front of everyone. The four of them chatted among themselves for a bit as I tried to make sense of the last few hours.

"Are you enjoying yourself?" Diego asked.

"Sorry, what was that?"

It was a bit too loud to speak, so Diego grabbed my hand and pulled me out to an empty bench on the patio as the others stayed behind to watch another drag act coming onstage.

"Much better. Now we can actually hear each other."

His friends' comments were lingering in my mind. I don't know whether it was the drinks, or a genuine feeling that I had nothing else to lose after losing you, but I was emboldened to be direct.

"Diego, why did you invite me out with you?"

"Well, you just got here, so I thought it would be good for you to make friends."

"But we literally just met. Isn't that a bit strange?"

His laugh was nervous. It was the first time that night he wasn't playing cool or acting overly confident. I watched as he sipped on his beer, bopping his head to the music playing inside.

"Do you want to be my friend?" I asked.

"I think so, yes."

"Do you know that I'm gay?"

"Yes, Daniel. I felt you might be a kindred spirit. Something about you at the party, a spark you could say, I felt between us. So I thought I might invite you out to get to know you more."

I was surprised by his candor. It threw me off for a moment, and so I took a big glug of my beer before asking what he meant by "more."

"You are an overthinker, aren't you, Daniel?"

"Honestly, it's been said before."

"What are you thinking about?"

"I'm just trying to make heads or tails of tonight. So you own this bar and your catering company, and you want to be my friend, and you don't warm to people too easily."

"I see the girls were speaking to you."

I turned from him to study the glimmering lights and listen to the sound of people walking up and down the street. The nighttime atmosphere was so electric and magical—and I was full of so much excitement—that I didn't even feel tired from my day of traveling. I just wanted to be among all that life. Inside, there was an impersonator singing along to Gloria Trevi's greatest hits. What I loved about this first night was how it was so similar to parties from my past year, but with a different color, a different texture. I was around people who looked like me, who were potentially queer like me. I was seated next to a man, a handsome man, a brown man, a man named Diego. So much of the setting was familiar, and yet all of it felt overwhelming because I was existing openly in a city in which I thought I'd need to be invisible. I was already being challenged by the possibility that things could be far better than I'd thought.

"I like you, Daniel, and I hope you might like me too. I didn't tell you about the bar because it's very rough and ready, but I own it and I'm proud of it. It's like a pet project, something I can do outside my family's hospitality business. I wasn't hiding it from you. But you know, sometimes, especially in this city, people only like you when they know what you have. Inviting you out was a spur-of-the-moment thing because, like I said, I felt a spark and I needed to see what it was about. I hope you understand."

"Totally, I appreciate your honesty."

"Good to know. You have beautiful eyes, by the way."

I nodded in agreement, slightly buzzed, not really listening to what he was saying as he moved in closer. He looked deep into my eyes and then he kissed me. Just like that. No hesitation or vagueness or yearlong will-they-won't-they. His lips tasted like sweet lager and smoky mezcal.

"That was nice. I'd been wanting to do it all night."

"A bit of a surprise for my first day here, if I'm honest."

He laughed at this, his face lit by a streetlamp and the rest of his body and mine cast in the dark shadow of the patio wall. Sitting there, it felt clear that there was a heat between us, but something was telling me not to rush anything. I wasn't going to get over you in a day, and rushing from one bed to the next wouldn't do me any good. But that didn't mean I couldn't stay here, in this moment, next to this man who brought about my smile.

"Can I kiss you again?" he asked.

"Yes, you can."

So he kissed me again, this time more softly. Just like that. It didn't take weeks between first kiss and second. It didn't require tears or existential crises. Diego then grabbed my hand and hoisted me up, wrapping his arm around me as we walked through the patio into the bar. We joined his friends for the rest of the night, dancing in the sweaty, dingy, effervescent bar. We danced to Thalía, Shakira, and Paulina Rubio, songs I'd grown up with but on that first night enjoyed in new contexts. Under the strobe lights of a rough-and-ready gay bar in the homeland of my parents, I was the most alive I'd been in a long while.

At two in the morning, Diego drove me home, his truck my gilded carriage and the whole night my Cinderella story. As we drove, I couldn't help but marvel at how that night was an unexpected bookend to a day that began with heartbreak.

He parked outside my great-aunt's house, in the complete stillness of the street. His hands reached for me in the safety of the quiet darkness, and he kissed me one final time, hungrily so. Eventually, we parted, and I said my goodbyes and made promises to text him soon. Diego had stopped drinking those last few hours and been sober enough to drive, but as I fumbled with the door keys I quickly realized how drunk I was. I didn't regret it. I knew the kissing, the touching, the desire came from a sober place, a lucid place of wanting to be free that summer.

I tiptoed quietly to the kitchen to fill up a glass of water and made my way to my bedroom. A soft light fell through the netted curtains of my window, but everything else was steeped in darkness. I stepped gingerly toward the bed, climbed in, and began to replay the events of the day. It was hard to grasp that I'd left my small hometown earlier that morning and been driven to the airport by my parents, only to receive your breakup email mid-journey and then arrive in México—all in the past twenty-four hours or so. The last time I was in Chihuahua I was twelve, very much unaware of who I'd grow up to be, who I'd grow up to love. But there I was, nineteen years old, a man who had just kissed a man named Diego after saying goodbye to a man named Sam. I thought about how, for so much of my life, I'd survived by staying quiet, making myself small enough to fly under the radar. I decided then that I no longer wanted to be quiet. I wanted to be loud and colorful and every piece of myself at any one time.

As I lay there, I began to dream of all the ways I'd allow myself to flourish in the land of my people, how I'd learn to take up space and bring that understanding with me back to Ithaca when the autumn winds began their return. I'd spend the summer nurturing my roots, boring into the desert earth, and in turn would see all the parts of myself begin to flower.

I fell asleep imagining beautiful desert plants: the shin-digging lechuguilla; agave azul, which can be magicked into tequila; la candelilla and the ancestors of mine who understood its medicinal properties. All around me, as I slept, flora continued to thrive, understanding how to flourish in the harshest of situations—something I, too, would have to learn—but just then I had no way of knowing what was waiting for me, out there in the distance.

JUNIO

Today is Sonia's eighteenth birthday. I can't believe the day has come when she's no longer a child. My little sister is an adult. I asked her what she wanted for her birthday, and she surprised me by saying, "To see you happy, Daniel." I was so caught off guard I couldn't say anything back, so she filled the silence: "I don't think you've been happy for a while, hermano, and I am worried about you." Here she was with a prescient awareness of my emotions, me not having said a word . . . it stunned me. I wanted to tell her, "I want to be happy." I wanted to tell her, "If happiness were a destination, I'd need a map." But instead I hugged her and told her I loved her, hoping that those words would be enough.

—D.M.

I hope you understand my reasons for choosing to share my summer in México with you, how the aim is not to make you jealous, or shove in your face the beauty of those seven weeks before the news about you came hurtling toward me. I want you to see it as a means of sharing with you what I'd have shared had we remained friends. I hope you can see it as honest and truthful, as what really happened. It is important to me that you know what went on between the time you sent your email cutting me out of your life and the day your mom called to tell me you had been taken from us. You see, Sam, there were forty-eight days in which you were there with me in the same plane of time, days in which there existed the possibility of reaching out. There were a few weeks in there when I thought that just maybe, come August, we might rekindle our friendship. We might even learn to quiet our love and our desire and, instead, accept friendship as being enough.

Looking back, I now understand just how distraught I was upon arriving in México. Then I met Diego. Sweet, sweet Diego. For a little while, my hurt was quelled because I was caught up in the thrill of something new—the possibility of love, a spark of attraction. It was enough not to think of you, at least for a little while. But a little while could only last so long.

The next time I saw Diego was when we ran into each other outside Sunday mass. We had texted a bit, but nothing serious, and I was totally fine with that. Those early days were about finding my footing and spending time with Abuelo. It was while receiving a blessing from the priest (at my grandfather's personal request to him) that I caught sight of Diego, standing next to a beautiful woman a few years older than me. When I was done with my blessing, I went over to say hello, leaving Abuelo and my aunts, Tía Marta and Tía Yoli, who had a laundry list of prayer requests for the father. It was like a competition between them, spouting off the most loved ones in need of God's divine intercession.

The bright sunshine and buzz from the street vendors selling raspas and tacos added such a rich color to the morning. Children were running up and down the street, joyous and free from the strict reverence of the church behind us. I walked with a new lightness as I made my way through the crowd to a smiling Diego.

He introduced me to his younger sister, Yesika, saying she was his business partner, right-hand woman, the brains of the operation—all things that made her laugh. She then asked me my thoughts on her brother's cooking, Bar Gloria, and Chihuahua before being called over by a client. As she walked away, many a stranger's eye followed her movements. She was as beautiful as her brother was handsome, I thought.

"Did you enjoy our night out together?"

"Yes, all of it was great. If not a bit random," I said, laughing.

It was strange to be talking with someone I had kissed only a few days prior, someone I didn't really know. It was even stranger to be doing so in front of a Catholic church, only a stone's throw from my grandfather, but there I was.

"Glad to hear. That was my intention," Diego said. He leaned in closer. "Can we see each other soon so I can get in a few more kisses?"

"I'll have to think about it," I said, with just enough coyness.

"Oh, is that how you're going to be?"

"Maybe. I'm still trying to get my lay of the land."

"Why of course . . ."

The way the light hit his eyes made all their shades of brown come to life. His features were so much a foil to yours, and perhaps that was also what drew me to him. The idea of two men in their two brown bodies, in the spring of their attraction . . . yes, I think that's what excited me about Diego.

"But yes, I'd love to see you soon. Text me, okay?"

We hugged each other and I went to save the priest from being further inundated with my relatives' prayer requests. I was feeling a sense of unbridled happiness rivaled only by the sugar high of the children running in circles around us. Summer was looking hopeful, and I wanted as much of that hopefulness as I could get my hands on. I was ready to open myself to all the good things that might come from being a braver version of myself.

I spent the following morning reading the Sandra Cisneros book that I'd gotten in Ithaca. As I opened it, I thought about the old man who'd gifted it to me, how he had chosen it because he felt it could show me something I needed to see. I was enthralled by Cisneros's depiction of her colorful barrio in *The House on Mango Street*—its rich mezcla of characters and language, the seamless lyricism with which she weaves Spanish and English together. Reading her words, it dawned on me that I had never read a character that looked like me. How strange to love books so much and only find myself in one at nineteen?

At some point, my grandfather had to come pull me out of Cisneros's world and back into the present. He said we were going on a trip, but wouldn't tell me where to. When I pressed him for details, all he said was that he had something to show me.

I got dressed quickly and joined my grandfather in his faithful pickup truck to drive through parts of the city that were new to me, areas I had no memory of. Throughout the journey he shared more stories of his life in Chihuahua, a life before I, or the United States, were part of his world. We passed streets that carried family stories, buildings that had not existed prior to his emigration. He pointed out the factory where he and my dad had worked just after my parents married, before all of them migrated north of the border. The building was imposing, with barely any windows, and the sun shone brightly against its white metal walls. He pointed out the small green church where he and my grandmother had married. The church looked oddly out of place against all the new apartment buildings on both sides of it. Then he pointed out the hospital where my mother and my uncle were born, its façade covered in a mural of the Virgin Mary with her hands open, as if welcoming the masses.

"Has it changed much?"

"The city? Yes, quite a bit. It feels very modern now."

"It's not at all how I remember it from childhood."

"Imagine how I feel, mijo. I left in my forties, and in those twenty-odd years, it is like the Chihuahua of my past was changed overnight. All around us I see a thriving metropolis, which is wonderful, but also so very different from the city I left."

It was strange to hear my grandfather speak so openly about the past and all these landmarks brimming with memories, especially those of my uncle. I'd spent my childhood with little ever said about Tío Daniel. All I was told was that one day he went to visit his best friend at work. His friend had just inherited an antique pistol from the Mexican Revolution and was showing it off in the way young men do with one another. As the story went, a shot was accidentally fired, then a stray bullet ricocheted off a steel beam and lodged in my uncle's head, killing him instantly. I memorized those details from a young age because they were all I had of the man whose name I carried, whose face stared back at me in the mirror. In a second, my family's dynamic changed completely, and the city that had been ours for generations became too much for my mom and grandparents. His memory was everywhere.

"We're here, mijo."

We pulled into an empty parking lot and Abuelo turned off the engine. Outside the truck I could see a derelict building and tired gas station pump, and next to it was the small kiosk where one could pay for gas or buy beer and cigarettes. Everything was eerily still.

"This is the place I wanted to show you."

"Is this where it happened?"

"Yes, mijo."

We got out of the truck and began walking around. No one was working that day and the mechanic's shop was chained shut. As I moved about, I tried to think of something to say to my grandfather, but nothing felt worthy of this moment. It was strange to realize I'd likely passed this gas station during previous trips and no one had ever pointed out its significance. It was ordinary, rundown even, and this made it all the sadder. The place where my uncle had died was virtually indistinguishable from any number of other gas stations in the city. Did anyone even remember what had happened here? Did anyone know I now carried this man's name? Did anyone even give a shit? I wanted it to look grander, or for there to be some plaque—anything to mark its importance.

"I thought it was time you finally visited, since you were named after him."

"You all never spoke much about him."

My grandfather stood there thinking seriously before responding.

"It's hard, Daniel. I think, as a father, I felt the need to be strong for your mom, and as a husband, for your grandmother. It hurt me, but for your mom, she loved him so much, and he was her only sibling. When he died it was too painful for her to stick around, and when your dad had the opportunity to go to the United States, well, your mom was the first to pack her bags."

The outside of the kiosk was covered in vintage cigarette ads and hand-painted signs for deals on beer and tequila and bags of ice. The lights inside were off, with no sign of life. I closed my eyes, trying to listen to the noise of traffic. I imagined him walking here to greet his best friend, who would go on to accidentally kill him. I listened for the echoes of their conversation prior to his friend showing off the gun, prior to the misfire, the loss of life. I tried to imagine where Tío Daniel might have planned to go after, had he been able to go somewhere else that day. I took what little I knew of him and built this world, because it was all I could do to bridge the real Daniel with the one I imagined.

"What happened to his friend?"

"He served a few years, but I never wanted him to go to jail. It was an accident, mijo, we all knew that. We were angry, of course, but we did not want two families to suffer. When the police told us what happened, we asked to speak with him. It was a painful encounter; I felt like two young men died that day."

"What's his name?"

"Luis Menchaca. He was your uncle's best friend from childhood."

"I wonder if it still haunts him."

"I'm not sure, mijo. I hope not. Everyone deserves to have peace in this life. I forgave Luis long, long ago. The boy suffered enough by losing the most important friend in his life. I don't want him to be plagued by guilt. I'd never wish such darkness on anyone."

I closed my eyes, trying to visualize my uncle in his final moments as it dawned on him that he was dying, the bullet lodged in his brain. I longed to know what he felt those last few seconds as his life slipped from his hands, what he wished he could still do, what he wanted to get off his chest, who he wished to see. It felt important. As important as sharing his name.

"I think you would have liked him, mijo."

"I wish we could have met."

"He was smart, Daniel."

"That's what Abuela always used to say."

"It's true. He was always reading great big books, questioning everything. I think he believed he was living in a world that did not understand him. Do you know what I mean?"

I studied my grandfather for a moment. My heart began beating loudly as I took in those words so weighted with meaning, a bridge across time, a way of connecting both of his Daniels. I wasn't confident I totally understood his inferences, but I could tell he was sharing with me something vitally important.

"I think so."

His eyes went glassy, and his moustache began to twitch ever so slightly. He held his hand over his mouth to stop any more pain from surfacing. I wrapped my arms around his shoulders, hugging him fiercely. His crying was muffled by my hug, my shirt wet with his tears, and I thought of what it was to hold someone in their sadness. Love could be softness, but it could also be strength.

"I love you, Daniel. You know that, right?"

"Of course, Abuelo."

"I want you to be happy in this life. No matter what or who it is that brings you happiness. I will always love you, ¿me entiendes?"

As the sun caught my eyes, I saw my Abuelo in a different light. I saw him as someone who was more in tune with the world than I'd ever realized. Looking around at this place where Tío Daniel died, with his father in my arms, and me, the nephew who carries his name, things started to make sense. I didn't push the conversation any further that morning, but let what he said settle within the space between us. In time, I'd be brave enough to show him all my facets, share all my truth.

A few days later Diego reached out to me, and we agreed to meet for dinner downtown. I was honest with Abuelo about where I was going but didn't confirm whether or not it was a date. I still needed a bit more time to process what I believed my grandfather was telling me: that Tío Daniel had been gay, and he suspected I was too. It was a lot, and I needed to wait for the right moment to return to it. On the night of the date, I asked my cousin Marisol for a ride into town, as she was already picking up Analyse from my Tía Carmen's.

In those days after visiting the gas station, I was desperate to share what was weighing on my mind with someone, and the truth is, the person I wanted to speak to about it the most was you. Of course, I never did reach out. I sometimes wonder what that conversation would've looked like, what it would have been like to pick up a phone and call you. What it would have felt like for you to be surprised by my caller ID on your screen.

"Hello . . . Daniel? Is that you?" you'd answer hesitantly.

"Yeah, it is. Sorry to bug you . . ."

We'd let a few seconds pass between us, deciding who'd have the next line.

"Umm . . . that's okay, I guess. Are you all right?"

"I think my uncle was gay."

I'd rush out with it but leave it to you to move us along to the next bit.

"*What? Sorry, I don't know what you're talking about.*"

"*I think my dead uncle was gay, the one who died young. And I'm afraid of dying too, before coming out. I need to come out, Sam, before I die. I need to be free.*"

"*I see . . . I'm sure that's a lot to be dealing with.*"

"*Do you ever get plagued by that need? Do you ever wonder where it comes from? This panic of being out or not being out or forever being a secret. Does it scare you like it scares me?*"

"*Daniel . . .*"

"*Do you ever think happiness might be a place that will elude you for the rest of your life?*"

"*Daniel . . .*"

"*Because I think it might elude us both and that scares me. That really fucking scares me.*"

But of course, you know as well as I do that this call never happened. I didn't have you to confide in, and I didn't want to bother Rob and Mona with my family drama while they were enjoying their summer of music festivals and backpacking across Europe. So instead I kept it all inside, allowing the anxiety to creep in during what was honestly, otherwise, a happy few weeks of my life.

On the night of my date, Marisol sent me a text to let me know she was outside my Tía Carmen's house. I quickly said goodbye to my grandfather and aunt and uncle, then rushed outside with little Analse. I was excited and nervous in equal measure. I didn't know what to expect. As I got in the car, it dawned on me: I'd never actually gone out with anyone before. This was wild. I'd feared my summer would be one in which I'd have to hide part of myself, but I was having more opportunities to flourish here than I could've ever begun to dream of.

"Hola, Marisol."

"Hola, Daniel. Is my little chickadee already sleeping? Poor mamas, being five must be such a tiring existence, no?"

I turned around to find Analyse already passed out, having only just been buckled into her car seat.

"Yes, she was playing jump rope outside for hours this afternoon. Thanks for agreeing to drive me, by the way."

"No problem, mijo. My pleasure. I feel like I haven't been able to hang out with you at all so far, work has been a bit mad lately."

"Marisol, why do you always call me 'mijo' when you're only, like, eight years older than me?"

"Because you're my primito. I even changed your diapers when Sonia and Chavo would visit. You will always be 'mijo.'"

This made me laugh.

"How about some music?"

"Will Analyse wake up?"

"Oh no, homegirl is five going on seventy. She sleeps through anything."

Marisol gestured toward a Maná greatest hits CD tucked in the passenger door, and I put it in as she pulled onto the main avenue in town.

"So, Daniel, rumor has it you're off to hang out with Diego Salazar?"

"Yes, we're meeting up for dinner."

"You know, he's kind of a big deal in this town."

"Oh, really? How so?"

"Some say he is Chihuahua's most eligible bachelor. I mean, truth be told, not my type, but his family are pretty well off if you catch my drift."

"Oh, well . . . he is very nice. Money or not."

"You're right. He is sweet. His father and our cousin Edgar have been friends since elementary school. Their family are always helping cater quinces, or weddings, or whatnot for ours."

I was feeling a bit more nervous now that we were so close to the restaurant and began to silently pray I didn't do anything stupid to embarrass myself. I didn't want to come off as awkward or inexperienced, and the six-year age difference scared me.

"Mijo, can I ask you a question?"

"Go for it," I said, unsure what she'd ask me.

"This wouldn't be a date, would it?"

She had the most conspiratorial grin on her face. I wasn't surprised. Marisol was in tune enough with things to have figured this out. However, I was surprised at how very little her question worried me—if anything, I felt relieved. It was reassuring to have someone else know it was, in fact, a date, so much so that I felt comfortable sharing with Marisol how I'd gone out with Diego after my welcome party. I even told her about the kiss, and how he'd said he wanted to take me on a proper date like this. It all came pouring out, and I felt lighter afterward for having shared.

"Well, I hope you have a wonderful night, mijo. You deserve a bit of fun."

"Thanks, Marisol. I really appreciate it. And, if you don't mind, can we keep this a secret between us both? I just haven't had time to tell Abuelo or my parents about, you know, being gay and all."

"Of course, mijo. My lips are sealed."

"I love you, prima. Thanks for everything."

"If you need anything, I'm just a phone call away."

I got out of the car and walked the rest of the way. I sent Diego a message to let him know I was en route before checking my reflection in a large store window. Staring back at me was a Daniel quite different from the one who'd left Ithaca only a few weeks prior. I was surprised by my square face; my shoulders, which had widened in the past few months; my frame, which was now a little bit more muscled. Overall, my body was more grown-up looking. I was staring at Daniel, but a Daniel still evolving, still with so much growth within him. It made me happy to know I was capable of so much change still.

I made my way to the restaurant and, realizing I'd beat Diego there, went to order a drink at the bar. Thrilled at being legal this side of the border, I walked up to the barman with a slight bravado, grateful I didn't have to rely on a fake ID to be served. The inside of the restaurant was gorgeous, with original wooden beams framing the high ceilings. I tried taking a photo, but it was too dark, and I couldn't quite capture the age and allure of the space. As I reviewed the photos on my phone, I felt a tap on my shoulder and turned to find Diego dressed ever so handsomely, holding a bouquet of flowers. He smiled and kissed me gently on the cheek. It was thrilling to kiss a man so openly.

"Don't you look ever the handsome date?"

"Thank you, Diego."

"You are welcome, mi querido."

"These flowers are beautiful. I think this might be the first time anyone has ever bought me flowers."

"A small gift to say thank you for an incredible first date."

"It's just started," I said jokingly.

"A preemptive gesture then," he said, giving my shoulder a squeeze.

Diego and I were seated near a window with views of the avenue below, bustling with those just off work and buskers playing a cacophony of instruments, some with commendable talent and others who sounded more like drunk street cats—but to me, it was all magical. I took the opportunity to study Diego as he reviewed the menu with the expertise of someone who made his living from cooking. It reminded me of how I'd spend hours in our small living room watching you. Is there anything more intimate than watching someone when they don't realize they're being watched? Studying his face in the candlelight, the curve of his nose and the precise shape of his almond eyes, I saw a kind of manly beauty not a part of my world in Ithaca. The thickness of his eyebrows, the fullness of his eyelashes—it astonished me because he looked like me, with his brown skin and jet-black hair.

Throughout the date, Diego asked loads of questions about my life, and I appreciated his genuine interest in getting to know me. Over the starter, I attempted to explain my future ambitions. I shared how I wanted to publish poetry collections and go to grad school, how I wanted to see my name on the cover of books in Barnes & Noble. I told him I wanted to waltz into my former high school with a published book and let all the teachers who supported me know that I'd done it, that my dream had come true. As the words poured out, I saw Diego take in each and every sentence, and take them all seriously. With him listening, I didn't feel silly or naïve. I felt like it was all possible.

"I can't wait to buy your book."

"I'll sign it for you, but no freebies. I've got bills to pay."

His laugh was deep and honey-like, and I felt myself trapped in each of its reverberations. He told me he wanted to expand his catering company and grow his team; he even had dreams of opening a restaurant in El Paso that celebrated food from both sides of the Chihuahuan desert. When the mains came, we moved on from future ambitions to relationship history, which felt inevitable but was still not the easiest subject for me to broach.

"Have you ever been in love?"

I weighed the question, a vortex I could easily get lost in if I wasn't careful.

"Not yet, I don't think."

I don't know why I lied. It might have been because I didn't want to be in love with you just then. I wanted to be free of you in the same way I believed you had freed yourself of me.

"Well, you're young. I'm sure love is not far off for you yet."

He smiled before taking a sip of his water. Little did he know of my past year, of the real answer I was not ready to give him. You see now, I carried you everywhere with me. Even if I didn't say it aloud to Diego, it was no less real. I had been in love, and I was desperate to fall out of love and move on with my life because it's what I figured you wanted. It's basically what you'd instructed me to do—or so I allowed myself to believe.

When we finished our meal, it was quickly cleared away, and a second bottle of wine was brought out without us even ordering it. Everyone was treating us with so much care that it started to catch my attention. It sounds weird, but it dawned on me then that we hadn't even ordered before, they'd just brought out the food as if they'd known what Diego was going to ask for. The manager even walked over to pour the wine himself, which was strange to me.

"Hola jefe, how was the meal?"

"Lovely as ever, Ernesto. Please tell Salomon I send my regards."

"Of course. Enjoy the rest of your evening, chicos."

He winked at me as he meandered back to the bar, where I noticed some of the waitstaff watching us and gossiping away like a gaggle of geese.

"Diego, does your family own this restaurant?"

"Surprise! Yes—well, my aunt, to be fair—but I started my career here working every low-ranking job in the kitchen. The staff still jokingly refer to me as 'The Boss.'"

I thought about what Marisol had shared with me in the car, how Diego was seen as Chihuahua's most eligible bachelor. I thought about the people staring at our table and sizing me up. Were they assuming I was some twink, a brainless gold digger? Some parasite going after their city's gay Prince Charming? Was Diego just as much my polar opposite as you had been? The reality was, Diego was rich—like, really rich. He owned a catering company, he'd co-financed an incubator bar with his sister, his family owned restaurants across the city. He wined and dined with politicians. The more I thought about it, the more I couldn't shake the idea that he and I were mismatched.

"Did you enjoy the food?"

"Yes, it was lovely," I said, but then I couldn't stop myself. "But, sorry, I'm just a little thrown off right now."

I didn't want to make this a whole thing, but I needed to find out more about him. To my mind, it made no sense that this man was interested in me. I felt like I had nothing to offer him at nineteen years old, still so very much a kid.

"What else do you want to know?"

"Why are you interested in me, Diego?"

"What do you mean, guapo?"

"Diego, you realize we're from two completely different worlds. My parents are blue-collar workers back in America. No matter if my family seems nice and middle class here in Chihuahua—this isn't the case for me across the border. So I just don't get why you'd be pursuing someone like me . . . maybe you have a false impression of who I am?"

I felt like I was repeating previous bad habits, reacting to Diego's interest exactly as I'd reacted to yours. My need for clarity was driven by heightened emotions and overthinking, but I needed to state my piece.

"I just don't understand how you can possibly be interested in me, knowing that."

"Why does it matter?"

"Why does what matter?"

"Why does it matter if I come from money, and you don't?"

"I just feel like a silly little kid in your presence. I mean, I can't even afford to pay for this meal."

"But you don't have to."

"That's not the point. The point is, like, I just . . . I'm sorry. I feel a bit uncertain about all of this now. It has nothing to do with you. I think I'm working through some things, and they are having an effect on me and you've caught me off guard."

I had made things awkward, and it was clear Diego had no idea what to do with me. *Of all the times to sabotage myself*, I thought, *why now?* Why was it so difficult for me to be normal around someone I was attracted to? I hated that I'd fallen into this cliché of thinking myself unworthy of someone who came from the better side of the tracks, the opposite side of a border.

We got up and exited the restaurant. It was obvious I had really stuck my foot in it. We walked for a good while in complete silence before Diego stopped in the middle of a busy avenue. He turned to me with a serious look on his face and I braced myself for impact, to be yelled at, to be told I was a brat, to be punished for being the overthinker I was.

"Daniel, now I have something I need to get off my chest."

"Yes?"

"I'm not interested in you because I think you come from this or that type of family. I'm interested in you because you come off as very smart and ambitious. It also helps that you're handsome, and in spite of what I believe to be a default position of an overactive mind, you seem like someone I want to continue to get to know."

"But you must have your pick of any guy in this city? Why do you want to go out with an awkward guy like me?"

"Because you're so different from anyone I've ever met. Let me be real with you: I grew up here. This city is full of boring losers and social climbers. Guys I went to school with who don't aspire to anything because they live comfortably off their parents' money, and their comfort breeds their own apathy. At my age, I am already tired of people who have no drive. I hope you can let go of the fact that I come from money, because it is not my fault. I know that sounds like a cop-out, but I was born into this family. I did not choose them. That said, I'd like to think we are good people and never judge others. Does that make sense?"

"Yes, it does. I'm sorry if it seemed like I was judging you. My friends have told me I sometimes jump to conclusions too easily."

This made him laugh, which put me at ease. I hadn't completely ruined things.

"You don't need to apologize."

"I'm sorry. It's a habit."

"I get it. You totally have a right to ask me these questions, but please know I like you—like, really, really like you."

"And I like you."

"Good to know."

My heart felt full again. I was finally with someone who did not hesitate to bare his heart and make clear his intentions. Perhaps this was what growing up was: learning to not skirt around issues, but address them head-on with clarity and grace. Whatever it was, I felt better. I knew I hadn't fucked things up, I had just gotten a bit emotional, but emotions were not the enemy—as long as I didn't run from them.

"Now, can I treat you to dessert?" Diego asked, broaching the divide.

I looked up to where he was pointing. Unbeknownst to me, we had stopped in front of those familiar Golden Arches, now gleaming in the orange-and-purple summertime dusk. No matter where you were in the world, McDonald's was not far off. I couldn't stop myself from laughing to the point of tears at this turn of events. Maybe his invitation was a tongue-in-cheek joke at my concerns about money, or maybe Diego was just wanting something easy. I didn't ask, but instead simply accepted and followed him inside, where I ordered my childhood favorite: soft-serve ice cream with caramel sauce. Diego ordered the same, and with our ice creams in hand we walked outside to sit on a bench and observe the throngs of people going up and down the avenidas. I relished the hordes of families and teenagers speaking Spanish, the soundscape of this homeland of mine; these people who looked like me but also represented all types of social classes, life experiences. I turned to that handsome man beside me who really, really liked me, and for a few more hours, let myself exist within this city without worrying about what was to come or what others might think, putting to rest, at least for now, all the other questions bubbling near the surface.

JULIO

JULY 20, 1990

We went to visit my abuelos today to celebrate my bisabuelo's eighty-fifth birthday. My abuelos were hosting a huge fiesta on the ranch to mark this momentous occasion. The party stretched into the long hours of night. Around a fire we sang songs while my cousins played the bajo sexto and guitarrón. My bisabuelo sat in the middle of it all like a king at his throne, surrounded by family. I'd say he looked content, fearless even, as if staring the end of his life in the face, whatever time he had remaining. As we danced and sang and drank, I imagined my bisabuelo was pondering all the happiness he'd held throughout his past eighty-five years. I prayed that at his age I could have just some of that happiness. When it is my turn to blow out eighty-five candles, God willing, I pray that I only have happy memories to look back on and that I am fearless in the face of death.

—D.M.

So you now know how I spent my first few weeks in Chihuahua. They weren't what I'd envisaged for myself on the plane ride over, but they were very much what my heart needed. I'd left the US believing I might never move beyond you, afraid that my ability to open myself up to other men would be forever mired by your memory. But in those early days with Diego, I found myself at the border of your hurting me and his healing, and as I did, I fought the urge to look backward. You didn't want me, that's what you wrote, so I focused on the present, on a man who really, really liked me.

Sometimes I found it strange to be in Chihuahua without my parents, but I began to lean into the freedom of being on my own. I learned how to move through the city with my own eyes, my own desire, and how to fill my days with my own plans—sometimes with Abuelo's company, sometimes with my cousins, but also not. I'd wake up early while it was still relatively cool out and go on long runs through the mezcla of avenidas with their candy-colored houses, heat rising from the asphalt, dogs barking behind tall iron fences, chickens clucking from urban chicken coops. All of it was so different from our lives in Ithaca, and from my quiet home-town in California. Those summer months felt the closest I'd ever get to understanding my parents' life before the US. Each day, I attempted to map their former selves to the sights and sounds, the spice and sweetness all around that city.

One of the coordinates I discovered was gifted to me by my grandfather. You see, a few days after my date with Diego, my grandfather took me on a long drive outside the city. It took us over an hour in the hot midmorning sun to get to where we were going. As we drove with the windows down, letting the breeze offer us some small relief from the ninety-plus-degree heat, I hung my hand out, trying to glide along the currents. As a kid, I used to believe that if I could catch enough wind, my arm might grow into a wing, and if I could do that then maybe I'd be able to fly above the moving car. But try as I might, I never did learn how to become a bird. I stayed a boy dreaming, hand in the wind, head in the sky.

After an hour of only the wide desert's company, we pulled off the highway and onto a lone single-track road surrounded by dry plains on both sides. The dirt was the color of gold, the texture of brown sugar, a bountiful, beautiful arid treasure stretching out for miles. In the distance I could see tall green nopales and matorrales, which thrived in the harsh environment. As we got closer, I noticed the fence guarding what was obviously some kind of cattle ranch. My grandfather's last name hung above the entrance, each letter welded together from hot iron: "El Rancho Maldonado."

"Is this it?" I asked Abuelo.

"Yes, mijo, this is another place I have been wanting to bring you back to."

"I have been here before?"

"Yes, when you were very, very young."

His nephew Edgar greeted us and took us around the once-bustling farm, which I learned had been in our family for generations but was about to be sold. My grandfather had spent his childhood learning how to work this land until he got an apprenticeship at a factory at a time when many American companies were setting up shop in Chihuahua. But, Edgar reminded Abuelo, despite his move to the city, deep in our blood we were all rancheros. As we walked along the pens of the cattle that remained, I couldn't feel one iota of my family's past here. My clothes stained with sweat, and shoes caked in dust— nothing about it felt intrinsic or natural to me. My body felt out of place in the dirt and heat, amid the rusted iron and splintered wood, and though I knew it was all a time capsule of my family's lineage, I had the feeling that I didn't belong. I let Edgar and my grandfather wander off to the compound of houses where Abuelo lived long ago. I wanted to do my own exploring.

I entered the empty stables, and dusty light peeked through the slatted roof, painting parts of the interior in amber and leaving others hauntingly black. It smelled of hay and horse manure, with notes of citrus blowing through from the outside lemon trees. I tried hard to imagine walking through this building a dozen or so years ago as a little boy. I wanted to know what that Daniel had thought of this place—if he'd sensed some deeper connection here than I did at nineteen. Did any of it call out to him, inviting him to root into the copper dirt? I bent down to finger the grains of sand, hoping something might pour from inside me, but nothing came. So I walked further. The ranch was quiet and mostly empty. Edgar had sold most of their cattle stock and only a few horses were left. What I was seeing was a skeleton of this ranch's former self. I closed my eyes, trying to listen for echoes of the past. I wanted to understand this place as my grandfather did, and as his father had, and his father's father. I wanted to know the land like they'd known it, to be confident enough to lay claim to it and reap from it what they could sow. I longed to be still, to learn to grow something hearty and resilient, able to survive in the harshest of places.

"Daniel? Mijo, where are you?"

"Abuelo, I'm inside the horse's stable."

He was by himself, nursing a bottle of water, when he joined me. His collar was damp with sweat. I took a swig as he wiped his brow with a handkerchief. For a moment, I saw him not as my grandfather, but as a man at home in the desert, finding himself once again in the soil that bore him.

"What have you been doing?"

"Just exploring the grounds, trying to imagine what this was like when it was a working farm."

"Oh, it was a beautiful place to grow up. My father ran it along with his four brothers, and my grandparents lived alongside us all. The ranch used to spread out for miles in every direction before the younger generation started selling off the land."

"I can't imagine growing up among horses and cattle."

"Every day was a new adventure, mijo. I'd follow my grandfather and uncles around mending fences and feeding the animals.

My father taught me how to groom the horses and care for every living thing we had."

It all sounded so outside of the man I knew as my grandfather.

"Do you miss that life, ever?"

"I am grateful for it, but knew your grandmother would never have dreamed of living on a ranch. She was too much of a city girl, and my cousins were better suited to take it over."

Just then, a cock began to crow from atop the big chicken coop. Its call rang loudly in the otherwise noiseless expanse. We paused for a few seconds, listening, and when it tired from its crowing, I noticed the babbling of a brook not far off. Its calming trickle flowed over stones and twigs, leading to a man-made lake that Abuelo offered to show me. To get there, we had to walk through thickets of barren bushes, basically giant tumbleweeds. Little brown birds slid along the path as if leading us to the water, and it reminded me of when you and I hiked to Rainbow Falls in the company of sparrows. How much I wanted to send you a photo, and how very much I wanted not to as well.

Upon seeing it, I was astounded by how big the lake was, at least a mile wide. The water was crystal clear on account of the brook's rainwater, which rushed off the nearby mountains. I remember feeling so tempted to strip off my clothes and jump into the cold water, just as we'd planned to do back on the banks of Seneca Lake. As I stood watching the placid scenery, Abuelo shared Edgar's plans for selling off the land and putting an end to our family's cattle ranch. He had some interest from an American cattle business looking to expand into México.

"Any interest in buying a ranch, mijo?"

"I don't think I'm cut out for that life, Abuelo. Lo siento."

He laughed at this and pulled me into his arms, hugging me fervently. Every day I woke up to an even happier Abuelo, and it brought me so much comfort. He felt peace in his homeland, and even if I didn't feel a deep connection to México, I at least was deeply rooted to him. That love between us carried us along the dusty path back to Edgar's house, where we said goodbye, not only to our family but also to the land. As we drove back down the lonely road toward the highway, I thought of my ambitions, my studies, my dream of becoming a writer, and how truly opposite those things were to the land I was looking at then. If a cow was ill, or the stable roof needed to be repaired, if a new ditch needed to be dug, I wouldn't know where to start; but I could put down in words what was happening. I could write the heat into metaphor, turn the birdsong into verse. I could keep our family's land going longer in story.

I knew my grandfather was sad he was losing another bit of his family's history, but now, as an adult, I was starting to understand that life was a matter of deciding what to keep alive and what to let die. Personal dreams, family ranches, first loves, summer flings— all these things have a life span. As much as I was learning to let go, I was also learning to welcome new knowledge into my life. So as June bled into July, I spent each day trying to learn more about what it was like to be Daniel—a son, a cousin, a grandson, a lover. Every day I woke up and had something new I could learn. I found a rhythm to life and was able to fill my time, able to map more of myself and my history.

I had my runs, I had my adventures with Abuelo, my dates with Diego, and our hangouts with his friends at the bar. I went to Sunday mass with my family; I spoke to my parents every week. I even taught them how to Skype so the rest of the family could see them on camera. These routines moved me from being a mere visitor to building a sort of life in Chihuahua, at least for a season. I was happy and began to genuinely feel that things would be all right. July promised brightness, sunshine, heat, and endless joy, so that is how I went into the month. Then came a big surprise: my invitation to the mountains, where Diego planned to share another part of my homeland with me, a place that would help me build an even deeper connection to tierra madre.

It's funny when I think about it. The men in my life were always taking me into the wilderness to help me reach a kind of primal part of myself. Do you understand what I'm talking about? Do you remember our drunk dancing around fires, how we touched skin in the cool of night? Do you remember how ridiculous we were, shouting our dreams into the ether? Because I do. All of it was so powerful, and I remember everything. I know I'm meant to be showing you what I was doing between leaving you in Ithaca and learning of your passing, but there is a voice reverberating within me. As I sit here, writing to you, it keeps asking me questions, longing to know what you were up to. This voice tells me that knowing will help me to properly say goodbye. Is that crazy? Yet I hear it. So tell me, Sam, what were your eyes seeing as time was winding down? What were you up to? Was your heart vibrating in a forest with another man's? It's okay if so, you can tell me. I won't be hurt. Maybe, I keep thinking, even if we were both with other people, there was a point in our time left together on this earth in which our rhythms were in sync, totally in tune with the love we were still carrying. Maybe there was a night in which we both looked up to the stars and thought about the language we shared, how we'd mapped ourselves to our ancestors. Because even as I made room for another, you were still there, buried in my heart. I couldn't totally leave you. I kept seeing the world through your eyes and longed to show you what I saw.

It was toward the end of the month when Diego and I took our trip to the Sierra Madre mountains, and as I sat in the car while he drove us the half day's journey from Chihuahua, I was thinking of you. I was thinking of you because Diego and I were about to spend a long weekend together alone in a hotel in the same bed. Do you get where I'm going with this? We had been seeing each other for a few weeks now, and I knew it was likely we would move beyond kissing and heavy petting. I wanted Diego and he wanted me, but my body had only known yours in that way prior to this point. Again, I couldn't totally let you go even when you had moved on (or at least when I thought you had). I was excited at the possibility of being intimate with another man but was afraid of what it would mean for us, or what it might say about me. Was this my way of finally saying goodbye? Would I ever get you back if I gave myself to someone else? Was I a bad person, immoral for being in love with one man but learning the body of another? These questions followed me from my family's sleepy neighborhood deep into the mountains' shadow.

Do you remember the final time we slept together? It was the last time—at least for me—in which everything felt indestructible, but it was also the moment when I felt you letting go. We were stripped to our underwear in your bed; it was so humid those final weeks of May. The curtains were drawn but the window was cracked open, letting in a slight breeze. We had fallen asleep together and woken up in each other's arms. I could hardly believe it, and still sometimes had to pinch myself. We had gone from accidental spooning in the company of wilderness to intentionally sharing the same bed. My heart was so full, but my mind was trying to prepare for when we'd have to say goodbye. Of course, at that time I didn't know it would be forever, and not just for a season.

We lay there in the quiet hum of morning. I was counting the beats per minute your heart was making as my ear was pressed against your chest, my hand playing with the tufts of hair from your happy trail down to your crotch. There I was with the most beautiful man in the world, a man who happened to be my best friend and the love of my life. So many emotions were pulsing through me, and I knew I needed to say something to you, even if I was afraid to confront the bigger things, like what we were, or what would happen when you moved into your frat house and I lived elsewhere. Even though I was afraid, I couldn't let the moment pass without speaking deeply and honestly to you.

"I'm going to miss you."

Do you understand how scared I was, having said that? It felt like the most intimate thing I could've shared, and I was desperate for you to give me something back. You pulled me closer to you, your hand gripping my forearm.

"Summer's not that long."

I thought about it. June, July, August—only a few short months and then I'd be reunited with you, or so I hoped, but I still didn't know where we stood. I didn't know if you'd save yourself for me over summer, or if you'd give yourself to others, men or women, something serious or just a fling. There was so much I didn't know, and that not-knowing created a bigger chasm between us.

"You're right, I guess."

"It's not like we aren't going to see each other come August."

But you had chosen a different path. A house full of young men who felt a world away from me, from the parts of you you'd shared with me that made us more similar than different. Minutes passed with you caressing my arm, but no further words were shared, and this silence scared me. My mind could not put to rest what it longed to—no, what it needed to—know.

"Can I ask you something?"

"Go for it."

"Will you miss me?"

You laughed for a while before turning to me with a serious look, studying my expression, and I tried not to break. I tried not to let my face give too much away: my worries, my fear, my doubts. My need for you to tell me, confirm for me, that I mattered.

"Have you been waiting for me to respond this whole time?"

"I just want to know, Sam."

"Always overthinking . . ."

You were right, but I had my reasons, and although I was embarrassed, I was mostly happy you understood how my mind worked. How this overthinking never scared you, never made you run away. So I nestled into the crook of your arm, waiting for an answer.

"Of course I will, Daniel. Annoyingly, I think about you quite a bit."

"Annoyingly?"

"Umm, yeah. I have finals and shit. I can't be thinking about Daniel de La Luna 24/7. Give my mind a rest."

"You think of me 24/7?"

"Maybe not 24/7 . . . maybe like 16/7?"

"16/7?"

"Well, I do have to sleep."

"Do you ever dream about me?"

You pulled my head up by my chin and looked deep into my eyes. "Annoyingly, Daniel, I dream about you a lot."

I kissed you then, and you kissed me back, and we kept kissing. But I held on to what you said; in retrospect, those words have so much more meaning. Had it become too much too soon? Did the fact that you thought about me every minute of every hour scare you? Perhaps you started to realize that it might mean we were something more, something bigger than you'd ever expected. Whatever it was, in the days that followed you began to retreat into the shadows, leaving me alone and confused, both wanting you even more and wishing we had never crossed that threshold of knowing how two bodies work as one.

As Diego and I drove along the long, winding road leading us out of the city, I imagined what it would be like to stand naked in front of him. But each time I could only think of what it was like to stand in front of you. Your hot mouth on my skin, your hands grabbing every part of me, your body filling my body with all of your hunger. My entire understanding of sex was tied to you, and I remember feeling like I needed to free myself. I had no reason to believe you still thought of me every waking hour of your days, no reason to believe you still dreamt of me. And yet despite all that, despite the hurt you had caused me, I was, annoyingly, still thinking of you.

As we drove further, I took in the outside view of the forest road leading us toward the mountains and canyon. In all the times I had come to Chihuahua, I had never made it up that high. My memories of that part of the world were of an arid desert, but outside the car window everything was green and mountainous. The cliffs were covered in tall trees that went on for miles, more tree than rock. I hadn't discussed where we were going in any detail with my aunts and grandfather, and so had no idea who else in my family had ventured this far. Had my mother come to the mountains as a child? Did she and my uncle run up the jagged rocks, racing each other to the top? Did my ancestors ever forage the cliffside for food? I closed my eyes and tried to listen for echoes from the past, as I had at the cattle ranch; for anything that might give me clues to my connection to the land.

"I can't wait till this drive is over so I can finally kiss you."

There I was, seated next to a beautiful man who wanted to kiss me, who wanted to share more of my homeland with me so I might learn something. There was a kindness in his eyes that made me desperate to give my all to him, desperate to free myself from your hold. But I couldn't let go of you. Something was keeping me on the other side of that border. It was me, I realize now. Standing on the threshold between knowing one man's body and preparing to map the curves and grooves of another's, I was holding back. But it was time to let go.

"Kiss me, did you say?"

"Yes. Kiss you."

"Where?"

"Hmm . . . let me think. There, and there, and there," he said, pointing to many places only you had tasted.

"You know what I'm excited to do once this drive is over?"

"Dimelo," he said, taking the bait.

"Take a long piss."

"Very funny, cabrón, and here I am trying to be romantic with you."

I winked at him before pulling down my sunglasses and settling into our journey ahead, allowing the wind to carry you away from me so I was left only with what I'd soon share with Diego. I reached for his hand as a peace offering. As I fingered the lines of his tattoos with my thumb, I thought about the evening to come, questioning whether, when I looked up to see the constellations, my mind would see them with a new perspective or still feel tethered to you, the man who had given me the names for those stars. As we continued driving, I closed my eyes and kept my hand in Diego's grip.

When we arrived, I spent the first few hours by myself out on the patio of our hotel. Diego was rightfully exhausted from all that driving. As you might remember, I don't drive. It never seemed pertinent when I didn't have the money for a car. This meant, of course, that I was dependent on others to drive me when going further than my feet could carry me. So, as he took a nap, I sat outside looking onto the canyon the hotel was built on—or more so, into. Trees and shrubs and cactus stood proud and green against the coppery red rock. I closed my eyes and listened out for birdcalls, for anything that might help me let go of you. Hawks were circling above in search of prey hiding within the thick brush all around the canyon walls, and their squawks were piercing and menacing as they swooped down at many miles an hour, gliding dangerously close to the canyon ridge. When I opened my eyes, I caught sight of one hawk with a freshly mangled hare in its beak, bloody and hot with death. I feared this was a metaphor for you and me.

"Ay, pobre conejo. It never stood a chance."

I turned to find Diego standing behind me, holding two bottles of cold beer. It made me smile, how he had greeted me in very much the same way when I'd spoken to him for the first time only a month prior. He gave me a kiss on the lips before opening my bottle of beer. I pulled him close as he handed me the bottle. I breathed in the leathery scent of his musk and salty sweat, letting my olfactory system work its magic to build an archive of the moment.

"I am glad you joined me, querido."

"Thanks for bringing me. It's beautiful . . . I was just listening for the different birdcalls."

"What a magical place to tune into nature."

We sat there silently, drinking our beers under the humid gray clouds. He reached out for my hand, and we created a bridge to one another. As his fingers rubbed my palm, I released myself from the hours I'd spent out there alone, thinking of you. I wanted Diego to know I was present with him. I wanted him to know how grateful I was for the drive, the trip, for sharing this incredible mountain range with me. We made a toast to our trip and to each other, and then decided to play a game of who could spot the most birds. I wasn't really a bird-watcher, so Diego did much better than me. He spotted hummingbirds, orioles, woodpeckers, and was even able to distinguish the various hawks circling above. That afternoon he taught me their names in Spanish, and with each name I felt myself regaining part of my mother tongue that I'd lost to time. We soon ran out of birds, and I had to concede.

"What's the plan before dinner?"

"What would you like to do, guapo?"

"Let me think for a second . . ."

Something in me shifted. Maybe it was because an opportunity had presented itself. Maybe it was wanting to actually move on with my life, and maybe moving on at the time meant physically. No matter the reason, I got up and sauntered through the patio door and climbed onto the bed without totally knowing what I was doing. Diego was quick to follow my lead. I laughed as he downed the rest of his beer and then made his way to our room, plopping himself beside me. He was so handsome, and I wanted to share what I believed he was craving—what I too craved but was too scared to give just yet.

I gently combed his hair with my fingers and pressed my forehead against him. It was easier if I wasn't looking directly into his eyes. There was something calling from inside me, a need to give him a piece of myself. There, in the safety of our hotel room, it wasn't about giving him my body, but giving him part of my mind, the part that had been weighing on me.

"I want to be honest with you about something."

"Go ahead," he said cautiously.

"I feel like I need to share with you that I've only ever had sex with one other person before. It happened two months ago."

"Okay . . . well, we don't have to do anything you don't want to."

"I just needed you to know that. Not because I'm ashamed of my lack of experience. But I feel it's important to be up front if we're going to . . . you know . . . do that eventually."

"Thank you for that, querido. I appreciate you."

"Thank you for making me feel safe enough to be honest."

The bed creaked with our weight, which quickly lightened the mood. We laughed and just held each other, but I knew there was more to share, and I did not know exactly how to get there. The words were somewhere in the air, and I needed to piece them back together. I closed my eyes and took in a deep breath, exhaling what had been pressing down on me, releasing it with the carbon dioxide.

"Another thing . . . I think my uncle was gay."

"What?"

"The one who died," I clarified. "My mom's only sibling. He died about two years before I was born."

I was alone with no best friend to ask me how I felt about what was going on or how I was processing being back in México. Pouring my soul out to Diego just sort of happened. All I had been holding on to, or most of it, came flooding into that room.

"This uncle of mine—I'm pretty certain he was gay."

"I see . . . And how do you know this, Daniel?"

"My grandfather told me. Well, he kind of alluded to it the other day."

I had played our conversation over and over again in my head, trying to pick through my grandfather's words, sifting through the subtext as if I were panning for gold in Yosemite.

"Anyway, ever since that conversation with my grandfather, I've been thinking more about coming out to my parents. It's been weighing on me pretty heavily . . . I'm sorry if I'm just off-loading onto you."

"You've no reason to be sorry."

"Maybe I hope that by sharing this with someone a bit older, I might glean some tips or get a bit of advice—not that I'm saying you're old . . . oh God, sorry, my words are getting all fucked up."

"Ay, Daniel, I totally get what you mean."

"It's just strange, you know? Everyone tells me how much I look like him, but no one speaks about him. Not in a meaningful or concrete way. Who was he? What was he like? Was he someone I should be proud to look like, to be named after? Would he have even wanted me to share his name?"

"I can't imagine how strange that is to deal with. Especially how strange it would've been to deal with as a child."

"Maybe I still feel like a child. Like they're keeping something from me to protect me. I don't know if that makes sense, but it's how I feel."

He pulled me close to him as we fell back onto the pristinely made bed. I felt his breath on my neck, felt the rise and fall of his chest against my body. He was so kind, and let me blabber on and on until I had nothing more to say, until my brain felt exhausted from speaking for so long. Diego pressed tighter against me and told me how much I meant to him, how he was so grateful that I felt close enough to him to share these heavy thoughts, and in that moment

it felt like my heart was opening up more. I remember he told me
I would know when the time was right to tell my parents, and only
then would it be the right time, and somehow that made sense. He
then kissed me on the cheek and then the lips and then the neck,
and my body felt freer from having shared so much with him.

After our meal, we went for a walk around the hotel grounds.
We happened upon the pool, which was completely empty but had
an amazing view of the night sky. We sat on the lounge chairs and
took in the stars, out in their thousands. The sky was a purple-
black I had never witnessed before, and I tried to remember the
constellations you had taught me. I could see Orion's Belt, Ursa
Minor, and Ursa Major. I asked Diego if he knew any of their
names, but he was not as well versed as you. We then decided
to name the stars after famous Mexican musicians: Selena "La
Leyenda," Gloria Trevi, Paulina Rubio, Julieta Venegas, Los
Tigres del Norte, and Vicente Fernández. We laughed as we made
up myths about each of them.

As the temperature cooled, Diego insisted I come join him in
his chair, and we cuddled close. I felt safe there in his arms with his
breath on my cheek, listening to his heartbeat. I was remembering
what it was to make another human feel something, send blood
pumping through his body. As we lay there together in the purple
dark, a shooting star passed above us. It was so beautiful we froze
in awe; then Diego whispered in my ear to make a wish. I pressed
my eyes shut, praying. My heart began to beat loudly, but I did not
open my eyes to see the rest of the star's trail. I concentrated on letting go of each of those letters, spelling out my wish: to be free to
move on with my life. I let the sound of the wind rustling through
the trees carry them upward, toward an ever-watchful God, as we
continued to lie under the stars. I knew that when I finally opened
my eyes, my heart would know what to do.

We decided to head back to our room as the evening began
to cool down. The stars were now blanketed by big, heavy clouds

that had rolled in quickly. This was the first rainstorm of its kind I had seen since arriving more than a month ago, and it was unlike anything I'd ever witnessed. The heavens opened up completely before we even made it to our room, and thunder cracked loudly and fiercely as we rushed through the patio door. The noise of the rain was epic, all-consuming, and we entered the room completely soaked, our feet leaving a trail of watery footprints on the terra-cotta floor.

We stripped out of our soggy clothes, and as I took off my last bit of clothing, a final change in my body occurred. I turned to Diego, whose brown skin seemed painted a kind of blue in the light from the torrential sky outside, the dark shadows from various lamps making his tattoos appear almost alive. For some reason, I did not feel shy standing there with only rain droplets covering my skin. I walked over to him and pressed my lips into his with a strength I did not know I had. Whatever had been previously holding me back had ebbed, making way for something urgent and vital.

"I'm ready," I said to him, and I meant it.

"Are you sure?"

"Yes, mi querido. But only if you want to."

"Of course, oh God, Daniel, yes. I am very ready."

I led him by the hand into the most massive shower I had ever been inside and turned the taps on, letting the water warm up and steam the bathroom mirror. Diego kissed me gently on the neck, on each of my shoulder blades, then my clavicles. I grabbed the soap and lathered him up. I lifted each arm up one at a time, scrubbing gently underneath, making sure to clean all around his chest and down his stomach. He did the same for me. Next, he pumped some shampoo into his hand and massaged my scalp. This cleaning of each other's bodies was like a new love language I was learning. He followed with conditioner, and I rinsed and repeated the process for him.

"Do you want me to wash the other half of you?" he asked, staring down at my ass.

I nodded, turning toward the shower wall and spreading my legs. He gently glided the bar of soap down from my shoulder blades, over my back, to my ass, massaging gently into my cheeks until suds began to wash down the drain.

Once dried, we walked hand in hand back to our bed. He lifted me onto the mattress like you had not long before, but instead of getting stuck in that memory of you, I was fully present with Diego as he climbed on top of me. As I prepared for his body to enter mine, I quieted my mind, making way for this man before me and freeing myself from what had held me back for too long. That night, my body learned to bend and fold to someone new, and my mind allowed itself to be in the moment. As the rain continued to pour down, drowning out our passionate cries, I found a way to move forward. I finally learned how to let go.

We drove back two days later, after morning hikes and afternoon swims, days spent learning how our bodies worked together. We laughed and sang along to the radio; we stole kisses through mountain passages and along desert bush. What I wanted—all that growth, the ability to root myself somewhere else—it was all happening, and for a short while I was riding the waves of euphoria, at least until I arrived back at my Tía Carmen's house. I had been back all of thirty seconds when my phone began ringing nonstop. I chose to ignore it at first and set my bag on the living room floor.

I remember joining my family in the kitchen, as some of my cousins from down south were visiting my Tía Carmen and her husband. Marisol had even come over with Analyse. Everyone was asking about my trip, wanting to know what I saw up in the mountains, but our conversation kept being interrupted by the phone's incessant buzzing.

I remember my grandfather wouldn't stop bugging me about it, saying it could be an emergency and I should see who was trying to reach me. The number wasn't one I recognized, but it was the same one each time. Calling back, then back again. After ten minutes, I had no choice but to go and deal with it.

"Sorry about this," I said to my family.

"Don't worry, mijo. Feel free to answer it," Marisol insisted.

"No need to apologize, Daniel—just go, please," begged my grandfather.

"Sí, Abuelo. Ya me voy."

His concern made me concerned, not because I believed it was anyone important calling, but because I didn't like seeing my grandfather so worked up, with dread on his face. So I excused myself from the table. I remember making it halfway down the hall before finally hitting the answer button, standing in front of that painting of San Sebastián, when everything changed.

Where were you, Sam, in this moment? Do you remember? Because I swear you came to me as I chose to finally accept the call.

"Hello?"

"Daniel, sweetie, is that you?"

I recognized your mom's dulcet suburban voice in an instant, remembered the countless conversations we'd had with your parents on speakerphone, how you never minded me being the fourth wheel to your family catch-ups. We'd sit on the couch with the TV on mute, updating Martha and Ed on classes, our friends, and the changing weather during this brief period of my life when I was part of a perfect all-American family. Then even more came rushing back: the drive to the mall on arrivals day, the dinner on the lake, the care packages your mom had sent throughout the year, one for each of us. I remembered hugging her in the parking lot on that first day like she was my own mother, a mother leaving me to the wild wolf pack of freshman year with the responsibility of watching over you, her only begotten son.

"Mrs. Morris, is that you?"

"Yes, Daniel. I'm so sorry to be calling you during your family trip."

"It's okay, I'm fine to talk. How are you?"

"Oh my God, I don't even know how to say this . . ."

"Is everything all right?"

The line went quiet, and for a moment I wondered if the call had dropped. But then I heard her speaking again. Her voice was a mixture of drawn-out words and rushed phrases, and something about her sounded unsettled, manic, but it was also happening so quickly I didn't totally understand what was going on. I didn't know my world was about to break.

"It has been so hard to think who to tell or when to do it. But I wanted to call you because of how close you and Sam were, so close and . . . again, my brain has been a complete mess, I cannot speak properly . . . I asked his friends not to post anything because I needed time to deal with things. I needed time to figure out what to do."

She was crying, and I felt resolute in the fact that whatever she was about to tell me would be bad. My heart knew that her choice to call me in that moment hadn't been for the purpose of chatting about how well the Giants were doing, or asking for a recipe, or even to tell me her son was still madly in love with me. No, my heart knew, Sam, that for her to call me, instead of having you call yourself, meant something had gone horribly, horribly wrong.

"Mrs. Morris, is it Sam?"

"Daniel . . ."

"Please . . . tell me what's wrong."

"Daniel . . ."

"It's all right, I promise you can tell me. Please . . ."

I was going crazy. I wanted to scream. I wanted to cry. I was frozen there, willing your mother to speak.

"Sam's dead, sweetie. I'm so sorry to have to tell you like this."

"What?"

My mouth wanted to move, but none of my languages would work. *This can't be true,* I told myself. *This has to be some cruel fucking joke you somehow convinced your mother to make.* I stood there waiting for the big reveal, but it never came. I stood there waiting for you, Sam, but you never fucking came. I wanted to scream. I wanted to cry. But I was frozen.

"How? How did it happen?"

"He was out with friends and was drinking, and, well, the driver was drinking too, and they got in an accident . . . a very, very bad accident. There were others, his friends, who were pretty badly beaten up, but he, my Samuel, he wasn't wearing a seat belt . . . he, he, he . . ." Each second she took felt like a lifetime. "He was in a coma for a week and I thought, we thought . . . he'd get better . . . but we lost him a few days ago. He is gone . . . my sweet Samuel is gone," she said, almost screaming, and I wanted to scream with her, but my mouth wouldn't move. The ice was building up around me and I felt so cold and so alone, floating in a dark, tumultuous sea.

I turned left and right, looking for you in that hallway. You weren't there, so I looked for you in all the memories rushing toward me, a wave of nostalgia and pain about to completely blow my life to smithereens. I thought of the first time I saw you standing in front of me, how truly beautiful you were. I thought of our first kiss, how the moon was hanging above us, reflecting itself in that quiet brook of the gorge. I thought of all the mornings I woke up to find you in our small kitchen, a cup of coffee in hand and one poured out for me. I thought of all your smiles, the ones just for me. How you smiled differently for me. I thought of all the things I still had to say to you, how I was on the cusp of learning to speak from my heart. All of these things I thought, Sam, but none of them I could say aloud.

"Daniel, are you still there?"

"I'm so sorry, Mrs. Morris. I'm so sorry . . . I don't know what else to say. I'm so, so sorry for your and Mr. Morris's loss. He was such a great person . . . I am so sorry."

"He loved you very much, Daniel. You were one of his best friends. I know you made his time at Cayuga amazing and meaningful. I will forever be grateful he had you there to keep him right and be his support."

It was as she was speaking that you appeared to me. I swear to God, Sam, you were there. Walking straight through the house's walls, it was you, stopping and standing before me in all your glory. You were beautiful like an angel painted in some grand church, golden and completely naked, and you stood there staring at me and telling me to follow you, inviting me to leave this place behind. I wanted to go after you, but I was afraid.

"When he came back, he hung up all these photos of you both in his room. I loved staring at them and seeing his first year through both your eyes."

I was fighting tears as I listened to her, and all I could think was, *Fuck, Martha, why are you being so nice to me right now? You lost your fucking son! I'm no one. I'm fucking no one. He didn't want me. He didn't want to love me anymore, all the hours of every day. He let go of me and now I'm left to face this. What am I meant to do, Martha? What am I meant to fucking do?*

"He loved you so much, Daniel . . . I am so sorry. I don't know what else I can say."

I couldn't think of anything else either. My body had left me, and you had disappeared from the hallway too. I was floating in the ether, just limbs and bones and blood, standing there as I hung up the phone. Then a dark, angry cloud came over me and I started screaming. My grandfather, my cousins, Marisol, my aunt and uncle, everyone rushed into the hall. They were trying to ask what was wrong, they were shaking me, and all I could do was scream and cry and thrash about. It was like I was possessed. I let the phone slip from my grip, its screen cracking from the fall. I let my mind pour onto the floor.

"I never wrote him back. I never fucking wrote him back. I never got to speak to him one last time. He is gone. He is fucking gone. What the fuck am I going to do?"

"Mijo, you have to tell us what's happened so we can help you," Marisol kept saying. She tried desperately to pacify me as Analyse watched, crying, afraid of her cousin who was losing his fucking mind. My aunt swept her away into the kitchen along with our visiting family and closed the door as little Analyse kept asking what was wrong. My uncle tried to calm my grandfather as he watched his only grandchild fall apart.

"Sam. Sam's dead," I said, over and over again. "Sam's dead."

I couldn't stop crying as they pinned me down. I kept punching the air and yelling over and over that you were gone until I exhausted every last bit of will I had and relinquished myself to my grandfather. I allowed him to hold me in his arms and stroke my head, whispering softly how everything was going to be fine, you were going to be fine—Abuelo doing all of this as my cousin and my uncle began praying over me and praying over you. But I didn't hear their prayers or Abuelo's soothing or the phone call my aunt made to my parents. All I could hear was your mother's voice: "Sam's dead, sweetie."

As I focused on those three words circling around me, I resigned myself to the waves crashing down, the dark waters filling the house that no one else could see. I willed my body to get pulled into the riptide, longing for it to pin me to the ocean floor in hopes that I might stay there until the air inside me evaporated— until I might join you wherever you were in that moment, until I might finally be dead too.

brain, and lungs remained; a body in motion, no soul, no vitals, on autopilot. In that first week, I was numb from the tears, the terror of waking up, because when I did, I instantly recalled you were now dead. In that first week, my only goal was to remember to breathe, to not forget to breathe. That's all I could manage on my own. Everything else required the strength of others: being fed, being held, being consoled. I was afraid of being left alone, afraid of what sadness could do to a mind. Looking back, I see too how all-encompassing that sadness was, its power to devastate not just the individual in mourning but everyone around him; how such devastation can spread for miles, across borders, across time zones.

On the first day after the call, I obsessively read your email at least a dozen times. I thought there might be some small clue, some kind of foreshadowing of what was to come, something I might have missed. I wanted logic. I wanted your death not to have been so fucking random. I wanted to know that you knew deep down what was going to happen before it did, because to die at nineteen, out of nowhere, because of one stupid drunken mistake felt like the cruelest way to go. My finger ached from scrolling, zooming in, zooming out, closing and reopening the email. My eyes grew sore from the tears and blue light, from trying to search for something that wasn't there. No matter how I looked at it, I couldn't see anything other than a goodbye email. But why would it be anything else? I mean, youth is going through life think-ing you are invincible. Isn't that what you'd done? Isn't that why you didn't give a second thought to getting in the car of a drunk driver? Isn't that why you all coasted down the highway, oblivious to the consequences or their aftermath? One final night of living with abandon, unaware of the pain you'd cause—you couldn't have known, right? You wouldn't have done it if you had. Still, I cried myself to sleep, fixated on each question.

But on the second day, I allowed Marisol to come into my darkened den. I allowed her to crack a window open to air out the stench of sadness. I allowed her to sit on the bed with me and cradle me in her arms like Michelangelo's *Pietà*. It was as if I had been taken down from my crucifixion. I was dead inside. I was awaiting resurrection. I was praying you had not forsaken me. But you didn't return three days later; there would be no miracles. I would just be a broken body in the hands of a woman trying to calm me back to sleep. On that third day, I sent one long text to Diego, closed my phone, and then went off-grid. In the text to Diego, I mapped out everything—our friendship turned romance, our kisses, our sex—and then I jumped forward in time to your death, shared how you died because you were a big fucking idiot who did a fucking stupid thing. I told it all to him because I felt I owed Diego that much, at least. As I wrote the text, I felt like I was in confession and he was the priest. Upon hitting send, I began my penance.

Day four bled into day five with little sleep and little reprieve from sadness. In truth, I cried, then cried some more, until finally I released my pent-up anger by screaming into a pillow. I bit down hard, trying to muffle my anguish. Sometime late on day five, I also spoke to my parents, no longer able to hold off the phone call. It was strange to be speaking to my own mom over the phone when, only four days before, your mother had been the last person I spoke to that way. I hated phone calls just then. They only brought about destruction. And try as she might, my mom could do nothing to save me from the pain. I wanted nothing more than for her to reach through the phone with some magic eraser and swipe the page clean. But she couldn't, because this was real life and you had really died. It wasn't make-believe. Again, there would be no miracles.

On day six, Abuelo knocked firmly on the bedroom door. It was time to retrieve me. It wasn't healthy, what I was doing. It wasn't right. It was dangerous to be left to brew in loss. All of this I heard him say to Marisol, to Tía Carmen and Tío Hector, to my parents on the phone. So on that day he marched in and threw open the curtains. As Marisol and my aunt stripped the bed, and my uncle collected the detritus of used cups, glasses, and plates of half-eaten food, Abuelo took me into the bathroom. He turned the water on high, tested it for me, told me it was time to shower. He hugged me as I cried.

"This will be good for you, Daniel."

"It hurts so much."

"I know, mijo, trust me, I know."

I listened to the running water. It reminded me of the rain. It reminded me of my tears. It reminded me of the swelling waves of loss.

"It's time to get out into the world, so please shower. We have somewhere to go."

"Okay."

"You have a half hour."

"Yes, Abuelo."

"Trust me, Daniel. This is what you need."

The room began to fill with steam and a cloud of mist enveloped us, masking the tears we were both shedding.

"No more hiding by yourself."

"Yes, Abuelo," I repeated.

"I love you, Daniel, so, so much."

He reached through the fog to hug me. I could feel him, but I couldn't see him through the mist and tears.

"I know, Abuelo. I know."

I wanted the cloud of vapor to carry me elsewhere. I no longer wanted my body.

"I know you're still hurting, but it's time."

"I know, Abuelo."

And it was time, but I didn't know if I was ready.

Under the hot showerhead, I moved through the motions of cleansing my body. I had accumulated a week's worth of sebum, crusted snot, and tears. I scrubbed with real vigor, and as I did, I let my tears mix with the water, because I was at a point when just the thought of you was my undoing. I slid against the tiled wall onto the shower floor and sat against the cool, wet stone and convulsed. I felt more alone than I had ever felt in my life. Although my grandfather and cousin, my other relatives, were there for me, although my parents were only a phone call away, I felt isolated in grief. How was I supposed to accept that you were now gone? In seven weeks, I'd gone from having you cut out of my life to physically losing you. It felt unfathomable. At nineteen, I couldn't comprehend death's finality, not when it involved someone so young. The pain was so immense, too much for me.

I turned off the water, then wrapped my body in a towel and looked upon my own reflection for the first time in days. I wiped the steam from the mirror, and there you were. I swear to you, Sam. You were standing right behind me, completely naked. Your skin had an iridescent sheen, like an angel, and yet you were exactly how I remembered: stunning, with eyes a luminescent blue. I thought to myself, *Wow, for a short while that man's body and my body did things I've never done with anybody else.* I thought to myself, *Wow, for nearly a year that man was the love of my life, is still the love of my life, but is gone.* Do you remember being there? Was it even you?

Your face was the only part of you that was not exactly as I remembered it. There were red gashes and bruises on your skin, but despite the signs of a car crash, you were still magnificently beautiful. I walked up to you and touched your cheeks, careful not to hurt you. I feared my touch might be painful, but you didn't wince at all. I was angry with you. I was so, so, so fucking angry with you, but I couldn't say it aloud. I didn't want to let my anger out into the world.

You wrapped your arms around me, and I cried. I cried for so long as you held me. You stroked my hair and kept telling me

I was going to be fine, but I told you I didn't think I would be. I remember reaching for every part of you, so afraid you would vanish. I began to kiss you maniacally. Your chest muscles, your flank, the salt of your thighs. You bent down so we were both prostrate in prayer, and you kissed me fiercely. The taste of your lips was so intoxicating that I had to close my eyes. But when I opened them, you were gone, and I was alone on the bathroom floor, left to deal with my unraveling mind.

As I stood and got dressed, I let my body zone out. I allowed my mind to go somewhere else, gave it a reprieve from thinking. It was a survival technique I had gotten used to. While speaking with my parents, while eating the breakfast my Tía Carmen served me, as Analyse showed me the *Feel Better* card she'd drawn for me, I was there and not there. I let the minutes slip away until, eventually, I got in the truck with my grandfather and we made our way to the barrio where he'd raised my mom and uncle. As he drove, he kept telling me not to hide from the world. He said it was important not to let the pain of grief prevent me from living my life. He said this from experience, reminding me he'd lost his wife and only son, and also a country. I knew he was sharing these things not to make me feel bad, but to try and show me the universality of mourning; how all of us, at some point, will grieve.

We walked under bougainvillea branches shaded by tall palm trees, in the company of families going about their mornings. Abuelo wrapped his arm around me, and together we walked. A grandson and a grandfather; two men who had lost so much. The air was thick with heat, the sky immensely bright, and I was not dying. Being out in public had not killed me yet. I willed my body to keep moving: One foot, two feet, step, step. One breath, two breaths, inhale, exhale. I was out in the world where I belonged. I was no longer in the shadows of isolation.

"It will get easier, mijo. I need you to know that."

"How?"

"Time, Daniel. Time heals all things. You will need time, but you will learn to move forward."

"I never spoke to him after we left Ithaca. I didn't even write him back."

"You couldn't have known."

"Still, I could have tried. I could have listened to myself."

"You can't do that, Daniel. Trust me. It's a very dangerous game to get caught in, these what-ifs or things we could have done. The only thing you can do now is wake up each day and try to live your life for Sam and for yourself. You have to fight that darkness, the thing calling you into the shadows, because whatever it might tell you, it is not your friend."

His words were like a gut punch, ringing true. I couldn't think of anything worth saying back, so instead I just focused on the ground below me, finding comfort in its uneven patches of grass, pebbles, and dirt marking the treads of the hundreds of people who regularly walked along it. This neighborhood didn't look at all the way I'd thought it would. Growing up, I'd imagined my mom had left behind a life of gritty poverty, but her childhood barrio was pleasant and had everything you'd need to lead a happy life. Standing there, though, I thought back to what my grandfather had said on the first day I'd arrived in Chihuahua: that after my uncle passed away, there was not much worth staying for.

"Does it still hurt being back here, all these years later?"

"There is a pain still lingering there," he said, pointing to his heart. "But if I am honest, it is not the gravity of pain I felt in the early days of not having him around."

I held on to his answer as we walked further around the neighborhood, passing houses, a row of tiny shops, and a small playground with children running around, laughing and playing. I was desperate to see into the future. I needed to see the day when the pain I carried would not weigh me down, the moment when such intense grief might release me from its grip. My heart needed to understand that sadness was not a permanent state of being, that there was a time before this and there would be a time after.

"You're going to have your good days and bad ones."

"I just can't imagine it not hurting like this forever. I'm genuinely afraid of being sad for the rest of my life."

"I know what you mean, Daniel. I think it is because you are having to contend with the loss of someone so young. When death takes the young it hurts even worse, because for the old, at least, you are prepared in some way to say goodbye. But we are never prepared to say goodbye to a life unlived."

We stopped at a bench a bit away from the playground and took respite under a tree. I appreciated the privacy, as I needed the space to reflect on my grandfather's words. When my grandmother died, it hurt, but she was old to my teenage mind. You were the same age as me, and that was, I think, the crux of my sadness and anxiety. Through you, I had now been confronted with the impermanence of life. I had to face the fact that you would not be returning to Cayuga with me and our fellow sophomores. I would not have the chance to make amends with you. I would never have the chance to find a way forward through friendship or reconciliation. If I'm honest, the hardest thing to wrap my mind around was the sheer absoluteness of death—how your memory, even a week on, was starting to feel like it was crumbling around me. I also had the sense that it was just me who held on to those memories. With my grandmother, I at least had my parents and grandfather to share stories with and to remind me of things I might go on to forget. We had a house full of her photos, and I had so many concrete places in which her memory was present. But with you, with your memory, I was starting to understand that it was tied to a place that wouldn't be mine forever, meaning that, at some point, I'd lose you completely.

"Do you ever forget things?"

"About your tío?"

I nodded while looking at children swinging as high as possible. Their laughter in the summer sun felt an entire world away.

"Sometimes, yes. Sometimes your grandmother and I would have to remind ourselves of parts of his character. Help each other to remember."

"Like what?"

"How he would say things or how he would react to things. What happiness looked like on him, or sadness, how we could annoy him during his teenage years. All those things that make a person. But then, mijo, when you started getting older, we saw more and more of him in you. And that was a kind of salve for us. It meant he wasn't totally gone. It meant we didn't totally forget. We had our Daniel back and that was . . . that was a blessing we could've never thought to wish for."

"I think what scares me is not having others to help. With remembering, I mean."

"I know, mijo. It is not easy—but what is worth remembering, you have to trust your heart will hold on to that."

My grandfather wrapped his arms around me, pulling me close to his chest. He rubbed my hair just like he had when I was a little boy in his arms, crying from a beesting or stubbing my toe on a chair. But this time the pain was so much greater. It was intangible. It was purely emotional. A hurricane's eye hanging above us. It was the idea of something being there and then gone. This is what I was facing without you in those first few days.

"I'm sorry, Abuelo."

"Never apologize, Daniel, for how you feel."

"I don't know how to handle any of this."

"You owe no one any explanation for the pain you are feeling. This is yours to carry, but I am here for you always."

"I can't stop feeling guilty. He was my best friend, and I didn't say goodbye. I know the last time he wrote me, he wasn't looking for a response, but I could've sent one anyway because something inside was telling me to. There was something calling out to me, but I didn't listen. What if I had . . . actually said everything I'd been holding in? Then he'd at least have died knowing the truth—but he died thinking I didn't care enough to try and save our friendship. How can I live with that?"

"He knew, Daniel. I am sure he knew how much you cared about him."

"I hope so, Abuelo, because I can't carry this guilt anymore. It's too much. It's killing me a little more each day I wake up. I'm haunted by the idea that he died thinking he meant nothing to me."

"You have to believe he did. Do you understand me? You have to remember how deep your friendship was, and when you do, it will all make sense. It's the only way to survive this. Even if he is no longer here, you still have the ability to look back and remember all those beautiful times you shared. So you must tell yourself this—say, 'Yes, Daniel, of course he knew.'"

I looked around me. There was so much life and color, so much summer joy on all sides of Abuelo and me. He had returned to a source of pain. He had shown me what it is to face the absence of a son, without his wife, to stare down the barrel at his former life and survive. I had to believe that I, too, could do this. I had to believe you knew how much I loved you. I had to believe there was a purpose to moving forward and someday I'd find it.

When we returned home, my aunt and uncle told me there was a gift in my room. They did not say from whom, just that it was waiting for me. It felt strange to have spent so many days in a row being sad to now be slightly excited at the prospect of a gift. I was unsure if Abuelo had organized something for me while we were out, or my parents or Marisol. I remember cautiously opening the door. Immediately, I noticed how clean the bedroom now was: the crisp white sheets, the colorful serape neatly tucked into the corners, everything put back in order. Light was pouring in through the netted curtains. It did not look like a bedroom that had held so much sadness, but rather like a calming sanctuary. On the dresser, there was a bouquet of flowers and a jewelry box. I opened the small red envelope buried among the roses, lilies, and baby's breath.

DEAREST DANIEL,

I am so sorry you are going through this right now. I have been thinking of you each day. I hope you have felt my prayers. When you are ready, I would love to see you, to learn more about Sam and help you as you grieve. You mean so much to me.

WITH LOVE,
YOUR DIEGO

I opened the jewelry box, which was long and rectangular. Inside was a gold bracelet. *Thank God*, I thought, because anything else would've been a major misstep on Diego's part, given the circumstances. On one side of the bracelet was an etching that read *Chihuahua, MX*, and on the reverse, the coordinates *28°49'N 106°26'W.* The latitude and longitude of the city. I closed the box and tucked the card back in its envelope, then closed the door and climbed onto the bed. I turned on my phone, which I had left off since last speaking with my parents. As soon as I did, I was flooded with notifications of missed calls, voicemails, numerous texts and WhatsApp messages from Mona and Rob and Diego and Marisol. But I chose to ignore them all and instead opened my email. I needed to read your message again. This time I didn't cry reading your words, because, like my grandfather said, I had to believe you knew how much I loved you. I had to believe you always knew how much I loved you. I have to believe you will always know how much I love you. This time I listened for you. I imagined you saying those things aloud. I could still remember the timbre of your voice, and that was a small salve.

Outside the window of my room, birds were chirping loudly. The world's natural cycle of life was continuing on, and I felt a slight comfort in that. The scent of flowers warmed by sunshine blew through the opened window and, again, there was comfort in knowing beautiful things could still exist in spite of sadness. I listened to my aunt's singing as she scrubbed the tile of the outside patio. Her voice was dulcet but reserved, the kind of singing that comes when the performer believes they're totally alone and thus most free. She rinsed the mop and continued cleaning, moving further away from my window until her voice was only a tiny echo. The rest of the house was quiet, and I suspected my grandfather was resting in his bedroom.

Still not feeling ready just yet to say anything to Diego about the bracelet, I decided to open my suitcase to see the books I'd brought. There was the collection of Gabriel García Márquez's novellas, the Sandra Cisneros novel I'd already finished, and *Dreaming in Cuban* by Cristina García, which Naomi had recommended to me. I elected to start *Leaf Storm* by Márquez and, in an effort to not be a loner, ventured outside to read. My aunt had now made her way to the front of the house and so I knew I wouldn't be disturbing her, but I wouldn't be hiding in my room either, which was important. I wanted Abuelo to know I was done with hiding. So I clambered into the hammock strung up under a pergola. The green-and-yellow netting wrapped around me like a cocoon, and there was something invigorating about being snuggled against something other than my tear-stained sheets. Maybe by the end of the afternoon I'd come out a butterfly, renewed and refreshed.

I got halfway through the novella before the sun began to set. My arms were marked in diamond patterns from the netting. Getting out of the hammock was a lot harder than getting in, and I had to sort of lob myself forward and use the momentum to launch off of it. It was messy and awkward, and made me laugh out loud, and I realized, while laughing, that this was the first time I had laughed in a week. There I was alone, with no one to share the moment with, but I had laughed, and that was a form of healing.

I entered a very quiet house with no sign of my aunt or uncle. I figured they had gone out to visit Marisol and Analyse or any number of my other family members. There was no sign of Abuelo, either, but he wouldn't have left without telling me. I checked the clock in the living room; three hours had passed while I was reading outside. I started to worry he had gone out without me, thinking perhaps that I was doing much better, fine enough to be left on my own. My huaraches clapped loudly against the tile floor as I went in search of him, each click-clack of the sandals sending a shudder through my spine. I felt like a little boy again, afraid of being left alone. He wasn't in the kitchen or living room, but I could see through the front window that his truck was still parked outside. I stopped for a second to listen for him, but there was no sound beyond my own breathing.

"Abuelo!" I called out.

Nothing again but my own voice, echoing down the hall.

"Abuelo, are you here?"

I was starting to freak out. I worried maybe he had left because he needed a break. I worried that this was the reason my aunt and uncle were also out. I worried that for days now I had driven everyone to the limit of their patience. I went back outside and walked around the perimeter of the house and then looked in all the bedrooms and bathrooms, but he wasn't there. I went to the kitchen and then back into the living room, but no matter where I searched, I could not find my grandfather. The house felt big and empty and lonely. Just then, the door latch clicked and there he was, standing with a cardboard box in his hands. We just looked at each other for a moment, not saying anything. I think he knew I had been looking for him, as my face was all shock and distress. I willed myself not to cry. He put the box down in the doorway and came over to me and gave me a big hug. He apologized for not telling me he'd hitched a ride with my aunt and uncle to visit one of his sisters.

"I was worried. Please don't do that again."

"I am so sorry, mijo, but I am here now."

I kissed him on the cheek and told him it was fine. I was glad he was back and grateful the anxiety was beginning to dissipate. He asked me to put on a pot of coffee and then to take a seat.

"I have something to show you, but I need to go to my room first."

I returned to the kitchen and filled the machine with coffee grounds, then topped it up with water. As I waited for my grandfather, I pulled out mugs and a tray of cookies, grateful for a task to alleviate the anxiety that had colored the past half hour. When the coffee was ready, I poured it out and brought everything to the kitchen table. I didn't know what I was waiting for, but I was happy to have my grandfather's company.

Abuelo came into the kitchen holding a small green wooden box with snakes carved into it. He placed it right in front of me when I looked up at him. He was smiling and indicated I should open it. I remember the clasp was a bit rusty, making it difficult to unlock. Abuelo just stood there watching me, which made me more nervous about accidentally breaking the clasp. With a bit more fiddling, I managed to get it open. Inside, I found notebooks, some badges, flyers for meetups, pamphlets, and photos of a very handsome-looking group of men. I picked up one of the photos as my grandfather sat quietly watching. The men were holding placards written in Spanish that read AIDS *Is Spread by Fear* and *Hate Is a Disease*. In the middle of the group was Tío Daniel, standing proudly with a sign that said *Not One More*. As I studied the signs, it dawned on me that these were photos from some type of AIDS awareness demonstration.

I opened one of the notebooks, full of dates with short diary entries. This was, I realized, my uncle's diary; the place he kept his personal musings, his innermost secrets. I felt stunned. What a gift to have this portal into his world, the man I never got to meet. I was face-to-face with someone who had put pen to paper to share his own observations of the world around him—what he hungered for, the dreams he had for himself. I asked if I could read some of it, and Abuelo nodded. He had earmarked an entry halfway through, which appeared to be one of the last:

AUGUST 19, 1991

I have decided (finally, after months of back-and-forth with myself) what I am going to do. I have decided happiness does exist, and it is a place I can get to. I have decided to move to D.F. I have done my research and saved money and will start afresh. Maybe finally enroll in university. Whatever I do there, I know I need more to life. I need to see the world and I need to live somewhere I can thrive in all my glory. I have saved up enough money for a bus ticket and a few months' worth of rent and will tell my parents soon, before my birthday next month. It is time. I promise myself this with every ounce of strength I have inside this body. I will get there. I will reach my dream place and I will be happy. I will finally be able to live freely, as I am; will know what it is to have a body fully at peace with itself. I will know what it is to love the life you are living. Now is the time for a life full of color, desire, love—both given and received. I am ready.

He would die two months later. All the evidence was there. Not about his death, but about who he was. I now understood how my uncle and I were cut from the same cloth—a cloth you, too, were cut from. I didn't know whether my uncle had ever told his parents or my mom, but the truth was that I wasn't the only gay person in my family. Sitting there, processing this news, I felt grateful.

It was like seeing myself reflected back, but in another person's words—finding another coordinate on the map of what it meant to be Daniel. Seeing all these bits of history alluding to a bold, enraged, passionate young man was another form of healing.

My grandfather told me he wanted me to keep the box, explaining it was time for someone else to hold vigil over it. He hoped it might help me as I worked through my own loss, and that I'd choose to write about my uncle one day. For my stories, he indicated.

"Where did you find it?"

"I've had it ever since he passed away, mijo. We left some things behind with family because we felt it was important to have roots in Chihuahua, but I always planned on giving you some of his stuff. I was just waiting for the time to be right."

"Did he ever tell you he was gay?"

"No, mijo. We never had the opportunity to have that discussion."

"But did you know, Abuelo?"

"Part of me did, I believe, yes. There are some things that are understood, and I knew Daniel was a very special young man living in his own world."

I took in a deep breath, counted to five, then released it. There was a shift in that moment, and I felt on the cusp of freedom. When I opened my eyes, I knew what I needed to say. I finally had the right words in the right moment. I no longer felt afraid.

"And you know I am gay?"

"Mijo, I've always known you live in a world a little different from mine too. Something closer to your uncle's, if that makes sense. I don't know why or how I knew this, but I want you to know I love you no matter what. I want you to be free. Rereading his words, I understand your uncle did not always feel he was capable of such freedom."

I studied Abuelo, whose hand was resting on my leg, gripping it tightly. I sensed that although he was relieved to finally share more of my uncle with me, all of this was still difficult. Resurfacing a past he had for so long kept quiet must've been painful. There I was, the one who carried his son's name, and he was giving me a gift, a deeper understanding of my namesake. He was widening my world, allowing me to understand that I wasn't as alone as I'd allowed myself to believe.

"I don't want you to feel like you have to run away," he said softly. "Do you understand?"

His body felt utterly frail, as if it could've dissolved in front of me, as I hugged him with all the strength I had left.

"I love you, Abuelo. So much."

"I love you too, Daniel. I'm so proud to be your grandfather."

We spent the rest of the evening drinking coffee and eating cookies and reading bits of my uncle's diary. Some entries made my grandfather laugh, some made him somber, but mostly I think it made him happy to hear his grandson bring his son's words to life.

Later that night, I walked back to my room carrying this holy grail of a box. I placed it gently atop the chest of drawers in the corner, then noticed my laptop resting on top of my suitcase. I hadn't used it much that summer and felt like it was time to slowly take the steps to ready myself for sophomore year. Summer would be over soon, and the reality was that I had a life to get back to. So I logged on to my Cayuga email account, intending to see whether there were any updates on my scholarship disbursement. My day with Abuelo had lifted my mood so much, and I wanted to ride that wave of optimism, be productive, and begin to look toward the future with hope. My grandfather had shown me it was possible to build a life back up after loss, and I had to believe I was capable of it.

So much junk had flooded my student inbox ahead of fall semester, but I couldn't see anything related to the scholarship. I decided to look in my spam folder, and that's when I saw it: the last piece of our story's puzzle.

[MORRIS Sam: I am sorry (please read!!!)]

I can't even begin to explain to you what happened to me in that moment. It was like I was actually having an out-of-body experience. My heart dropped to the floor and my mouth went completely dry. I couldn't believe it, Sam. I thought I had received an email from a ghost. I remember how quickly my hands began to shake, my body convulsing and almost ready to throw up. *What the fuck is happening?* I asked myself. I chucked the laptop onto my bed and rushed to the bathroom to throw water on my face. I braced myself for the mirror, looking to see if you were there as you'd been earlier, but of course that had been a hallucination. You'd never been there—but you were here now, or at least your words were. There was your email waiting for me, and I knew I had to read it, but I was so scared.

I willed my body to move: one foot, two feet, step, step. I reminded my body to breathe: one breath, two breaths, inhale, exhale. I sat down on the bed and began to read a letter from a ghost.

DANIEL,

I cannot even begin to apologize for that last email. I was a coward. For days, I have been freaking out about sending it. I even Googled how to reverse send an email, but it was too late, I waited too long. I am so sorry. It is the honest truth, I really fucked up, but please know I did not mean any of the stuff I wrote. I don't want us to stop being a part of each other's lives— that would be terrible! I cannot lose you. God, you are one of my best friends and Cayuga would not be the same for me if you weren't in my life. Again, I am so sorry for being a dick to you during the last few days of the semester, for not being brave enough to really talk about what was happening, especially after you shared so much with me, shared how you really felt. I am so angry with myself that I left without saying goodbye to you. Please forgive me. I miss you . . . can I call you? Is there a number

at your aunt's I can reach you at or can I call your phone directly?
Will it charge you? I love you, Daniel, I really do. Again, I am
sorry . . . can we talk please? I know I fucked up, but I hope you
can forgive me, and I hope you know how much you mean to
me. I have so much to still work through, but I know we can
get through this together. I understand now. I am not afraid
anymore. I am ready.

—SAM

I reread the date. You'd sent it three days after the first email, but it had gotten lost in the spam folder of my Cayuga email. Why did you do that? Why did you send the first to my Gmail account and the second to my Cayuga one? I was losing my fucking mind. All these weeks it was waiting there, and all the while you were still on earth, and all the while the world was fucking me over and over and over again. But you wrote to me. You had reached out after all. And for a second time, I hadn't responded.

It was then that my heart began to hurt, straining from how fast I was thinking, and I remembered how you'd described a panic attack to me and realized one was happening just then. I wanted to call out to my grandfather, but I couldn't. My mouth was so dry; my ears were ringing loudly. My brain was pushing hard against my skull with dull thuds. I ran back to the bathroom to look at myself in the mirror. There were so many tears, but I didn't feel like I was crying. It was as if I was watching everything happen to me, a car crash on a giant movie screen—but I was the only audience member and it was my own life, once again, that was falling apart.

I navigated to my other email account to read your first email again and compare it to this final one. I don't know what I was attempting to achieve. I think I was trying to verify that it really was you who had sent both emails; perhaps I was proving to myself that I had, in the end, gotten everything I wanted. It was all there in twelve-point Calibri font, single-spaced. You, Sam Morris, had finally told me what I wanted to hear, one long paragraph containing all I'd ever dreamed of. For that whole paragraph, I had the possibility of spending the rest of my life with you, and then I didn't. There in my inbox was my second chance, but I had lost it before I'd even known it existed.

I love you, Daniel, I really do.

It was incomprehensible. What had I done in my life to deserve this? Do you know? Because if you do, please tell me. Even now, I can't wrap my head around it. You, Sam Morris, actually loved me, but it was too fucking late. Everything in my life was a series of things happening too fucking late. Finding out about an uncle who was like a kindred spirit, a gay elder, but he had died at twenty-two. How fucking cruel? There was someone who shared my blood, my lineage, who understood the world in a way I did, but I would never meet him. Then there was this, the olive branch you'd sent, but I'd known nothing about it. I could have called you. I could have heard you say it into my ear, those words: *I love you, Daniel de La Luna.* But no, all of it was too fucking late.

I sank into my pillows, muffling my tears as my mind floundered into even deeper waves of sadness. It was like I had lost you all over again. I willed myself to be flooded over, wanting to drown in that dark sadness because I had no positivity left in me just then. The world had truly fucked me. I had lost you and then lost you once more. You weren't there, and then you were, and now it was too late. It was always too fucking late.

I love you, Daniel.

I know, Sam, but now what?

DÍA 59

I drove to the coast today with Luis. It took us over fifteen hours. We left in the early cover of dawn. I told him I needed to feel the salt in my hair. He called me crazy but said he would go with me if that's what I wanted. I told him it wasn't what I wanted—I said, "Compa, it's what I need. Quiero ver el mar y las olas . . . tú sabes. I need something beyond this desert." So we drove, and as soon as we got to this small seaside town, we parked the car, ran down the rocky shore, and stripped into our birthday suits. We were screaming like banshees as we dove into the water. The fishermen kept a close watch on us "dos locos" as they put out their nets for the nighttime catch. Their boats looked like floating candles in a darkened tub. The cold Pacific against my skin was invigorating, everything I could have hoped for. While paddling into the choppy waves, I finally understood how very much I'd needed this reminder of what it was to be alive. To appreciate what it meant to come up for air and breathe in all that beauty.

—D.M.

It's strange to look back on what I've written and remember this was all only a few weeks ago. It's like my brain has added on extra time as a mode of survival. Now it's just the end of August and it was in the last days of July that I received your mom's calls. It's crazy, really, how little time has passed. I can't begin to imagine what time is like for you, wherever you are. I keep telling myself it's only the end of this season of our lives. Even as September inches ever closer and a new school year begins without you, somehow, someway, I'll find a path back to you—I promise you this.

Before I share this last chapter detailing what remained of my time in México, I want to tell you a bit more about the present, because I think it will be good for you to hear how I'm doing right now. I signed up for therapy. It was Naomi's suggestion when I met up with her the other day for a coffee. I told her about losing you, about my summer in tierra madre, about facing a new year in the midst of mourning. She was kind and attentive. She let me go on for as long as I needed and then casually reminded me that students get ten free sessions with a campus therapist each year. There was no judgment, no insinuation, just a kind reminder for me to then decide what I'd do.

I also reached out to Bernie-Bernice. We spoke for quite a while over the phone after I shared the news with him, which was strange. I mean, he'd never met you, but in some way, he'd followed our story, its ups and downs. I also shared our actual story, how I am writing it all down, using it as a way to process. He invited me to join this writing group he runs at the Rainbow Center. Bernie-Bernice told me there's no obligation to share what I am writing right now, but that it might be good to meet other queer people, to hear their stories and share mine if I ever feel compelled. I might join, or I might not, I'm still deciding. But I know one day I'll need to learn to open up to new people, to be okay with that.

As harrowing as those first days of August might read, as alone as I felt in México, I want you to remember I survived them. I am surviving—living, actually—no longer hiding from the world. I have my parents and Abuelo, I have Naomi, Bernie-Bernice, and, of course, Rob and Mona, who have been wonderful. I have our story. I have this city. I'm learning to rely on others. I'm learning not to run from the light; I'm learning to face it. I wanted to say all of this before presenting you with the final part of this story so you can remind yourself: *He is okay, he will survive it.* What's to come isn't pretty. What's to come is quite painful. But all of it is true. Truth and honesty were always important to us, so I will show you what happened even if it hurts.

You have to remember where we left off: I had lost you twice over. For a few sentences, a whole paragraph, I had you in my life once again—but then I didn't. All I could think about was how, in the end, you did love me, but I'd never had a chance to hear you say it.

As the next two weeks passed, I regressed to hiding myself from the world, convinced everything was out to get me. I thought maybe I had done something as a child to deserve what had happened, and began spending hours in bed conducting an audit of my life. Had I bullied anyone growing up? No. Had I ever stolen anything? No. Had I ever killed someone? No. So what was it then? How could I have been so unlucky to have lost you in a few short weeks in so many ways? Was it a family curse I'd inherited from my uncle? Had he done something truly bad in his life before dying? I was desperate to pin blame on something tangible. I read more from his diary and all I could find was a young man full of so much promise, a deep longing for more in his life. More happiness, more adventure, more love.

"Daniel, you need to eat."

"Daniel, you need to shower."

"Daniel, your parents are on the phone. You need to speak to them."

"Daniel, Diego is here. He'd like to speak with you."

I don't remember much about that last one. I know I walked out into the hall and he was standing there. His face was sullen; he had not shaved in a while. Light was pouring in from outside, but the hall was dark in the way houses in hot places are built to keep cool and shaded. It must've been morning, but time meant nothing to me then. We walked outside to the back patio and sat. The tiles were slick with water, and I remember thinking that my aunt had to have woken early to wash the floors before the mercury rose. Abuelo brought out some coffee, patted me on the shoulder, then left. I felt like a patient in a sanatorium with his day visitor. I was there and not there.

"I'm sorry, Daniel."

I looked at him, his pained expression. It was as if he was also mourning you.

"I can't imagine what you're going through."

His mouth moved. Words came out, but all I could do was think of you.

"Death is such a cruel beast."

The birds were chirping. Bees were buzzing. The sky was bright. You were dead.

"I know this is hard. But there are so many people here for you."

You were dead. That's all I knew of the world.

"I'm here for you."

You were dead. So why was the sky so bright? Why were the bees supping on sweet nectar? Why were the birds singing in the morning calm? Why was the world so happy?

"Maybe it would be good, querido, for you to get out. You don't want to stay inside forever. I think it might help for you to hang with people."

"Okay."

He smiled at me.

"Bueno. It's settled."

I don't know why I did it, but I agreed to go out the following night with Diego and his friends. I think I agreed so I could get my grandfather off my back. I couldn't deal with anyone's well-meaning thoughts and prayers, so at least going out with people my age would look like I was doing fine—but the truth was, Sam, that I wasn't. I was spiraling down a dangerous well of sorrow and I didn't know if I'd ever climb back out. But I needed to do something. I prayed I could sleep away the rest of my time in México until I boarded a plane and left everything behind—the pain, the loss, the sadness. But the thing is, I couldn't. It would still be there to deal with, and I had to hold on to that pain until I was ready to actually do something about it.

So the next day, I woke up and commenced counting down the hours until the evening with Diego. I had begun to hide bottles of beer and liquor under the bed and in the chest of drawers, and I finished two beers that morning and a fourth of a handle of tequila as I lay on the bed. The electric fan buzzed with its metallic drone. I studied its slow pattern of movement, left to right, as it blew air from the corner into the rest of the room, causing the curtains to lightly dance. I watched for as long as possible, willing the clock to move faster, praying that I could just get the night over with. The light filtered through the curtains, casting lacy patterns on the wall and on my reflection in the mirror. I was captivated by my face, how tired and aged I looked, and I moved my hands slowly around my cheeks and the curve of my brow and nose. The man in the mirror was a ghost, someone I did not recognize. I wanted to tell him to go away. I wanted to say, *I choose not to see you.* But I just stood there staring, not saying anything until my eyes grew sore, my vision blurry from the heat and drink.

"You need to get ready."

I had to blink a few times to understand what was happening. There you were.

"You need to get ready, Daniel."

"I'm glad you came back. I thought I'd lost you forever."

"They're all trying to help you. Can't you see? Your family is trying to help you move on."

"I'm not ready yet . . ."

You stood there with a face full of disappointment, or was it sadness? I tried to reach for you, but you wouldn't let me. I wanted to feel you one final time.

"Can we hug?"

"Not now. You need to get ready."

"Please stay this time."

"Get ready, Daniel. It's time."

"I thought we had forever."

"I did too, but life doesn't always work like that."

"Were you happy?"

"I was."

"Were you happy with me?"

"I was."

"Did you love me?"

I asked you, but then I blinked and you were gone. You were there and then you weren't. So I let myself fall asleep a little while longer. I wanted to dream of you but all I dreamt of was waves making landfall, ready to crush me in their surge. Hours later, I was awoken by my aunt's singing. It poured out from the kitchen where she was making dinner for my uncle and grandfather. I could hear the laughter of the men in the living room watching something on the television playing low. It might have been a moment to turn things around, to go and join them, but instead I listened and thought to myself, *I hope they have a nice evening together free of my sadness, free of me. I hope the waves don't get them.* I decided to have one more beer to loosen up, because a dark shadow was whispering to me. I raised a toast.

"In honor of you, Sam."

I took the can and jabbed a key in the bottom, pulled the tab, and shotgunned it the way you'd taught me to. I chugged it all down in a matter of seconds, then chucked the can in the trash and went to brush my teeth. I didn't want my grandfather to smell the alcohol on my breath or in my sweat—I was still under the assumption, somehow, that I was managing to appear sober and compos mentis. In the bathroom, I looked for you in the mirror, but you weren't there. I combed my hair and you weren't there. I spritzed myself in cologne and you weren't there.

My phone began to buzz atop the dresser, and I went to check who it was. Diego was outside and said he was going to pop in quickly to say hello to my family. I grabbed my wallet and phone, taking my time to place each in my pockets. I walked past the vanity's mirror and diverted my eyes. I no longer wanted to see myself.

I crept down the hallway as quietly as possible. I think I was growing paranoid that others were judging me, so I wanted to eavesdrop, but to my surprise no one was talking about me. I wasn't the center of attention. I rounded the corner to find my grandfather and Diego in the kitchen, chatting over some mezcal. My grandfather offered me some, but I declined. Instead, I poured myself a glass of water. I thought that would make me look responsible. I drank it in one fell swoop, then poured myself another glass and drank it just as quickly. I was now waterlogged and had to excuse myself to the restroom. I ran to the bathroom and unleashed a torrent of dark amber piss. It was disgusting, and I was disgusting. How I was treating my body was disgusting. I see now all the pain I was harboring, how I was making choices that even today bring me shame. But it's what happened, and I'm choosing not to run from the truth of it all. I choose to show you.

"We should get going now, Daniel."

"Coming," I sang back.

As I walked outside the front door, I stumbled and almost went flying. My family rushed to me to ask if I was fine. All of them were there watching me and, again, the paranoia began to surface. Was I being examined? Had they been talking about me while I was in the bathroom? Did I look as drunk as I felt?

"Haven't eaten dinner," I said to them. "I'm sure it's just low blood sugar."

"Are you sure, Daniel?" my grandfather asked, his voice riddled with concern.

"Yes, Abuelo, don't worry. I will see you all later."

"Get him some food. He does not eat enough anymore. Que flaquito es este chico."

"Of course, Don Omar. We can eat something before we meet up with my friends."

I now worried I was visibly drunk. It was like a dozen eyes were watching my every move, sending thoughts to one another. *Pobre Daniel. He is truly falling apart.* I pushed through the swirling maelstrom and stood up straight, then walked purposefully to the passenger side of Diego's truck. I opened the door carefully and hopped in. *Pobre Daniel. He is such a mess these days.* I told myself to focus straight ahead and not to look toward the watchful eyes of Abuelo, Marisol, or my aunt and uncle. *Pobre Daniel. Should we lock him up?* I wanted more drink. I wanted anything to numb myself. I wanted to find you. I wanted a second chance. But I knew deep down I had run out of time, had no chances left. I needed to just get on with the night ahead.

"Ready to go?"

"Oops, need to put on my seat belt," I said, trying not to slur my words.

As we headed across town to meet Diego's friends, all I could think about was you. I felt you calling me, and I needed to reach you, but the truth was, it was the sadness calling me. It was asking me to join it. I needed to block it out. I was afraid what I'd do if I answered.

"Do you mind if we listen to some music?"

"Whatever you want, handsome," Diego said, passing me his phone.

I scrolled through his iTunes, which was mostly classic Mexican rock like Maná and Molotov. That wouldn't do—I needed something more saccharine, something to pump myself up. I kept scrolling till I found Rihanna. As the opening notes to "We Found Love" poured through the speakers, I turned the volume up as high as possible. Dancing there in my seat, I was somewhere else entirely—somewhere I believed, at least for a moment, I could live free from the pain rattling through me. As the crescendo erupted right before the beat dropped, Diego looked over.

"You doing good, guapo?"

"I'm out of the house, aren't I?"

I performed for him, singing loudly, swinging my head from shoulder to shoulder. As Diego pulled onto the highway, I continued riding the high. I could feel you there within arm's reach as we coasted, heard you calling to me to join you. I looked out the window at the city as the sun began to fade and fantasized about lighting the whole cruel fucking world on fire. I imagined a supernova exploding and wiping us all out, ending all this misery, all this death, then concentrated on the beer and liquor coursing through my veins as the beat got higher, my mind lighter. Your voice grew louder as it called to me from somewhere along that highway. I needed to find where your voice was coming from, I needed to reach you. I rolled the window down and stuck my hand out, trying to catch the currents and ride them like a sparrow, a falcon, the mighty eagle of both my countries . . .

"Daniel—"

Someone was calling to me from the distance. The angel Gabriel perhaps? My uncle? My grandmother? Or maybe it was you, Sam? As the call grew louder, I willed my hand to expand, morphing my arms into wings. I sprouted feathers, made myself more aerodynamic. I was a bird, finally answering your call. My tendons turned muscular but light, letting me fly higher. My nose morphed into a beak. I was the eagle with a snake in his mouth. I had finally found Tenochtitlán. I was going to return to you, to the valley of our people. My uncle would be there, he would welcome us, I knew this in the deepest part of me. We would all be safe from this world that wanted to dim our light. We would shine brightly and call out to others.

"Daniel, we're here."

Where were you just then? Where were you when I was drunk, trying to fly to you? Where had you gone to wait for us? The ones you left behind.

"Querido, it's time to get out."

I awoke to Diego waving his hand in front of me. The music had long stopped. I was no longer flying. The darkness had lulled me into a cruel dream. You weren't there. I hadn't reached our nest. Instead, I was in the cab of Diego's truck being instructed like a sleeping child who'd been awakened after a long road trip. But I wasn't anywhere exciting like Disneyland or Niagara Falls. Instead I was outside a pretentious-looking bar owned by one of Diego's family friends. I took in a deep breath and prepared myself for a night I was not up for. I was going through the motions at this point, and I desperately wanted to leave, but I had made my bed and now I needed to lie in it.

Diego, his friends, and I were seated in a private booth adorned with tall glass vases of orchids and other tropical flowers not native to the desert landscape. It was all glitz and glamour, and I did not feel like I belonged—not to mention the fact that I still felt tipsy. Trapped there in the middle of this group of Diego's, it seemed there was no escape. My only possible exit would have been to slide under the table like a puddle of water and flow below the stools and chairs, onto the street and down into the sewer where I belonged.

"So, Daniel, how much longer do you have in México?"

"Two weeks."

"Ay Dios Mio, the summer has flown by for you."

"Yes, it has."

"Well then, we need to get some drinks and send you off in style."

I could feel Diego's eyes searching for mine, willing me to look at him long enough that he could figure out what was happening, why I was being this way. You see, I hadn't mentioned it to him yet, how I knew the exact date I was leaving, and had known ever since asking my parents to book my ticket home. I'd decided that, despite this sadness I was carrying, I'd return to Cayuga and try to move forward. Although I felt resolute in this decision, I was still uncomfortable with having to tell Diego. I wasn't naïve. I knew how much he liked me, how much he hoped, even if he hadn't yet articulated it, that I'd be there in Chihuahua for longer than two more weeks. But in that moment, I didn't care if I was about to hurt him. I was ready to cause destruction.

The waiter brought over a tray of drinks and Yesika poured out the bottle of mezcal. I knew it would lead to no good, but I joined the others, shot for shot.

"¡Arriba, abajo, al centro, pa' dentro!"

The smoky, woody liquor gave way to sweet notes of honey and agave. It burned my throat until a warmth wrapped itself around me. It was like a friend meeting up with me after so long—but it hadn't been that long. I'd been drinking on and off for days, but still I thirsted for more of that numbness. I wanted to escape my mind for a bit. I wanted the night to be over. I wanted to return to you. But then a voice called out to me, reminding me that I needed to stay lucid enough to break up with Diego. I couldn't let myself forget to do that.

It was while Yesika was telling me about her and Diego's plans to expand their hospitality empire that a reggaetón song came on, and Yoli and Emilia demanded everyone get up and dance. I politely but firmly refused their invite, so they dragged Sebastián and Yesika off with them, leaving me and Diego behind.

"I'm going out for some air," I said.

"I'll join you. I want a cigarette as it is."

As we made our way through the crowd, I could feel Diego's hand resting on my backside, almost pushing me forward. Even though I was ahead of him, it felt as if he was leading me. I tried to shake away and dashed toward the first open table I could see. He called the waiter over and ordered himself a beer and a glass of wine for me. I remember thinking, *Wait a minute. He didn't even ask me what I wanted. He just did it.* I stewed in angry annoyance, adding this ordering to my list of reasons why I wanted to end things. He pulled out a pack of Marlboros and smacked it against the table to loosen the cigarettes. He took out an ornate gold lighter with an Aztec design and lit the cigarette with a flick of the wrist, mindlessly blowing smoke in my direction. As we waited for the drinks, he sat there smiling at me and rubbing my shoulder, which also annoyed me. I didn't want his touch and I hadn't given him permission to put his hands on me.

I had had enough, so I grabbed a different waiter's attention and ordered a bottle of Topo Chico. Although I didn't yet have a concrete plan, I knew I needed to sober up.

"It's good that you came out tonight, querido. I was getting worried about you."

"You don't have to worry about me."

"I know, but still . . . you can't hide forever, you know. It's not healthy."

"I don't know what that means."

"In your bedroom. Alone. It is just going to perpetuate sadness. You need to get out more. I'm sure your friend would want that."

I can't begin to explain to you the rage I was feeling. He did not know you. He had no right to begin to even dream up what you would think or want for me. I wanted to throttle him. Thankfully, the waiter returned with our drinks before he could say any more. When she set down the three glasses, Diego looked at the wine and then slid it my way as if coercing me to join him in drinking more. I fought off the idea of just saying fuck it and allowing myself more booze, more numbness. I reached for my water and took a long sip. The effervescent bubbles were refreshing in that oppressive desert heat. It was time to stop drinking; it was time to finally release myself from all the things that were holding me back. I knew everyone wanted me to find peace, but it was my responsibility to figure out how to get there.

As Diego blabbered on about expanding his catering business, I began to think through all the things that had happened in the past few weeks and how the person staring at me from the other side of the table wasn't the person I wanted to share any of it with. Diego was handsome. Diego was ambitious. Diego could provide a wonderful life for an eventual partner, but none of that was enough for me. My heart was tied to someone no longer here, and I needed time to work through that. You see, the thing that made it so clear to me was something so ordinary, and not overly profound—but it meant a whole lot. Even to this day, and especially during those dark days, whenever I saw something beautiful, you were the first person I wanted to share it with. You were the first person I wanted to take a picture for, send it to, and write, *I wish you were still here.* That desire to share my world with you confirmed to me that I needed to return to Ithaca, that I couldn't stay stuck in Chihuahua forever. This all sounds more poetic in my retelling, but in that very moment, seated across from Diego, I only wanted to run from him because I found him so fucking annoying. What once came across as sexy bravado now revealed itself to be closer to arrogance and pretense.

"You gonna drink that, querido?"

"I didn't order it."

"I know, but I got it for you."

He picked up my glass of wine, swirling it in the light to show what a nice vintage it was. I didn't say anything else because I felt a heat rising in me, a heat I feared I'd not be able to control. I watched as he took a giant sip.

"Shame for you to waste it."

He then finished it for me before stumping out his cigarette and flicking it in the glass. I watched as the paper filter bloomed a dark purple-red from the remaining drops of pinot noir. He shifted his chair closer. I was grateful there was a table between us because I could feel the heat turning into molten anger at the back of my neck. His face had gone slightly red and sweaty from the mezcal and beers.

"So querido, what have you enjoyed about your time here?"

Again, I was completely dumbfounded by his behavior. I mean, what a stupid question to ask given the circumstances. He knew about you. He knew I was going through a difficult time in my life. Did he think this would all just blow over? Did he think I would enjoy this earnest bullshit, this lovey-dovey persona? I was beside myself with anger as he just kept staring at me.

"Spending time with my grandfather," I said.

It was an honest answer. Despite the sadness I felt in my heart, despite the dark clouds blanketing so much of my trip, I was grateful for Abuelo, for our time together. I was grateful, too, for what he had gifted me: my uncle. In that moment, I wanted to run to Abuelo and apologize for everything. I wanted to tell him I was going to get better. I was going to survive this. I was going to be okay.

"Stay, Daniel."

I didn't know whether I was imagining what he had said, or whether what was happening was, in fact, happening. I sipped on my water. I didn't want to humor him. I was trying not to snap.

"You don't have to go back," he said, louder this time.

I told myself not to react.

"Two weeks is too soon to return to school and all that drama. You should take a year off and stay in Chihuahua. Give yourself room to breathe. Get your life back together."

"I have a scholarship, Diego," I said through gritted teeth.

"I am sure they will understand. I am sure if you reached out and shared with them that you need time to get better, they'd work with you."

"Who? Who will understand?"

"Your college."

"My life is there. I'm in the middle of a fucking degree."

"You can stay in Chihuahua, enroll in the local college instead, and move in with me. Please stay."

"I'm not from here. I mean, you get that, right?"

"You are though, Daniel. You are Mexican. This is your homeland. Stay in México, we can live together, we can keep dating. I will help you get through this."

"You can't be fucking serious."

"I am, Daniel."

He got up and moved to the chair closer to me. His eyes had grown wild with a kind of lust, a manic love I didn't have for him. I realized then that we had truly different understandings of where things were. For me, this was a summer fling. This was temporary. I was already a thousand miles away, somewhere else completely.

"Move in with me?"

My body froze as he pulled out a rectangular box like the first one he'd gifted me. He opened its clasp and revealed a shiny set of keys. I could sense the eyes of complete strangers watching us and suddenly felt like I was in some kind of TV show with a crowd of background actors in the periphery. People were smiling and pointing our way, whispering into their friends' ears.

"Give me the pleasure of being your boyfriend and stay here, and when the time is right, we can think about the next step."

He sat there looking at me with those hungry, stupid, drunk eyes. He sat there waiting for me to respond with something powerful, romantic; something to let him know we had a future together. But I couldn't move my mouth. It truly amazed me how off the mark he was, how truly deluded he must have been to think I would just give up everything and move in with him after two fucking months of sort-of dating. He pushed the opened box toward me. He said, "Look at it." He said, "Look at what I want to give you." But all I could think about was what he wanted me to give up. I looked down and his hand angered me so much, and I thought, *Enough already. Enough, Daniel!* I went to swipe away the stupid box, but accidentally ended up flinging all the empty glasses off the table. They came crashing down and smashed into hundreds of pieces on the floor. It was so loud, and the entire beer garden went quiet. Without thinking, I bent down to pick up the mess and ended up cutting myself on a large shard. The pain was fiery, and the blood began to pour hot and steady. Diego got up and reached for me.

"Get the fuck away from me!" I roared.

"Let me help you, Daniel. You're bleeding."

"I don't love you, Diego. I don't love you!"

"You need to calm down."

"I don't fucking love you, do you hear me?"

The words came flooding out of me. At this point, the audience of strangers was feigning a return to their conversations, pretending like they weren't, in fact, watching with horror what was unfolding before them.

"I think you need to be quiet and let me help you."

"No, Diego, don't you understand? I don't want to fucking be with you!"

"Okay, calm down. You're acting crazy."

"Wow, that's really rich coming from you."

I looked down at my clothes, soaked with beer and wine, and my hand still covered in blood. The ground was a minefield of glass shards and spilled booze. A waiter ran out with a broom and began sweeping up the mess, and our original waiter came over with a clean towel for me to wrap around my hand. People were murmuring around us, staring with eyes full of judgment. I could even see, from the corner of my eye, Diego's sister and friends watching from the door. I ignored them all and told Diego I needed to go.

"Go where?"

"Home," I said. "I need to go home."

Before he agreed to take me home, Diego demanded to inspect my hand. I relented, as the towel had gone bright red from all the blood. The cut was still quite painful and felt uncomfortable when he unwrapped it.

"This isn't deep," he informed me with mild annoyance. "It's just the alcohol in your system. Make sure you put pressure on it."

I went to grab my things as he threw money on the table before apologizing to all the staffers we passed. He led us out through a door at the side, so we wouldn't bump into his friends. Everyone just kept pretending to mind their own business, but I knew they were still watching us, all side-glances and whispers. Outside on the street, a valet driver ran up to Diego to ask if everything was all right. Diego gave him the ticket and said we were calling it a night. The truck pulled up within the blink of an eye, and Diego opened the passenger door and pointed at the seat, telling me to get in. From somewhere deep inside, a voice called to me and said: *Wake up, Daniel.* That's when it dawned on me: Diego had been drinking all night. Was it you, Sam? Was it your voice? Because in that moment I thought of the split-second decision you'd made to get into your friend's car. I finally felt lucid with clarity. I knew what I must do.

"Are you sober enough to drive right now?"

"What are you talking about?"

"You've been drinking, Diego. You shouldn't drive."

"I'm a grown man, Daniel. I can handle my drink. I'm not one of your silly college friends. Now get in the damn truck."

It was as if he'd slapped me in the face. I felt even angrier than I had before, but also afraid I might begin to cry in front of him. I knew he'd said it as a jab against you. I knew he was being cruel, intentionally so.

"No, you've been drinking. You can't drive."

The valet was watching us as his colleagues returned with more vehicles. A line of cars was building now, people waiting for us to vacate the spot. Drivers honked loudly and the parking staff looked uncomfortable, unsure what to do. It was obvious they were aware of the tension between me and Diego.

"Get in the truck now."

"No, you're fucking drunk," I repeated, more loudly this time.

"What did you say?"

"You must be drunk because you're acting like an insensitive asshole."

I stood firm. I told myself, *No matter what, Daniel, you will not get in that truck.* The valet came over to ask if everything was fine, and Diego shooed him away as if he were a fly, a nuisance, and not someone trying to do his job. The other drivers began honking more aggressively, unsure what was going on. Diego pleaded with me to get into his truck, begging me to stop making a scene.

"I know the owners of this place and you are embarrassing me now."

"No," I said. "I'll get a fucking taxi."

I kept repeating how he had been drinking, but he wouldn't listen to me. His face shifted and I could see he was now visibly angry. My words were being drowned out by the honking, and the manager of the bar finally stepped outside and asked what was going on. Diego told her we were fine and leaving immediately. He apologized to her, but his eyes were full of venom as they looked at me.

"I'm not getting in the car with a drunk."

"Get in the motherfucking truck, you spoiled brat!"

It came out of nowhere. I remember thinking, *Well, this anger is the only logical emotion he has displayed all night.* I resisted his commands, but he leapt out to grab me and drag me into his truck. His grip was strong and scared me. He squeezed on my cut hand, and I knew he was hurting me on purpose. I called for help, "¡Auxilio, socorro!" But no one came to my rescue. The few people on the street watched like this was a movie scene instead of real life, or perhaps they just chalked it up to two drunk men doing what drunk men do. Again, I pleaded for help, but the bystanders simply shrugged as if to say *This is your problem, man.* I told Diego he was hurting me, but he didn't listen, just kept trying to push me into his truck. I was freaking out, and he wasn't showing signs of relenting, so in that moment I did the only thing I could think of: from somewhere deep inside, I mustered the courage to actually fight back, and I kicked him hard in the balls. He fell back from the pain, and I was able to break free. Everyone was looking at me like I was the crazy one, and maybe I was. But I wasn't going to let Diego take me home.

Some smokers started chanting, "Fight, fight, fight," and as the valets ran over to help Diego up, I made my exit.

"Get in the car, you fucking piece of American shit," he screamed at me. "Come back here and get in the fucking car!"

I bolted as fast as I could and ran toward the traffic lights. I kept running past billboards, past neon signs from clubs lining the street, past taco stands and teenagers peddling weed. As I drove my body forward, it dawned on me that I wasn't managing well. I had lost that kind, loving person who was at the core of my being. I thought to myself, *You need to heal, Daniel. You need to heal yourself.* I thought, *You're not okay, but you're going to be one day. I promise.*

I kept running. I hauled ass and could feel Diego chasing after me. I could hear his angry words following me down the street, but my body pushed onward, following that voice of lightness:

Daniel, you need to learn to heal!

Step one for beginning your healing is not making other people's mistakes.

The lights and the sounds were all blurring, but I kept moving.

Step two is admitting when you're not happy with life.

Step three is running toward the light. To where it calls to you.

In the moment, I felt alive again. I felt like some magnet was pulling me away from the man still screaming behind me—a man who I can now see wasn't a monster, but was also not my savior. I needed to be my savior. I needed to trust myself once again. I knew that I'd used Diego during a period in which my life was stranded at the border between heartbreak and moving on, that I'd turned to him when I felt alone and jilted by you. We had each been what the other needed for a time, but I could no longer be part of his dream life. It was time to return to the reality of mine, to not hide any longer. So I kept going, running like I hadn't run in months—really, I hadn't run like this since all those mornings I would wake up in Ithaca and go in search of answers for what to do about you and me, those days in which gaining clarity could only happen by taking my body to complete exhaustion. Running farther, running faster.

I made it two, three, four blocks before the wind was completely knocked out of me. The road smelled of smog and summer heat, steaming off the black tarmac. Before me was a gas station that looked familiar, but I didn't know why. I was too delirious, too dizzy, too drunk to understand where I was as I walked over to the little kiosk to ask for help. My hand was still hurting but the bleeding had stopped. My head was pounding from all the booze, the loss of blood, and the running. Cars whizzed by near the main road as restaurants were closing and bars were putting out last calls. The scent of tacos al pastor was wafting in the air from all the stands set up to feed the drunk masses. Women in cheap heels clickety-clacked down the street next to men in cowboy boots and gallon hats. Everyone was going about their evening, looking happy and hopeful. I was a complete mess now, but I would get there too, again, I told myself. I would have that soon.

I opened the shop's door and the bell's singsong announced my arrival. It was completely empty of customers, but there was an older man working behind the counter. He looked up at me and I swear his face was like it had seen a ghost. I was afraid my bloody towel had scared him, and so I tried to quickly explain in slurred Spanish that I wasn't injured or there to cause trouble, that I just needed help calling a taxi. He had backed up against the wall behind him and was muttering something under his breath. Again, you'd have thought I was the devil himself. I tried to calm him down. I just wanted to go home. He was a nice-enough-looking man—handsome, even, with his hoop earring and thick-rimmed glasses. I remember thinking he looked like a Mexican Elvis.

"Can you help me?"

He just kept pointing at me and repeating something under his breath. I read his name tag: *Menchaca.* I tried enunciating my words this time in case he hadn't been able to hear me earlier.

"Señor Menchaca, can you please help me? I need the number of a taxi."

His mumbling grew louder, and for a second, I swore he was saying my name. But I was also exhausted and still very much drunk.

"If you just write down the number of a taxi company, then I'll be on my way. I don't want to bother you."

His hands were shaking as he wrote down a number and slid it under the glass partition that separated us. I thanked him and asked if he was all right, but he never responded. He just kept repeating what sounded like "Daniel," which freaked me out. I thanked him one last time and quickly took my leave. He continued to brace himself against the back wall of his little kiosk, watching me in fear until I left the shop.

Once outside, I took out my phone and dialed the number written on the small scrap of paper. When the taxi operator asked for my location, I realized I didn't know where I was. I searched around for the name of the gas station. That's when I looked up to see the weathered, hand-painted sign above the mechanic's garage: *Menchaca Mecánico.* I could barely make out the address below the shop's name. The floodlights above the gas pumps were shining so brightly, almost blinding me. As I looked around more, it finally hit me. I realized why I knew this place: it was the gas station where my uncle had died.

"¿Señor, usted está allí?"

"Sí, sí. I'm on Calle Garza at Menchaca Mecánico near the launderette."

"Okay, I know where you're at. Someone will be there in two minutes."

"Muchas gracias."

When I looked down at my hand I saw the bleeding had stopped, so I chucked the towel in a nearby trash can. I didn't want to draw any more attention to myself. The taxi arrived almost instantly, and I hopped inside and awkwardly buckled my seat belt with my uninjured hand. I gave the driver my aunt's address, then rested my head against the cool glass. From the highway, Chihuahua looked like floating candles in a dark bath, thousands of lit houses, streetlights, and shining billboards illuminating the night from afar as we coasted down the road. It was utterly intoxicating—beguiling, even—and all I wanted was to take a picture and send it to you. I would have written something like, *Look at this place that made me. One day I will bring you here.*

But of course, you know I couldn't do that. So I sat there with my head against the glass, looking up. I couldn't see many stars, but I could make out Ursa Minor and Ursa Major. I gently waved to the heavens, then closed my eyes. I knew somewhere out there you and my uncle were watching over me. Wrapped in the comfort of your guardianship, I let the sparse light guide me home.

EL ÚLTIMO DÍA

AUGUST 23, 1988

I am turning eighteen in a few weeks. This is an age at which I am told I'll be an adult. I wonder, when the clock strikes midnight, if I will experience a transformation going from boyhood into my manhood. How will the world treat my version of man? Will he be enough? Still to be decided. But I hope my version of man is centered in kindness. I hope my version of man is unafraid to love, that he carries with him all the joys of youth, all the wonders of childhood, all the ways in which life can be surprising. I don't want to be weighed down by the world, I want to float freely, soaring higher until I can eventually touch the sun.

—D.M.

On my final day, I returned to the gas station to meet Luis, my uncle's best friend: *Señor Menchaca*. It dawned on me when I woke up the following morning who he was, and this realization was like a mission given to me by my uncle, telling me I needed to reconnect my family to this man who once was so very much a part of their lives. After my night with Diego, I told my grandfather everything—and I do mean everything. I did not let myself dilute the truth of my past few weeks there in Chihuahua. I was honest about how I'd been numbing myself with beer and liquor, how the sadness was more destructive than I had let on. I told him how things had broken down with Diego and how I had fled into the night, leaving him behind. I needed my grandfather to know how I had lost myself ever since I had lost you, floating alone in the dark tumult of a storm. But I wasn't lost anymore. In my grandfather's room, seated on his bed, as the tears once more poured from me, I let him know I was going to be all right. I was going to find a way forward, had started to find a way.

When I phoned Luis and explained who I was, the line went silent for quite a while. I think he was afraid. Here I was, this ghost from his past reaching across time to ask to meet so I could learn more about his best friend, someone he'd lost at the hands of a freak accident, a negligent decision. I wanted him to understand that I wasn't coming from a place of anger but rather of wanting to know my uncle in all his color so I could help my family move forward. I wanted us to be unafraid in acknowledging what we had lost, and I hoped that, with Luis's memories, we might learn to build back the man my uncle was and, together, find a way to honor his life.

"I'd like to meet with him, Abuelo. I think it would be good for you to come."

"It's been so long, mijo. I'm not sure."

"If I have learned anything these last few weeks, Abuelo, it has been to not miss the opportunity to reconcile the past. I do hope you'll come with me when I go."

My words settled among us, nestling into the empty chair of the patio table.

"Mi niño hermoso. When did you become so wise?"

"Everything good and wise about me, I learned through you, Abuelo."

"My sweet, sweet Daniel. You are a much better man than me, and each day I am learning from you."

He took a few days to decide, but one afternoon while I was packing, Abuelo told me he'd come. Together, as we folded my clothes and wrapped my uncle's things in bubble wrap, we both allowed ourselves to be open, to face our pain in order to heal. He shared more with me about my uncle, like what he was like with my mom growing up. He told me about my uncle's teenage years, how he would blast rock music loudly in his room, how his brain was a sponge, always reading and learning from the world around him. The more I learned about my namesake, the more it felt as if vibrant color was returning to my life; as if I was learning, once again, to see the world for all its beauty. I even began to share details about you with my grandfather—of all our adventures, of the way in which you shared a city with me, opened up an entire world.

The morning we were to meet with Luis, Abuelo and I woke up early and first went to weekday mass. Abuelo wanted to spend time with God in their hallowed home and pray, and though it had been so long since I'd allowed myself to speak with my version of God and I was nervous, I agreed. So I went with my grandfather to ask forgiveness for these past few weeks, but not with a priest. No, I would face my God on my own, genuflect in a quiet pew and speak directly to them.

Together, my grandfather and I lit candles and prayed to La Virgen de Guadalupe, my ancestors, God, and in the quiet sanctuary of that church, I asked for help from all of them in moving out of the shadows. I then closed my eyes and allowed myself to feel my uncle's presence, the man I was finally beginning to know. I thought of what I could remember from reading his diary. I thought of each letter, each description, each carefully considered word—all of his writing. His words were part of my larger map, and as I connected the dots to learn who my uncle was, I was beginning to make my way back to Daniel—both the Daniel I was reading about and the one who is writing to you now. This journeying would not be complete on this day, my last one in México, but every journey needs a start, and that's what I was doing.

The drive to the gas station was quiet, and I knew my grandfather was nervous, a feeling I shared because I didn't know what to expect. I didn't know if opening up the past was the right thing to do—in part because, as much as he might have forgiven Luis, my grandfather still hadn't seen him in over twenty years. I told my grandfather that if he didn't feel comfortable, I would go myself, and he could drop me off down the block, no problem. But he told me he was ready. He had prayed, not to God, to my surprise, but to Tío Daniel and my grandmother. He'd asked for their advice, and he told me he needed to go. He needed to help our family open up this wound so it might truly heal this time around.

When we got there, the gas station was closed but the garage was open. It was just Luis standing in the cool shade among stacks of boxes and greasy car parts. We got out of the truck, and I made the first move and formally introduced myself.

"Hola, Luis. Soy Daniel, el sobrino de Daniel, hijo de Sonia. Mucho gusto."

"Ay Dios. You look just like him. You have his eyes. Those same brown-black irises."

"I have often been told that."

"It's true, Luis. I have long thought I'm looking at my son when I see Daniel. But now I also am seeing Daniel as his own man, someone I'm sure his uncle would be proud of."

Luis looked past me to my grandfather and it was like he was a young man all over again, afraid and unsure of what to do when confronted by Abuelo's voice. But my grandfather broached the divide. He walked over to Luis and took him in his arms, and I watched as two grown men allowed grief not to destroy them, but rather set them free. The sun was radiating brightly on the hot asphalt and I noticed a few families walking by, looking toward us. I let Luis and Abuelo have all the time they needed because, on this day, we had all the time in the world.

"Cálmate, mijo, no more tears, okay?" my grandfather said, gently rubbing Luis's back.

"Sí, Don Omar, you're right. I promised myself I'd hold it together today. I'm so sorry."

"It's a lot, I'm sure, but we are grateful you agreed to see us," I offered as an apology, afraid everything was starting to be too much for him.

"No, it's fine. Lo prometo. But, anyway, you said on the phone you wanted to ask me some questions?"

"Yes, if that's all right."

"Of course, anything I can help you with I'll do, mijo."

I smiled at him, this conduit to my family's past. I thought of everything I could ask, but narrowed it down to one first question: "I really just want to know who he was as a friend. What was he like when you were growing up?"

Luis's eyes grew bright. "He was very independent. We were so close, but Daniel was always dreaming and scheming. He pushed me and challenged me to question things about the world, things that I didn't think affected me at the time—or didn't want to be affected by."

"Like?"

"Well, I don't know if you or your grandfather knew . . ."

Luis looked at me and then my grandfather, and my grandfather and I turned to each other and nodded.

"Sí, mijo, I knew, and I've shared that with Daniel," Abuelo told him proudly. "There are no more secrets. No need for them. I want to honor Daniel as he was."

Luis nodded and considered what to say next. It was strange—if I'm honest, in that moment, I saw myself. What I mean, Sam, is that I saw what the future held for me. At some point I, God willing, would be an older man and I'd no doubt speak of you, and it would be like crossing time. I watched my uncle's best friend think of what to say next about this other Daniel, and couldn't help but see me, future Daniel, learning how to speak of the past.

"Well, I'm also gay, and, well, when your uncle and I were around your age, mijo, the world was a slightly different place. Very scary for us in what felt like a bubble out here in the desert. But Daniel was learning about things happening around the world—he'd watch the news and meet up with other gay men, read magazines, and, well, he envisaged a different world, a better world. He knew it was possible."

"I read some of his diary entries and looked through the pamphlets and flyers. It's amazing to see how much more alike we are than I could ever have thought. I mean, I think he was much braver and understandably angrier. But still, never could I imagine he was so close in spirit."

I watched as Luis took in my words. He smiled.

"Yes, well, when Daniel left high school, I think he felt the world around him was too flat. He wanted purpose. In his final few years of life, I think he found that in his sexuality. What I mean is, he found purpose in challenging this idea of having to hide, and instead learning how to fight loudly to exist fully as himself."

"Can I ask if you two were ever . . . you know?"

"Together? Oh, no. Definitely not. He was like an annoying brother. I loved your uncle, but we were very much friends—again, like siblings. I mean, ask your grandfather. Sometimes as little boys we'd try to tear each other's necks off if we didn't get our way. We'd drive our parents mad. We quelled our competitiveness once we were teenagers, but as little boys we could go from friends to enemies and back in a matter of seconds."

My grandfather laughed. It was lovely to hear him laugh about a memory of my uncle.

"Yes, there were times I didn't know if you hated each other or if you were afraid to leave one another's company. Your friendship was always intense and fierce to me. But you always forgave each other very quickly."

"Your abuelo is right, mijo. Our bond was so deep, and I think it was because of what we carried inside ourselves, what we could not articulate until we were much older. What I assume you were alluding to earlier"—I nodded as he continued to speak—"but I think where I wanted to thrive was in a world a bit more fun and frivolous than your uncle's. I was all about dancing and partying, where your uncle wanted truth. He needed something deeper, others who might challenge him to fight the powers that be—does that make sense?"

I nodded fervently.

"We had plans to move down to the capital. There was a lot going on in D.F. at the time in terms of activism, as well as a thriving queer scene, but . . . the accident." His voice cracked and the tears started once more. "Then, you know . . . he passed so young."

Luis was trying to wipe his eyes and continue, but the memory of that day must've still haunted him.

"He had so many plans. He had so many dreams. I'm so sorry for what happened."

"Don't be upset, Luis. You know he wouldn't want you to be. He would want you to find peace," my grandfather said firmly.

"I'm so, so sorry. I think of him every day. Te lo juro. I'm never not thinking of him."

This time I was the one who held Luis and tried to soothe him. Our losses may have been separated by many decades, but I knew what it was to lose your best friend, someone you loved so deeply, with every part of your being. I knew what it was to fall apart, and now was the time to help someone else piece himself back together.

"It's okay, Luis. It's okay. I know he is just so happy now that we are here and we are connecting. It means the world to meet someone who knew my uncle so well."

I could see my grandfather watching as I tried to calm Luis's tears. In that moment, what did we look like? Did he see me as his grandson, or was his past bleeding into the present? I don't know, I never asked him, but I remember a change in his expression as an idea came to him.

"Luis, mijo . . ." he said, broaching the pain still there.

"¿Sí, Don Omar?"

"If you're not busy right now, I wanted to take Daniel to one final place before he leaves Chihuahua tomorrow. I think it would be good for you to come."

"Yes, wherever. I'd love the chance to spend more time with Daniel's nephew."

"Great. Then it's settled. You can drive with us."

"Okay, let me just grab one thing and I can go."

As Luis went to lock the garage, I walked over to Abuelo and gave him the biggest hug. I thanked him for coming with me and for inviting Luis to our next and final destination. As the sun bore down on us, not a cloud in the sky, I knew we were in my uncle's favor, making him proud.

"This is for you, mijo. I'm sorry I didn't have anything better to put it all in."

"Thank you, Luis. What is it?"

"They're some things from your uncle. Things he'd given me or left at my house over the years, things my parents kept for me. I think it's time they returned to your family."

I looked through the plastic shopping bag and there was an envelope of photos, letters Luis had written my uncle in the years since his passing, and some band T-shirts of musicians who I assumed my uncle liked. I took out a beautiful shirt with colorful embroidery, a guayabera. I buried my nose in its crisp linen, and it was like I could smell his life. I felt grateful for having these treasures from a man who for so long was a mystery to me, nothing more than a memory. I now had him out in the open, bright, shining light of life. That's what I needed to do with you too, I realized. I needed to not keep your memory in darkness. I needed to not hide it away. I would not let myself do that to our story.

"Okay boys, let's get going."

I climbed into the back seat and let Luis sit up front with my grandfather. I scanned the letters as the three of us drove to a cemetery in the outskirts of Chihuahua, located on top of a hill that looks down onto the city. It was huge. But even though it was full of graves and people no longer on this earth, it didn't feel sad or scary. There was something comforting about the idea of remembering all these people who had existed at one point or another—people just like you, just like my uncle, just like any of us who walk this earth.

Under the wide blue sky were thousands of stone epitaphs, stretching for miles in shades of marbled white and gray. Together, we walked to find my uncle's, and as we stood by it I felt I had put the final piece in the puzzle of Daniel's story. There, in the presence of the man whose name I carry, next to his best friend and his father, I felt whole. Birds soared above us, riding invisible currents. I think this was the moment in which the cogs began to turn, the exact moment in which my idea for writing our story began to germinate. Standing beside his grave, I understood the importance of having something to return to, something to look back upon. I needed something physical, something of yours I could touch, could hold, could speak to.

I knelt down and kissed the cool stone of my uncle's grave. I whispered things I always wanted to tell him, stories of my childhood, questions I longed to ask him about the common threads we shared. I traced my finger along the carved letters of his name, of my name: D-A-N-I-E-L. I made him real because he was real, because he had walked this very earth under this very sky. I read the words my family had chosen to mark his life and I understood how this man had dreams, ambitions, so much to give the world.

How, in spite of leaving this earth at twenty-two, he had already done so much.

A quietness overcame the three of us, each man processing the moment in his own unique way. But even if we were alone in our thoughts, we were not alone in our bodies. We were bonded by this man, this Daniel before us—a Daniel who'd given my life a new start when I had all but given up.

"So, Don Omar, will you be staying around in Chihuahua?"

"No, Luis. I think it's time I returned home. My family needs me, and the truth is I need them."

"So you're going back, Abuelo?"

"Sí, mijo. It's time. There's so much I have left to do on this earth, and that begins with learning to speak about him with your mother. Learning not to be afraid to face the past."

"I'm so grateful to you, Abuelo. Hearing that just gives me so much peace."

"I'm glad, mijo, and I'm grateful to you for reminding me what it is to live. I think I'd forgotten, and that's no way to be." He paused. "Living is a blessing and I choose to honor it."

Looking upon the city so deeply tied to my family's history, a past just opening itself up to me, there in the heat of an August morning, I came to terms with one of life's truths: death cannot be undone. My uncle's and your death could not be undone, but I could live on your behalf—and his. Luis could learn to forgive himself. My mom could learn to speak her brother's name again and not be afraid. My family could open up to one another, acknowledging what we had lost while cherishing what we'd once had. This Daniel could choose to live a fully present life, and a bold one. That is what I could give you all, and that day, in the presence of my namesake, I promised to do it: To live. To be happy. To be free.

PART IV

DAY ONE

AUGUST 23, 1990

Today, Sonia told me she met a boy. His name is Salvador. She was starry-eyed. I asked her to describe him to me. She said, "Hermano, all I can say is Chavo is the person I am going to spend the rest of my life with." "How do you know?" I asked her. "Because when I look into his eyes, I see my future." I asked her what the future looked like. "Bright and never-ending. Like a sunset that is always followed by sunrise. The most perfect day. A day that never stops." "I hope he makes you happy," I said to her. She looked at me and said, "One day, Daniel. You will find someone like that for you, and when you do, I hope you only have the most perfect never-ending days for all of your life. I hope he gives you that." And I smiled at her, and she smiled at me, and we didn't need to say anything else because sometimes words are not needed. She saw me and she knew all of me and I was a little freer that day.

—D.M.

So we have reached the end, or at least the end of what I can share with you. Over the past seven days of nonstop writing, I've mapped out for you our story. I guess this endeavor was born from some manic need to prove we truly existed, a need for something more concrete than fading memories. But I now understand that there is so much more than just memories to our story. There is a whole city out there, a whole year to look back upon. Thinking about this past year of unfolding love, of heartbreak, and of what I believe to have ultimately been our redemption, I can see how we experienced a lifetime together, and how I could've written down a lifetime's worth of memories. But it's time I look forward, my friend. I can't narrate the future to you, or predict how this next year will go, but what I can tell you is, right now, I feel a sense of solace. I feel freer for having done this, written down our story.

Right now, what I can do is show you where I am in the present. I'll do that for you, but when the time is right, please know you can go. You can be free. I don't want to hold you back. I want you to feel able to pass on to wherever it is you will wait for us. You don't have to worry about me anymore. We will get through this, and we will find our way back to each other. When we are meant to, we will be reunited—I promise. But for now, this is what has been happening.

Aside from writing about us, what have I been up to? Well, some things I'll share now that didn't feel right to say during the heart of our own story: This morning I went to my first meetup with Bernie-Bernice at the Rainbow Center. I spent two hours with new people and I allowed myself to be present, putting pen to paper. I wrote about my final day in Chihuahua and shared parts of it with the group, and you want to know something, Sam? It was incredibly freeing. Bernie-Bernice invited all the participants to bring something from a queer elder, familial or historical, to write about. I chose a photo of Tío Daniel at his AIDS demonstration at the university in Chihuahua. I studied the photo as Bernie-Bernice led us in a free-write, and all I could think about was how the man in the photo was so brave. Brave at a time when bravery could cost you everything—and maybe that is what bravery is about. It is about risking it all for love, for your rights, for the ability to exist fully as yourself. I listened to others read poems and prose while talking about queer elders who have been pivotal to their journey, people like Miss Major, Audre Lorde, and Freddie Mercury. Some, like me, chose family members or friends, those who'd helped guide them toward acceptance, welcomed them in. Holding space and hearing their words this morning felt a bit like light at the end of this long tunnel. I realized I would not be alone this year. I do not have to be. I could learn to lean on community, nurture friendships, play a role in making life that little bit better for others.

I promised Bernie-Bernice and the group I'd be back, and I know I will. Having something of my own this year will be a good thing, I can feel it in my soul. I know it is early days, but I also know it is possible to create a life, a happy life, even after loss. I've seen it with my mother, and Abuelo, through all those I've met who've lost so much. It doesn't lessen the pain, but perhaps makes it a little more tolerable. Knowing there can and will be light at the end makes the pain less scary, and so I will walk proudly toward that light. I will not be afraid. I will no longer run.

What else is there to share with you, outside of our story? This may come as a shock to you, and sorry for sharing only now, but my grandfather arrived last night. I had known for a while he was coming, but again, it didn't feel right to bring that up just yet, not until I'd written the last chapter of our year. But, yes, he is here, and we are going to spend some time in the quiet start of my sophomore chapter exploring this city of mine. Before classes begin and I give myself to deadlines and my little nook in the main library, I will relish my grandfather's company because time is a gift, whatever amount we have left on this earth. I think Abuelo needed to see Ithaca for himself so he could feel closer not just to me, but to my uncle. He needed to understand why some people must leave a home to find themselves; how leaving isn't about cutting off roots but strengthening them so they can hold on tighter.

Abuelo loves how different Ithaca is from our small town in California: its Victorian houses with their wide wooden porches colored every pastel shade of the rainbow, our campus that looks like a scene from some Jane Austen novel, at least to our Mexican American eyes. I took him to this new place called For the Culture for lunch, and it might have been a step too far. I can't say he appreciates a lunch of fermented vegetables, yogurt, and kombucha. Afterward, we went for a slice of pizza, much more his scene. "Real food," he kept repeating as he tucked into a slice topped with chicken parmigiana, and I took a photo of him and sent it to my parents.

> MOM: *He looks happy, mijo. Thank you so much for sharing a bit of your life with him.*
>
> ME: *We love you so much, Mom. I can't wait for you to visit one day.*
>
> MOM: *Me too. But enjoy your time with him over the next few days and send lots of pics.*
>
> ME: *I will. Thank you again for everything, for your prayers, all your love.*
>
> MOM: *We are always here for you, Daniel, and thank you. You have given me the greatest gift: you have brought my brother back into my life, you have made our family whole again.*
>
> ME: *He did, Mom. Tío Daniel did it all.*
>
> MOM: *I know, mijo. I know.*

Maybe that is one of the biggest things I've learned to do these past few weeks: to share. To not hide from the world, or in my head, letting thought after thought pile up until it blocks the outside from ever reaching me. It may have taken something as grave as loss, but my family and I are learning to evolve. We will not hide from pain. Instead, together, we will learn to talk about all these facets of life, the heavy parts and the lighter ones. You and my uncle have given us that, so thank you. Honestly, Sam, thank you for showing me it's okay to move forward. Thank you for calling me out of the darkness.

What else can I tell you? Well, before meeting up with Rob and Mona to do something I thought of earlier, an idea I came up with to mark our end (yours and mine), I took Abuelo to a special place—to somewhere I needed to return to but wasn't quite ready for, especially not without company.

"Is this it?" Abuelo asked me.

"Yes. This is somewhere I have been wanting to come back to for a while."

"Thank you for choosing me to join you."

We stood there, looking up at that redbrick dormitory where you and I had existed for a whole ten months. Together with my grandfather, I treaded the path around our former home and the tall trees we'd seen from our living room. And do you want to know something, Sam? It did not hurt. Instead, it was like a salve. I realized there were so many physical places I could go to be with you, and that showing my grandfather our dorm was a way of offering another person a bit of you, meaning I didn't have to carry your memory on my own. Even after your death, I can still choose to share you with the world. I can keep you alive in that way, and so that is what I'll do.

Abuelo and I gave ourselves to the quiet of the afternoon, no longer afraid of our thoughts, of silences. As we stood there, I thought of all the happy times in which I'd open our door and you'd be there to greet me, saying my name aloud. In my mind, I said yours back, over and over, reciting it like a prayer, and I began to understand I could still do that. I could still call out to you. I would always have your name to hold close.

"Do you think he feels you here, mijo?"

"Yes, Abuelo. I know Sam does."

"Can I tell you something?"

"Of course."

"I feel your uncle right now. I know he is with us, watching over us as we do this. I know we are whole because of it."

"Me too, Abuelo. Me too."

Shortly after, we arrived at Rob's dorm to meet him and Mona, and the four of us drove to where I've chosen to see you off, making our way through the campus and down gridded streets to the only place that felt right. It's a spot I believed I could visit to say good-bye, knowing we would be okay, understanding endings aren't forever.

So where am I now? Well, right now, in these final moments of summer, Rob and Mona have gone with my grandfather to order ice cream for all of us from that little snack bar on Cayuga Lake, the one we went to in the depths of January's cold front. I am standing at the edge where the beach meets that giant lake. The evening is unimaginably warm even as the sun hangs low, prepared to set. There is humidity in the air, rolling off the lakeside, and a myriad of people enjoying the orange-dusted views, dozens of families and gangs of college students eating barbecued food and splashing about in the cool waters of Cayuga. There is a real sense that this could be the last summer day of the year. Standing here, there is something thrilling about seeing all these people lean into the revelry, and something heartwarming about seeing my grandfather in the distance, making small talk with my two best friends—these three wonderful humans who are helping me navigate something I could never have imagined I'd be dealing with at nineteen. But I now understand that loss does not discriminate; we all must face it at some point in our lives. I take comfort in the idea that, along with pain, beauty is universal, and together on this lakeside so many strangers have come together to watch a summer sunset.

In these final moments I have left to tell our story, I'll close my eyes and take in all this life around me: the music blasting from a stereo, the laughter of children as they run about the beach, the chatter of our peers enjoying one last night of freedom. All these joyous noises let me know that life goes on, and that idea doesn't scare me anymore. But can I tell you something? If I concentrate hard enough, I can hear you and me floating in the currents of the summer breeze. I can hear all the laughter we shared, can hear us howling at the October moon. I can hear all the ways in which you said my name, the ways you showed me how love can evolve between two friends. I can hear all the promises we made to each other. If I reach my hand out, I can even touch these words moving through this August zephyr.

I'm Sam   by the way   Sam Morris.

I am glad you found your way   to   Cayuga.

You or me   we all deserve   happiness.

You're like   my best friend   Daniel.

I wish   I had been   there with you.

I'm   glad   you're   here.

You're my compadre   always.

Annoyingly   Daniel   I dream about you   a lot.

Isn't it beautiful? All those memories are proof we existed together for an entire year. Even if others can't hear them while running up and down the beach, even if it's just me, it doesn't make it less true.

As the sun sets, I'll hold out for a little while longer. I don't need to open my eyes to know the light is fading and the purple-black of night is drawing near. I know you're leaving now. I know it's time. But I'm no longer afraid. The light no longer scares me because I understand it now. It's how I can connect with you. So let me listen

Note to Reader

It goes without saying that this is not a memoir, and I am not Daniel. Perhaps, to your potential disappointment, Sam never existed—at least not for me, and not as he does in this book. But the experiences that Daniel goes through, of being named after a family member he never met, and then losing a dear friend at the tender age of nineteen, are both truths that have shaped my own story. For me, love and loss are integral to my writing, and Daniel's journey has always been about honoring each of those human experiences. I am grateful for Daniel helping me to finally let go of the last of that pain and turn it into something meaningful. This is a story I have carried for nearly fifteen years, and I am in awe that it is now in your hands, dearest reader. So, if you'll humor me, I'd like to share a bit more about this book.

Many of the imagined conversations Daniel has with Sam after Sam's death were inspired by exchanges between Vladimir and Estragon in Samuel Beckett's seminal and existential play *Waiting for Godot*. For me, it was important to center Daniel's imaginations in a surreal, if painful, world, and I have always admired the relationship of Vladimir and Estragon, two people tasked with passing time in a lonely, uncertain place. Throughout the opening of Act II, Vladimir prods Estragon as to whether he is happy, and for me, Daniel's need to know if Sam is happy in the afterlife felt like an important parallel. I have always read Vladimir and

Estragon as queer, and whether Beckett would agree with that is not important. What is important to me is having the language to make sense of death and fear of the unknown. We may not know where we end up going to pass the time (if we go anywhere at all) as we wait for loved ones still on earth, but to Beckett, I will always be grateful for this inspiration.

If any character is based on a true experience of mine, then it is that of my maternal grandfather, Papá Filomeno, who inspired Abuelo Omar. My grandfather was a kind, loving, and generous man. I am so honored to be his grandson. I started writing this novel long before he passed away from COVID-19, and so his was another loss that shaped the story in profound ways. My grandfather (y mi abuela) gave me my first solid understanding of México, when they took me to where my maternal side of the family comes from. At ages ten and twelve, my sister and I went on a summer adventure around Chihuahua, and in so many ways that trip helped me to make sense and fill in missing puzzle pieces of who I am and where I come from. I will always be grateful to have gained that part of myself because of my grandfather. If it wasn't for Papá there'd be no Abuelo Omar, and the second half of this novel would not have been able to exist as it does.

And while Tío Daniel might not exist in my own life in the way he is written, I am immensely grateful to the legacy of activists across México for fighting for human rights of marginalized communities, queer people, women, and Indigenous people who have long called la tierra madre home. Tío Daniel's story was largely inspired by the exhibition *The Seropositive Files: Visualizing HIV in México* and its subsequent text written by Alejandro Brito Lemus, Oliver Debroise, Sol Henaro, Luis Matus, Alfonso Morcillo, and Rosa María Roffiel (Museo Universitario Arte Contemporáneo, UNAM, 2020). As a queer brown Mexican, it is important to me to highlight that AIDS activism is not solely a Western story, and that work was occurring throughout the Global Majority, and thus the research of these scholars, artists, and curators helped to inform my understanding of what activism looked like in México at the time Tío Daniel would have been alive. There are countless stories that need to be unearthed and shared so that we as Black and brown queer people can understand the legacies we are born from, the names we carry, and the words that can serve as guides. I would also like to acknowledge the inspiration I took from the activist language of feminist groups like Círculo Violeta and Ni Una Menos México, who work on behalf of women and non-binary people to combat femicide and corruptive powers in México. I was in México City during the 2020 Valentine's Day demonstrations and witnessed firsthand the direct action these women and non-binary people used to bring attention to the recent murders of Ingrid Escamilla, Fátima Cecilia Aldrighett Antón, and countless other young girls and women in México annually. Some of the language on the placards Tío Daniel carries in his photos take inspiration from signs I noticed while in the capital. For me, Tío Daniel represents those who refuse to remain silent, despite the danger it might present, and instead choose to live loudly and work fiercely for change and equality. To those who inspired his words, mil gracias y siempre tendrán todo mi apoyo.

To my own LGBTQ+ family members, I am so glad we exist, have always existed, and will continue to exist as branches of this ever-expanding family tree. And I hope this book might inspire you, reader, to unearth what hidden legacies are contained in your own story.

CON AMOR,
ANDRÉS

Acknowledgments

I would like to thank the judges of the Morley Lit Prize for Unpublished Writers of Colour and the Mo Siewcharran Prize, who shortlisted an earlier version of this novel for their respective awards. The attention I received from those shortlists helped me in more ways than I'll ever be able to articulate in full. To the subsequent editors, literary agents, and publishing professionals who gave me their time and feedback, I offer you my deepest gratitude.

I am grateful to the Scottish BPOC Writers Network for their continuous support and countless opportunities to improve my craft among other writers of color through workshops and master classes. To Jeda Pearl, Alycia Pirmohamed, Hannah Lavery, and the rest of the network, thank you one thousand times over.

Many writers have offered encouragement throughout the genesis of this novel and at critical moments of exhaustion or confusion—thank you to all of you. A few new names I'd like to mention: Nadine Aisha Jassat, Katie Goh, Etzali Hernández, Jess Brough, Yara Rodrigues Fowler, Jessica Gaitán Johannesson, Damian Barr, and Jenni Fagan. Whether it was advice shared during long walks along the North Sea, via Twitter DMs, over coffee, over pints, or during events, your kindness and knowledge of the literary industry has been instrumental in my own growth. Fiction writing is a solo act, but it never needs to be lonely.

Thank you to team Tin House for taking a chance on a debut like this one. To my astute editor, Elizabeth DeMeo, I am in awe of your care and attention to both language and the poetry of a sentence. Thank you for understanding Daniel and Sam and helping each to shine. To Beth Steidle, who designed the luminescent cover, and Sarah C. Allen for the original linocut that stars at its center, to Allison Dubinsky, who copyedited (and ensured I correctly named the local fauna and flora of each setting), and Lisa Dusenbery, who offered careful proofreading, my deepest thanks—it truly takes a village to produce a book.

I must offer my deepest thanks to Eduardo C. Corral, Zak Salih, Christopher Castellani, Eloisa Amezcua, Analicia Sotelo, and Richard Mirabella for offering to read and blurb an early version of my debut. Your words have buoyed me in the final stages of waiting to send this book out into the world and I am eternally grateful.

Caro, my dearest agent, you are one mighty champion of diverse voices—where would I be without you? You have never doubted my ability to craft the story I needed to write even when you signed me only having read three chapters (sorry for keeping you waiting, but hope it was worth it). Without you, I would not have produced the version of this novel that I knew was in me and for that I will always be grateful. Thank you for reminding me that there are bright lights in the publishing world.

To my friends, found family, and extended family, thank you so much for your love and support. I would particularly like to extend thanks to Lisset Luna Maldonado Sousa (mi tía materna) and my cousin Monica Maldonado Alarcon, who both shared important family stories I was able to use to add authenticity to Daniel's background. To other members of las familias Luna y Maldonado, muchísimas gracias. I hope you find joy in the parts of our family lore that have helped color these pages.

Acknowledgments

I would like to thank my own immediate family for their love, prayers, and personal stories that have informed my own craft. To my mother, Sonia, you are the best storyteller I have ever met. I hope one day you choose to put pen to paper and share all your brilliant memories of life, but, until then, I will always happily be your first listener. To my father, Salvador, thank you for teaching me that manhood does not require a silencing of emotions or heart. To my siblings, Salvador, Selyssa, and Enrique, you are the stars I will always map myself to. If Daniel were to have siblings, he would be so lucky to have you three.

Lastly, to my husband and first reader, Kevin, I could spend a lifetime writing of love, but I would never be able to capture quite so well what it is that makes our story better than fiction. Thank you for our lifetime of adventures, for your passion to make the world a better place, and for being a place I can return to, a place I choose to call home.

Reader's Guide

1. This story takes place over the course of a single year—why do you think author Andrés N. Ordorica chose this timeline?

2. During their first year at Cayuga, both Daniel and Sam experience challenges—did any of these challenges resonate with experiences in your own life, either those you've lived through or those you've witnessed?

3. Throughout the book, it's Daniel recounting the story of his and Sam's relationship—how do you think this story would be different if told from Sam's perspective?

4. Why do you think it is that Daniel is first drawn to Sam, and vice versa? What qualities do they bring out in each other?

5. For both Daniel and Sam, their relationship is one of first love. Do you think there is a special kind of power that a first love holds, in this book and in life?

6. What role does place play in this novel, and how do you think its characters would define the concept of home?

7. What did you think about the diary entries at the start of each chapter? Were you surprised when you learned which character had written them?

8. Writer Eduardo C. Corral describes Daniel's bond with his Abuelo as both impactful and instructive. What role do you see Daniel's Abuelo playing in his grandson's life, and how would you characterize the relationship between them?

9. Throughout the book, Daniel interacts with different men, whether friends, lovers, or family members—how do you think this book represents masculinity, especially masculinity across generations?

10. How, by book's end, do you think Daniel has grown?

Andrés N. Ordorica is a queer Latinx poet, writer, and educator. Drawing on his family's immigrant history and his own third-culture upbringing, his writing maps the journey of diaspora and unpacks what it means to be from ni de aquí, ni de allá (neither here, nor there). He is the author of the poetry collection *At Least This I Know* and currently resides in Edinburgh, Scotland.